Praise for Madelynne Ellis's
Enticement

"...an interesting glimpse into the heads of three well-drawn characters... worth a look if you are looking for a ménage a trois story with a solid emotional component."

~ *Mrs. Giggles*

"...at times I wondered if the pages were going to catch fire."

~ *Just Erotic Romance Reviews*

Enticement

Madelynne Ellis

SAMHAIN PUBLISHING

Samhain Publishing, Ltd.
11821 Mason Montgomery Road, 4B
Cincinnati, OH 45249
www.samhainpublishing.com

Enticement
Copyright © 2011 by Madelynne Ellis
Print ISBN: 978-1-60928-292-9
Digital ISBN: 978-1-60928-237-0

Editing by Tera Kleinfelter
Cover by Angie Waters

First Samhain Publishing, Ltd. electronic publication: November 2010
First Samhain Publishing, Ltd. print publication: October 2011

Dedication

To my monsters—life wouldn't be the same without your unique perspectives and all the riot and rumpus you cause.

Chapter One

"Ross—you home?"

Evie Latham dropped her keys on the kitchen table before poking her head around the living room door. Besides the single pool of warmth created by the standing lamp, there was no sign of Ross. He had to be home, though. There was no way Mr. Energy Conservationist would ever be caught leaving the lights on all day. She'd only just trained him out of unplugging the kettle after every cup of tea.

Upstairs, the exotic scent of his herbal shower gel suffused the corridor. Evie glanced at her watch. It wasn't like Ross to dive in the shower the moment he got home. He knew she liked the smell of him, all musky and hot, with a hint of the chemicals he used at work blended into the mix, and the powdery smears from the latex gloves still fresh on his fingertips. She loved to press her nose up tight to him, snuggle into the crook of his arm and breathe in his wonderful scent. Clearly, today had been gruelling. Possibly, he'd lost one. It sometimes happened. Animals he just couldn't save. Ross wasn't the sort to get all teary-eyed, but she could always tell how his day had gone from the timbre of his voice when he spoke. Too low and dry, and he was obviously choked up. Eight years as a vet and losses still bruised him.

Cheering up tactics would obviously be necessary.

Having shed her shoes at the bedroom door, Evie pressed on towards the bathroom, unbuttoning her white blouse as she went. Some things never failed. Just thinking of how delight would transform Ross's expression as she stepped into the shower with him fully clothed gave her butterflies.

Little transgressions. That pretty much summed him up. Wet clothes that clung to the skin and turned transparent being his number one thing. A curious one as kinks went, but far preferable to him admitting a love of spanking or borrowing her underwear. Each to his own, of course, but she thought she'd have a much harder time accepting either of those things.

Ross loved water. He loved being caught in the rain. While everyone else was hurrying by, he'd be the one dancing in the puddles or sauntering along sans coat and umbrella without a care in the world.

They'd met in the rain, in a thunderstorm, only a few yards from their current doorstep. She'd been wearing a floaty white dress that had turned transparent at the first touch of water and clung to her skin, accentuating every curve. She had a fair few of those, not all in the right places either. Ross had seen it all before they'd even exchanged names.

In her fantasy replays of that event, Evie liked to imagine their meeting had been an explosive coming together of yin and yang, a passionate melding of minds and bodies. The truth was that she'd gone arse over tit on the wet grass and slipped a disc. Ross had kindly called an ambulance and held her hand on the way to hospital while she screamed in pain.

The wet scent hit her like a blast of steam as she ploughed through the bathroom door. The normally shiny surfaces were reduced to fuzzy blurs by the wall of fog. Instinctively, she reached for the fan cord, and as the gentle whir began, the overhead light flickered on too. Even then, she could only just discern his outline through the steamed up glass bricks that screened the shower. Strong shoulders, dark hair, his cute tight-as-a-button arse. Her Ross. They'd been sharing a place with friends for so long it was good to think that, now they had their own place, he was entirely hers.

Evie dropped her jewellery and mobile on the edge of the

sink. The final button of her shirt undone to display her admirable cleavage, nicely framed by her new polka dot bra, she stepped under the shower spray behind him, and wrapped her arms around his waist. "How's this for a welcome home?"

There was something wrong.

Even before her hands closed upon his flesh, she knew it. His scent... Even masked by the citrus and wood of the shower gel, his underlying scent was different, as was the way their bodies folded together.

As if scalded, Evie jerked back, unleashing a blizzard of ungodly oaths. She scrambled out of the shower and pulled her wet clothes tight around her. "Who the fuck are you?"

He turned slowly. "Erm... Evie?"

She stared at him, all ripped smooth muscle and not a speck of hair on him anywhere besides his head, and failed to find any hint of familiarity. His two perfect penny-like nipples were all perked up and excited. "Start talking, mister. You've thirty seconds before I call the police." Assuming the local station didn't just laugh when she complained of having a gorgeous man in her shower.

Her fingers nervously twitched as she stretched her hand towards the washbasin and the phone, still blindly backing up.

"Evie," he said again.

Water droplets clung to his eyelashes, while his dark eyes—so dark she couldn't really tell what colour they were—smiled down at her. How did he know her name?

Cheeky bastard didn't even have the grace to look embarrassed.

Her phone exploded with sound. Evie made a grab for it, only for it to shoot from her hand like a bar of soap. It hit the wet tiles and skidded to a halt between the stranger's feet. With a squeal of alarm and frustration, she hopped back a little farther towards the bathroom door.

The stranger stepped from the shower and wrapped the skimpiest towel the bathroom had to offer around his hips. He

<caption>Madelynne Ellis</caption>

bent and retrieved her phone. He glanced at the face before lifting it to his ear. "You're too late, mate," he said into it. His voice rich and smooth like honey. "We've already met." He held out the phone to her. "It's Ross. He'd like a word."

Ross... Ross?

Evie snatched the cell from him and clamped it to her ear. "What in the blazes is going on?"

"Yeah...er... Hi, Evie." Ross's semi-apologetic tone washed a sense of calm into her ear. "Sorry to spring this on you, but, you remember my friend, Kit? I'm sure I've mentioned him before. Well, he's back in the country and I said it would be okay for him to crash with us until he sorts his place out. That's all right, isn't it?"

All right! Like hell it was. How could he even contemplate destroying their privacy after only two weeks? They'd been waiting months to get this place. They were barely settled. There were still boxes in the spare room they hadn't unpacked. Speechless, she just glared at the naked intruder.

"Evie? You all right?" Ross asked, an apprehensive edge creeping into his voice.

"I thought we moved so we could have some us time," she said.

There was a long pause on the other end of the line. "I know... It won't be for long, okay. I promise. Just a month or so."

"A month!"

"Evie, I did try to reach you at work. Your phone's been off. Look, it is okay, isn't it? He's not a scruffy lout or anything, and we go way back."

"I can see that." Not that they went way back, obviously, but that he wasn't scruffy. He'd started drying his hair with another skimpy hand towel as she talked, so that the muscles in his torso rippled with the movement. A lock of thick black hair flopped forward over his brow.

"We'll talk when I get in," said Ross.

Yes, they would. Not that there actually seemed all that much to negotiate. Kit was already here. She risked another glance at him. Yep, quite definitely here. Still mostly naked and making himself at home. He sniffed at a bottle of Ross's aftershave, but discarded it unused.

"Love you," Ross managed to squeeze in before she hung up.

Yeah, love you too she thought, still bitter but no longer quite so cross.

"That's some welcome technique you have." Kit glanced at the shower cubicle and smiled, so that the corners of his eyes crinkled and his lips parted to reveal slightly crooked teeth. "I'm sorry I shocked you. It is lovely to meet you at last." He offered her a hand.

"Kit?" she said, accepting it.

He nodded.

In the comfort of the master bedroom, Evie shrugged off her wet clothes and collapsed on the rumpled duvet in her dressing gown. Frigging crazy, they'd only been here a fortnight. Two weeks of harmonious bliss away from the inconvenience of housemates and ever-calling friends. No one was quite as keen to drive out to the village of an evening, as they'd been to just nip in when she and Ross were living above the town's finest take-away. The last thing they needed was a houseguest, gorgeous or otherwise. And he had been that. This move was supposed to be about them gaining some private time, not taking in waifs and strays.

Kit! She huffed out a sigh. She wasn't even sure she recalled Ross ever mentioning him. She'd met most of his mates. This one had to be from eons back.

There was a rap on the door. Evie sat up, a pillow clamped to her chest. "Yeah," she called.

Kit poked his head around the jamb. "Tea, coffee, foot massage," he offered. He was still showing far too much skin.

Judging by the way he leaned around the door, he probably only had on a pair of shorts.

"Get real."

He shrugged. "Just trying to apologize, and drinks is what I do best."

Her gaze flicked down over the perfectly buffed skin of his chest as he leaned a little farther around the door. Ross was sexy, but compact and rugged, more Sean Bean than GQ model. This guy was rangy and moulded, with lighter skin and a tattoo on his hip that just poked above the line of his shorts. His knees looked as if they'd seen a few scrapes. The skin upon them was silvered and ruddy.

Kit continued to stare at her expectantly from beneath his cloud of coal-dark hair.

He had to have some Asian or Romany ancestry. Had to. No one had hair that dark naturally without it, and of course there were his eyes to consider—equally dark, two pools of glowing temptation focused entirely upon her.

The first stirring prickle of arousal chased across her skin. Evie clutched the pillow a little more tightly. "Just put some clothes on, all right."

He seemed a little startled by her concern over his near-nakedness. "Okay." He dug his teeth into his bottom lip.

Really, there was only so much temptation one could accept in a houseguest and still permit him to stay. She sank back against the duvet once he closed the door. Kit was one hell of a package of smut. Not the sort of man boyfriends generally invited over to stay. Give it a few days and she'd probably have all her girlfriends driving over to check him out.

A little while later, back downstairs, Evie flicked on the TV and settled in front of the road traffic update. Another lorry had blown over on the A1 resulting in a twenty-mile stretch of it being closed. Ross called again to say he was stuck in the resulting tailbacks.

Kit cast a shadow over the sofa.

Evie glanced up at him. He'd finally dressed, although, actually that didn't stop her insides doing a little hop. She sat a little straighter and lifted her feet off the sofa. My God, was he dressed. She dusted the Kettle Chip crumbs from her dressing gown and refrained from putting another into her mouth. Leather trousers hugged his thighs and fell in tailored perfection to rest on leather boots, while a green silk shirt flowed over the contours of his chest, the top three buttons left undone. "Are you going out?"

Kit gave an eloquent shrug. "Figured I'd do some catching up. There are plenty of folks still around that I used to know."

Evie nodded. She kept looking him up and down as if she couldn't quite decide if he were real. "You do know there's only the pub in the village, right? No clubs or restaurants or anything. It's all a bit downbeat and homely really."

He shrugged again, a move that pulled the silk taut across his broad shoulders. "Sure. I know that."

"Oh!"

He cocked an eyebrow as if the remark required further qualifying.

"I just thought something more casual would, you know, fit in better with the jeans and jumpers crowd."

Kit looked down at what he was wearing with his eyes narrowed.

My god, she realized. This was Kit's version of casual. Heaven help her and the rest of the village's female population if he ever dressed like he meant business.

"I've never been much into jeans." He strolled over to the mirror that hung over the traditional fireplace, where he tweaked a few stray strands of dark hair into submission. "I'm sure they'll forgive my little eccentricity. They never worried about my aunt, and she wore three-piece suits made from her neighbour's old chintz curtains. They'll just think I'm following in her footsteps." He glanced down at himself again. "It's hardly that outrageous."

It wasn't. It just wasn't typical Yorkshire village haute couture either.

"So, where's this place of yours?" she asked, wondering how quickly she could slip away and pull on something less dowdy. Not that she particularly needed to impress him, but she didn't want him thinking her a total slob.

"Down the road." He came over and perched on the sofa in the space her feet had recently occupied.

"What, in the village?" There wasn't anywhere up for sale. She and Ross had had to wait five months for this place to become available just to rent. Kirkley wasn't really even a village, more of a hamlet. Just a few old cottages huddled around a green with a pub, a duck pond and a sort of post office. No church, no school, no streetlights.

"Rose Cottage. Do you know it? It was my great aunt's place. It's been going through probate and whatnot, but it's all sorted now."

"It's a fucking wreck!" she blurted before she thought better. There wasn't even a roof on it. Evie clamped her hand across her mouth. Okay, there was half a roof, and maybe three intact panes of glass in the entire building.

Kit's expression remained cheerful. "Yeah, I suppose it does need a fair bit doing to it." He rubbed at his scalp, mussing up the hair he'd just straightened in the mirror so that if flopped forward over his eyes. "Still, I reckon I can be out of your way once I've a couple of rooms fixed up. I don't need much. I can sleep in the kitchen once the Aga's fixed."

"Don't worry about it," Evie muttered.

His smile broadened to show off his slightly crooked canines. "Thanks, I appreciate it."

What was she saying? She couldn't live here with Mr. Enticement for months. What about space and chilling out? What about what he was doing to her heart rate? That smile of his was wicked, and his body to die for. She was going to have to poke her eyes out to stop herself gawping at him.

Ross, she bemoaned, what are you doing? I thought you loved me. Why are you throwing your handsome mates in the way?

Kit, she could sense just from his smile, was going to be trouble. They'd have to lay down some house rules.

Such as no bringing his dates home.

"Wow!" Ross stumbled through the front door forty minutes later carrying a briefcase and a cardboard animal carrier. "What's the occasion?" He stared dumbfounded at Evie's party dress and makeup before he dropped a kiss upon her upturned face and handed over the box. "Yet another addition to the family, I'm afraid. This one's just for tonight. Iris is taking her after, but she has her dance class tonight and didn't want to dump her in an empty house."

Evie peeped inside the box at what appeared to be a tabby ball of fur. She felt Ross's gaze upon her rear as she bent over.

"Are we due out somewhere?" he asked.

"Uh-uh. I just thought I'd make a bit of effort, seeing as we're suddenly entertaining." She reached into the container and scooped out the kitten. "Oh, she's cute." Maybe they could keep the kitten and send Kit to Iris's. Ross's secretary would probably appreciate a nice bit of man flesh to twirl her around the living room.

"She came in from one of the rescue centres, wound up in fishing twine. Some evil bastard had left her hanging from a tree in a plastic bag," said Ross about the cat.

"That's sick." Evie snuggled the kitten against her breast, then set it down on the floor.

"Yup." Ross picked up her discarded bag of Kettle Chips and helped himself to a handful. "So, where is he?"

"Who?"

"Kit, you dope. What have done with him? You've not banished him to the coal shed already, have you? He's my oldest mate."

"I think he's gone to the pub. He said he had lots of people to see."

"Yeah...suppose," Ross replied, an unfamiliar hint of disappointment in his voice. He swivelled on the spot, then seeing her, his face brightened, and a wolfish smile tweaked his lips. "Actually, that's a good thing," He drew out the last few syllables so that they rumbled in his throat. "Because there's a few things we need to address, right?"

"Right," Evie hesitantly agreed. There didn't seem any point in going over Kit's impromptu tenancy. The guy had already moved in.

"Like," Ross continued and he hooked a hand around her waist and pulled her into his arms, "what exactly I'm going to do with you in that dress."

"Ross." She raised a warning hand, but he brushed it aside.

"Come on. You know I've always liked this dress with its itty bitty straps and its scooped neckline." He traced one index finger over the top of her breasts as he pulled her tighter against his body. Slowly, he traced the top edge of her bra across to one of the straps, which he lowered off her shoulder.

"Ross!"

Grinning, he did the same to the other strap.

"Wouldn't you like something to eat first?"

"Just you." His lips brushed hers, lightly, flirtatiously, never quite delivering on the promised kiss, so that she soon craved the contact. Meanwhile, his palms skimmed over her ample bottom, then crept down towards the hemline of her dress. "I swear you're the sexiest woman I've ever met. And I want you." He bent his head and sucked the side of her neck, an act that always made her knees wobble.

Evie laughed, even as excitement zinged through her midriff, but the sensation of his lips upon her neck soon seduced her to his will. She felt the edge of his teeth, and the roar of her pulse echoed in her ears. He didn't bite, just sucked, but that alone was enough to set her squirming, even before his hand made contact with the bare expanse of her thigh. Two fingers traced the edge of her knickers. She squirmed against him, still not sure if she was encouraging him or suggesting he should wait.

"The body's willing, but...what's up?" He teased one finger beneath the lace and then slid his finger upwards to rub her clit.

Evie's breath caught. Her body softened, warmed. Two minutes with him and she was already slick with need and eager for him. It was always that way. Sometimes he didn't even need to touch her. He just had to look at her in the right way, raise his eyebrow slightly and fix his hot blue gaze on her.

"What if he comes back?" she gasped, already rolling her hips and forgetting Kit.

"Evie, he won't be back for hours."

"I don't know, Ross," she whispered against his shoulder, teasing him now. "Maybe upstairs would be best."

"Right here, right now." He kissed her lips, and stroked her clit a little more firmly. "I'm hard for you, baby." He placed her hand over his groin, and sure enough, the long length of him filled her hand. Ross moaned deep in his throat at the contact and stiffened a fraction more. "It's got to be now, Evie. Not upstairs. I want you here, on my lap, on the sofa." He edged backwards into a seated position and tugged her astride his knee, so that their bodies pressed up close. Through the layers of clothing she could feel him, hot and swollen, his cock begging for freedom with fractious little jerks.

The spectre of Kit loomed in her subconscious again and shot apprehensive prickles down her spine. She shrugged away the feeling. Kit would be in the pub for hours. The house was theirs. They could rub up against one another, cuddle and fuck wherever they liked until the clock struck midnight, when their houseguest would no doubt stumble in merry and bleary eyed. A time frame of five hours didn't seem so bad. Evie rocked a little harder against Ross's loins, rubbing her pussy lips up and down the length of his cocooned shaft. For too long sex had been performed behind a locked bedroom door to a death metal soundtrack for fear of being overheard. Now, they could talk dirty, or run about the house leaving behind a trail of clothing if the mood struck. They could make out in the bathroom, the pantry, on the sofa or the floor.

The lacy scrap of her knickers pulled taut against her needy clit as Ross tugged her closer still. They were moulded together, chest and loins pressed tight.

"You're such a tease." Ross nipped her earlobe. "Are you going to get me undressed or just bounce on my lap?"

She liked the way he sounded, all needy and hoarse. His cock gave another joyful little jump, almost as if greeting her before it filled her. She could picture the exact moment of their joining. Shivers raced across her body, so her breasts grew heavy and her nipples steepled.

"A tease?" Maybe she was. Of course, he liked it when she teased. She shuffled back off his lap and knelt on the floor. "You're right. We do need to get these undone." Her fingers worked at his fly and then his underwear. His cock rose, stiff and eager, from within the folds of fabric, and twitched against his stomach in response to each trace of her fingertips. Evie slowly circled the tip as she simultaneously licked her lips. Ross's resulting groan sent a ripple of excitement straight to her cunt. She withdrew the touch and rose to her feet, then let the image of him sitting rampant and exposed, burn into her memory. He looked fantastic—jacket and trousers open, his tie askew and just that single column of proudly rearing flesh exposed.

"Do it," she demanded, knowing that he'd understand. After three years together, Ross knew exactly how much she liked to watch him touch himself.

The skirt of her dress was already rucked up around her hips. Evie hitched it a little higher, and pulled the top a little lower, exposing the lacy cups of her bra. At the same time that Ross curled his fist around his shaft, she worked two fingers into the front of her knickers. Watching him stroke his cock always made her wet. It was something about the way his big palm wrapped so snugly around the shaft, and how he tugged far more forcefully than she ever dared. She loved the way he squeezed but never really touched the sensitive head except with the centre of his palm.

Sometimes she liked to just stand back and look at him, gaze at him as though he were an ornament not a living being. Other times, she'd admire him for what he was—a rampant male. Clothed and yet obscene.

Evie rubbed her clit a little faster, feeling her pulse begin to flutter as arousal knotted within her womb like belly ache. She swept her gaze to Ross's face; his eyes were closed, and concentration lined his brow. He kept telling her how much he liked the way her body moved when she touched herself, but always after a minute or two, his eyes closed, as if the visual stimulus combined with the smooth massage of his cock was too much to take at once.

His jaw went slack. "Evie," he sighed. His eyelids fluttered open and closed, out of sync with the demanding roll of his hips. "Don't make me come like this. I want to be in you."

"I don't know," she teased and bit her fingertip, holding her index finger between her teeth for a moment. "You did spoil things by inviting your mate to stay."

Ross's eyes flickered open and this time stayed wide. His gaze pinned her. "Kit won't spoil things. He won't spoil anything." She read a heartfelt promise in his gaze, and a sudden lightness lifted her up. "Please, Evie."

She held back a moment longer, just long enough to make him sweat. Ross troubled his plump upper lip with his teeth.

"Say please again." She straddled his lap.

"Please. Pretty please, and I'll let you keep the cat."

The cat! Evie laughed; she looked around and found the little kitten curled up on the window ledge above the radiator. "You know I think I might just have something for you." She held herself over him, until she was poised right over his cock, then shoved her knickers aside and sank down slowly.

Ross nuzzled against her breasts as she slid around him, taking him fully. He lifted her bra and let her breasts fall, heavy into his waiting palms. Thumbs and fingertips troubled the already peaked nipples, only to be replaced by the wet heat of his mouth.

"Yes," she hissed. Her nerves fizzled with the energy of joining. All her muscles pulled tight, then relaxed, letting him sink deep. She loved being on top like this, knowing she held the control. She loved the way his body worked in this position and when they fucked standing upright. The way his muscles pulled tight with each thrust, and he rose up, fighting gravity to make their bodies meet with a ferocious slap.

Evie clawed at Ross's shoulders. She thrust a hand between them and rubbed her clit. It was so sensitive, just petting it a little sent showers of fiery sparks streaking across her body. Ross clasped her bottom, his grip tightening and relaxing. He traced circles over the plump flesh, his fingers feathering into the channel between her cheeks.

"Ross," she squeaked when he circled her anus with a wetted fingertip. Shocked and excited, she moaned into his shoulder and rode him faster, already starting to climb. He met her increased pace and lifted them both off the seat with each thrust.

"Noooo-ooo!" she squealed, blinded by the sensation. Her groans grew louder and less coherent as his delicate tease continued to trouble her arse. It was enough to tip her over. Evie threw her head back, shoved her breasts in his face and came hard.

Ross held her and kept working his hips even as she sobbed into his shoulder. Just the tip of his little finger teasing her arse had lit up all the nerve-endings there so that her orgasm pulsed and pulsed. So many times he'd teased her. Told her he was going to fuck her there. Stick his nice hard cock into her voluptuous arse. The mere suggestion of it was enough to set her writhing.

Only who was he really tormenting—himself or her?

He got hard just imagining pressing his cock to her dark hole. Except, at this moment it wasn't his cock that he was imagining filling her. No, in fantasyland he was right where he was, deep in her cunt, feeling the crazy flutter of her muscles squeezing his shaft.

Kit stood in the kitchen doorway, his eyes as black as tar, only a million times more luminous. His black hair fell in a jumbled shadow over his face, partially concealing his expression, but when Ross looked into his eyes, he saw the shape of things to come, and things as they'd once been. For a split second, he wondered if he'd been wrong to invite Kit to stay. Not that he'd ever been able to say no to him. As teenagers they'd done a hell of a lot of fucked up stuff, experimenting, pushing boundaries. He'd never managed to turn his back on Kit.

Kit had been there the first time he'd lain with a girl. Sharon, her name was. Older than him, already self-assured at the grand age of twenty-three. It hadn't been pretty, just seedy really, looking back. Sandwiched together out the back of some nightclub, wedged between a drainpipe and a car exhaust. He'd felt like shit afterwards, but he'd stuck around, watched while Kit had her too.

Their gazes locked across the space of the living room.

Evie lay sated and lethargic in his arms, her head nuzzled into the crook of his neck, still crooning to herself.

"Come," Kit whispered.

One word, not even firmly spoken and his body leapt to do Kit's bidding, just as it had always done.

Breath ragged, Ross hid his face in Evie's shoulder as his balls gave up their load.

Chapter Two

"Kit!"

Ross's gasp tore through the contented peace of Evie's afterglow. The rhythm of Ross's motion changed, and she sensed a momentary lull in his attention before everything coalesced again and drove him over the edge.

Kit. He'd seen Kit. Had given her a warning, even as every nerve in his body had fused and fired as one.

Apprehensive flutters beat inside Evie's chest. She hardly dared look. Her fingers still curled around Ross's shoulders and hair, while his hands still supported her bottom. She didn't want to see Kit standing there, but was powerless to resist the truth.

Slowly, she turned her head.

Lean and rangy, Kit stood in the kitchen doorway, his firm butt resting against the doorframe, while his long legs stretched out before him. A steaming cup lay clasped within his palm.

He hadn't just arrived. He'd probably seen it all... Ross fingering her anus, her frigging her clit as their bodies slapped together. Evie's grip tightened around the short spikes of Ross's hair, provoking a whimper from him. Gut level anger brewed inside her, dashing icy water on the residual flames of her arousal. If Kit thought he had the right to intrude on them like that, he had another thing coming. There was no room for a Peeping Tom in her house.

"What are you doing back?" she growled, allowing her anger

to swallow whole her embarrassment. How dare he stand there so calm, without a trace of discomfiture about him, while inside she was mortified?

Kit swept his long fringe from his eyes and took a sip of his drink, as if standing watching people fuck were as commonplace as watching the telly. "I saw Ross's car pull up, and figured we had plenty of catching up to do without me propping up the bar for the night. 'Course—once I got here I realized you were kind of busy." He lifted the mug in a sort of salute, as if him making a cupper somehow detracted from the intrusion. "I'll just slip past if you're not done. We can always talk later." He nodded at Ross, who, to her astonishment, simply nodded back.

Kit slid across the living room and disappeared into the hall. The moment she heard his footsteps on the stairs, Evie scooted off Ross's lap and pulled her dress straight. "How long had he been there?" she demanded.

Ross sheepishly shook his head. His cock lay flaccid now, nestled against his thigh, still shiny with her dew. Normally, sex wouldn't have ended here. She'd have taken him gently in her mouth, got herself all worked up on the combined taste of their bodies, and sucked him until he stood proud again. They'd have rolled upon the floor together, or chased upstairs for a joint shower.

"How long, Ross?"

"I'm not sure. Maybe a minute or two, my attention was kind of elsewhere."

"Damnit!" she cut him off. It hadn't been only a minute or two, not if Kit had come straight back when he'd seen the car pull up, and he'd had time to make a brew. More than likely, he'd seen the lot. Absolutely everything. Evie didn't consider herself a prude, but sex was something couples did in private. Exhibitionism held no appeal. She hated performing. It's why she had the equivalent of a desk job where she worked, rather than one of the more showy roles.

Her cheeks blazed as she sought reassurance in Ross's face. There was none to be found. All he gave her was a wry smile and a shrug. That was it. It was over, done with, nothing to fret about in Ross's world. He wouldn't have sought out an audience, but it was no big deal to him that there'd turned out to be one.

"Let it go," he said, stretching his hand out towards her to pull her back onto his lap. "It's no big deal. What's the big fuss, Evie? We're a couple in our own home."

"He stood and watched is the problem. I'm not having him spy on us like that." She neatly sidestepped to avoid Ross's grasp.

"What, so you'd rather he'd coughed or something so we could run up to the bedroom and cower?"

"I'd rather he wasn't here in the first place." She stomped towards the stairs.

"Evie, where are you going?" Ross followed her a few steps.

"We need rules. I'm going to spell them out. It's my home and I'd like to be treated with respect."

Ross clasped the doorframe. He stayed just over the threshold and watched her mount the stairs. "Okay. Whatever. Go and say your piece."

The guest room door was closed. Evie knocked and walked straight into a pit of darkness. Boxes of unpacked knickknacks lay stacked just inside the entrance, draped with an old Guns N' Roses wall hanging. A pile of coat hangers clacked and scattered as she marched past, the light from the corridor illuminating the way to a neat stack of five unfamiliar suitcases.

"Let's get things straight, mister," she began before she'd even spotted him. "There are rules to adhere to if you're going to stay here. I don't like being spied on. If you come across us doing anything, anything at all, you take a hike right out of the door. You don't get comfy and watch."

"I'm on the bed," he said. The lamp flicked on as she turned towards what seconds ago had been the darkest portion of the room. "You know you shouldn't feel bad about being seen. You look damn good together."

"I—" she began, then stopped. Mouth agape, she stared at him. Kit lay stretched upon his back on the narrow guest bed, his upper body supported by a pile of pillows. The neck of his shirt was undone, as was a section over his stomach, while his leather trousers were pushed down around his thighs. Her gaze fastened upon the tantalizing glimpses of cream-colored skin, and his left hand wrapped around his cock, the skin of which was a good few shades darker.

"Oh my god! I'm sorry," she blurted automatically as she clasped her hand to her mouth.

"Don't be."

She took a hasty step back. He'd seen her and Ross and then he'd come up here and was... She couldn't even say it in her head, even though the sight of him spread before her like a banquet made everything totally apparent. He'd seen her, and now he was doing that.

"Stay right there." Kit pinned her with his gaze from behind the long shadows of his fringe. "I guess we're sort of even now. What was it you wanted to say?"

"Nothing."

He didn't stop touching himself even though she was staring him. Hard as she tried she couldn't quite tear her gaze away. He held himself differently than Ross, used his fingers more, instead of just relying on his wrist.

"You like watching, don't you?" His tongue tip flickered against his full lower lip, and the corners of his mouth turned upwards into a smile. He patted the duvet. "You can come closer. I don't mind. "

He looked like an indie rock god sprawled there, caught inflagrante and totally cool with it. Evie pressed her tongue to her upper lip and watched his long fingers play upon his shaft, vaguely aware that the motion was turning her on. She knew she ought to say something, maybe even summon more outrage and storm out, slamming the door, but the way he looked at her, so full of promises, sucked all the words of anger from her.

Ross had blue eyes—ocean-like, azure pools. Blue like the desert sky. Blue like a tropical storm. Kit's eyes were like dark mirrors, wickedness and playfulness the only clear emotions writ within their silvered depths. He shifted slightly, causing the edges of his shirt to part farther, giving her another glimpse of muscle and the tattoo upon his hip.

Realization dawned that Kit was not the sort of man a boyfriend typically invited to stay. He was too confident and enticing. Nicely packed too, handsome even, if you liked your men a little on the pretty side.

Evie pressed her tongue to her upper lip, her gaze still fastened upon his cock as he drew his looped finger and thumb up and down the shaft. This was more than just her barging in on him now. It had turned into a performance. If she'd been single, that would have been fine, but she wasn't. She was with Ross, and this guy was supposedly his oldest friend. It'd be best if she said her piece and left right now. Only, when she tried to speak, all that came out was a mute little croak.

She swallowed, wet her dry lips and tried again.

"You don't have to say anything. I won't intrude again. Sorry never really cuts it, does it? And I'm not, by the way. How can I be sorry about such a visual treat?" he said.

His gently spoken words made him sound like the voice of reason. He'd seen her at her most vulnerable; therefore it was only fair she saw him similarly exposed. Not that Kit seemed remotely vulnerable as he toyed with himself. His movements were too comfortable and precise. When she'd first asked Ross if she could watch him masturbate, he'd agreed but his cheeks had burned the whole time and his movements had been incredibly jerky. Through repetition, he'd learned to relax and had worn away the sense of embarrassment. Kit possessed no such fragility, or coyness of motion. He touched himself with the confidence of someone who was used to performing, and knew they looked good doing it. Each languid, feathered caress was designed to elicit a slow burn. There was no frenzy, just a soft whisper of enticement.

Evie refused his offer of a perch upon the bed and shuffled away from him until she found herself backed up against the stack of cardboard boxes. Probably best if she stayed out of his reach lest he suggested more than just watching. Frighteningly, she could imagine touching him. Not his cock per se, but definitely pressing her palm to his abdomen, and perhaps sliding it over his warm skin. Her eyes briefly closed, as she replayed how he'd felt against her when she'd wrapped her arms around him in the shower. She relived the jolt of fear and the fluttery feeling of panic, the latter so akin to the tingle of arousal she felt zipping through her now.

Ross... She loved Ross. He made her insides flutter and her heart race. She ought to be watching him, not this man with a devil's smile.

Her eyes snapped open again. "That's enough."

A refutal flared within the dark depths of his eyes, and then he moved his hands away from his body. "As you wish."

"No more watching," she said, just to make sure she'd been completely understood. "And no other guests, either. I don't want a stream of strangers traipsing through."

"That's fine."

"Good. I'm glad we understand each other."

"Perfectly." He grinned and settled himself more comfortably with his hands clasped behind his head.

Evie sidestepped around the mound of boxes and left, closing the door behind her. At the top of the stairs she paused and swallowed a ragged breath. Two dichotomous images of Kit lay etched inside her head, one of him naked with a hand-towel clamped over his loins, and the other of him spread out upon the bed, clothed, but with his cock exposed, and that after he'd been in the house only a few hours. Lord knows what other havoc he'd wreak given a month.

Ross had moved from his spot on the sofa when she got downstairs. She found him in the kitchen, scribbling answers into the newspaper Sudoku with a sandwich clamped between his teeth and the kettle in his free hand. Evie wrapped her arms around his waist and pressed up tight to his shoulder blades, taking comfort in the heat and strength of his body. There was no denying her encounter with Kit had left her more than a little horny.

Ross put down the pen and sandwich. "Everything all right?" he asked.

"Fine." She snuggled closer, breathed in his scent and rocked her hips against his bum.

"You didn't lay down the law too hard, did you? I haven't seen him in ages, and I'd like a chance to talk to him."

"It was all very amiable," she said and then clammed up. She'd fully intended to explain exactly what had happened to Ross, but somehow she couldn't. Blurting it out would seem too much like a confession, which it wasn't, and besides, Ross had a whimsical look about him, as though he was looking at his past through rose-tinted spectacles, and she didn't want to spoil it for him. Having your oldest friend turn up and flash his cock at your girlfriend, regardless of how it happened or for what reason, generally didn't result in anything but discord. Especially—a wry frown troubled her brow—when it had happened twice in one day.

Kit closed his eyes when Evie left the room. He unfolded his hands from behind his head and rested them palm up upon the duvet. For several minutes, he stared at the ceiling, replaying every moment he'd spent with her over in his head, while his cock continued to buck against his stomach, seeking additional stimulus. When it bucked a little too eagerly, leaving behind a wet thread of precome, he pushed himself up off the bed.

He was done with jerking off, for now at least, despite an awareness that he could come very quickly if the fancy took him. But the moment had passed. Evie had gone, his tit for tat apology half-accepted.

"*Shimatta!*" he swore. The lady no doubt thought he was a complete prick now, and she'd be right. Certainly there were better ways to impress a woman than giving her an eyeful. Sure, women liked cocks, but generally they preferred them with a brain attached. In the absence of higher functioning, they tended to opt for a nice whizzy toy in place of a dunce.

Engage brain not cock next time, he chastised himself. Although in the middle of a wank wasn't generally when he did his best reasoning.

Kit fastened his trousers over his hard-on. His cock strained against the leather, leaving him feeling uncomfortable, but it seemed fair punishment somehow. He'd known Ross wouldn't bat an eyelid at him watching, but he should have checked out the lady more thoroughly before indulging his voyeuristic streak, made sure she felt the same way.

A fractured glimpse of another pretty woman peeped briefly out of the mirrored wardrobe door at him before he pressed his forehead to the cool surface. He chased the thoughts of her as best as he could from his head. Maybe it had been a mistake coming back here so soon. Six years had seemed an eon on the flight from Japan, but it really wasn't that long at all.

Working in Kabukicho, he'd been isolated. No close friends, no real relationships and no troubles, just a nice, safe cocoon. The only demons he'd faced wore designer skirt suits and stiletto heels. If there were dark memories lurking in the shadows they were only of pointless fucks in dingy alleyways, nothing more hurtful than being paid to screw, even if it was in a round-about way. Here, time hadn't moved on. Kirkley was as it was the day he left. Same people, same chocolate-box façade, same red phone box nestled beside an overgrown hedge on the corner of the green.

"Hey, in there." Ross, unlike his girlfriend didn't bother to knock. He just barged in and struggled past the wall of boxes. His gaze swept Kit's body in one smooth glance and settled upon his face. Okay, Ross had changed. That his friend had lost about a foot of hair was the most obvious one. He'd filled out too, no longer a lanky youth who didn't quite have control of his limbs. Ross's increased bulk suited him well, especially as it appeared to be all muscle.

Gone was the rumpled sex-stained work suit, and in its place he wore a pair of faded black jeans and a tired grey jumper, mended at the cuff with silver embroidery thread and still familiar from six years ago. He sensed Ross's gaze too, probably ringing all the changes in him. There weren't many; it was just polish mostly, a nice glossy shine designed to win favour in the bar he'd worked.

"Thought I'd better come up and make sure she hadn't left any marks. Evie can be wicked cruel if you rub her the wrong way," Ross said.

Kit rubbed the melancholy film from his eyes. Too many times he'd wished that things had turned out differently. "Women were never my strong point."

"Yeah, right!" Ross gave an explosive snort. He sagged onto the bed and rested his elbow upon his knees. "As I recall, they were your only strong point. And looking at you I'm guessing that hasn't changed. Any chance of you slumming it, so I look a bit less of a tramp?"

"I suppose." Kit stripped off his green shirt and rummaged in the topmost suitcase for T-shirt. The one he pulled on was black, ripped at the neck and had "Sukebe 69" emblazoned across the front in white. He pulled a leather thong from a pocket too, and dangled a pewter skull pendant around his neck so it lay in the space where the T-shirt was torn.

"So, are you gonna come down and eat? I'm cooking," Ross said.

"Depends—I think I should tell you what I've been doing first. See if you still want me around."

"Kit, I know what you've been doing. Who'd you think told the probate people where to find you? I live in Yorkshire, not on the moon. I've seen your ugly mug plastered all over YouTube. It doesn't matter. I'm glad to see you."

Ross stood and clapped a hand on Kit's shoulder. He gave him a gentle shove towards the door. "I bet you were raking it in."

"I did okay." Kit allowed himself to be guided onto the landing. He'd kind of suspected that Ross knew he'd been working as a host. It might have been mostly innocent, but that didn't mean that people here wouldn't get the wrong end of the stick and think he'd been prostituting himself. He sighed. It was just something else they could hate him for.

"Yeah, well get downstairs and work your schmoozy host bar tricks on Evie, so I don't have to spend the next millennia apologizing for saying you could crash here," said Ross.

"I can get a room at the pub. As for the tricks—they involve alcohol and a hell of a lot of flirting."

"We have beer and wine. Alcohol isn't an issue."

Kit turned his head and gave Ross a shrewd glance. "Anyone would think you wanted me to seduce your girlfriend?"

"I don't think there's much chance of that, Mr. Intruder Man."

"She's already seen my cock. Twice," said Kit.

Ross just smiled at the admission. There wasn't even a momentary furrowing of his brow. Instead, he calmly leaned against the banister and gently shook his head. "I'm not giving you an excuse, Kit. It's up to you if you stick around or go. I just hope you realize that the only bogeyman here is the one that lurks in your head. No one ever blamed you..."

Shutting his ears to the sound, Kit continued down the stairs. It didn't really matter if no one else blamed him. He blamed himself. He should have been a gentleman that night, not a sod.

"Oh, for crying out loud, let it go," said Ross. "It's ancient history. Time to move on."

"I'm here, aren't I?" Kit retorted. He snapped his mouth

closed without saying anything else as Evie appeared at the bottom of the stairs.

"I was just coming to get you," she said to Ross, completely ignoring Kit. "The water's boiling and I assume you want to put something in it. Oh, and I think the kitten's hungry. He's meowing a lot."

"She," corrected Ross.

"What kitten?" Kit asked. He'd swear there hadn't been a cat earlier. He wasn't so good with animals.

"The one you clearly didn't notice cause you were too busy staring at my butt," Evie snapped, although she broke into a smile immediately afterwards, flashing a hint of teeth and a smidgen of a challenge. That spark jolted him out of his looming doldrums. She hadn't forgiven him yet for spying or being overly suggestive, but she was open to accepting him.

"I brought her home from the practice," Ross explained. He prodded Kit in the back again, urging him down the last few steps, whereupon he pushed past him and headed for the kitchen door. "There are some kitten pouches in my workbag."

Kit shadowed him into the kitchen.

"Is pasta okay with everyone?" Ross asked as he rummaged through the pantry. "It'd better be, because it's all we've got."

"So, what happens once you've done up the house?" Evie asked. Dinner had dragged on into late evening, followed by coffee and now several whisky chasers, as they lay sprawled across the living room furniture. She lifted her head from Ross's lap to peer at Kit. He'd taken the sofa by the window that she and Ross had made out on earlier, leaving her and Ross the joy of the threadbare, foldout sofa bed, which groaned like a banshee every time anyone moved near it. "Will you be sticking around or moving on?"

Although there remained a part of her that resented Kit's intrusion into their lives, she'd warmed to him over the course of dinner. Unlike most of Ross's mates, he grasped the fact that conversation was a two-way thing, and he didn't insist on putting vinegar and ketchup on everything.

Kit rested his chin in the palm of his hand, his elbow propped upon the arm of the sofa. "It's a lot of effort to go to, to just sell up."

"So, you'll be sticking around."

Kit pulled his eyebrows down low over his dark eyes. "Suppose. I haven't really thought that far."

"Leave him be. He's just got into town, Evie." Ross stroked a hand through the front of her hair. "Not everyone has their life mapped out the way you do."

"I just like to be organized," she retaliated. Her pursed lipped smile elongated into a yawn. "Think I'd better call it a night soon."

"Why don't you go on up to bed?" said Ross, giving her a friendly bump up off the sofa. "Kit and I can handle the dishes."

She glanced between the two men and clapped her hands. "I'm not arguing with that. Okay, goodnight." Having ensured the kitten was comfortable in the basket they normally used for kindling, by lining it with one of Ross's old fleece jackets, Evie left the two men to the washing up. She could still hear the low purr of the contented kitten and the rumble of the men's voices as she trekked up the stairs to bed.

Tea towel in hand, Ross lingered by the kitchen table, listening for the sound of Evie's footsteps upon the stairs. His gaze remained fastened upon the broad expanse of Kit's shoulders. Above the torn neckline of his friend's T-shirt lay the smooth expanse of his neck. The ends of his jet-black hair were shorn close, probably razor cut. The remainder of his hair was thicker, and of course, the front remained long enough to cover half his face.

"Get tired of brushing the back?" Ross asked.

Kit reached a soapsuds-covered hand out of the washing up bowl and rubbed the back of his neck, leaving behind a film of white bubbles. "You've lost a bit yourself," he retaliated. Not turning, but meeting the gaze of Ross's reflection in the kitchen window.

For a moment, they just looked at one another, then Kit put his hands back in the washing up water and started scrubbing again. Ross drew closer and began drying a plate. "So, why did you really scuttle back from the pub so fast?"

Kit's head remained tilted downwards towards the sink. "Why do you think? I never even reached the place. I got halfway across the green and saw Tony go in the door. That's one reunion I can live without."

"It's a long..." He was going to say time ago, but Kit turned and gripped the front of his jumper, leaving it wet, with several rivulets running towards his waistband and puddle of dishwater between them on the floor.

"It'll never be long enough. Don't pretend any different. I didn't come back because I thought everything would have blown over. I came back because..." Kit paused; he tilted his head upwards slightly, so that he was staring at Ross's mouth. "Because..." He licked his lips. "There are things that need to be said."

"What things?" The muscles of Ross's stomach cramped in anticipation of the reply. He placed his hand over Kit's fist, but his friend's grip didn't loosen.

"We left things at an awkward point."

"You mean, you did."

Kit jerked away at the accusation, and stalked across the kitchen. He paused by the pantry door and snatched up a towel with which to dry his hands. "Maybe I could have handled things better, but it seemed best not to embroil you in the media circus."

"But leaving without so much as a goodbye, let alone a postal address. That was uncalled for."

"Call it guilt. I had to, Ross. I couldn't stay."

"I'd have left with you."

"Gone into exile. That would just have made us both look guilty."

Dark storm clouds billowed across the coal-dark surface of Kit's eyes. Ross chucked aside the tea-towel and closed the gap between them again. He touched Kit's arm, where his bicep peeked from beneath his sleeve.

"You were training, Ross. You've a practice now. This place is right for you. Always has been. I couldn't steal you away from that."

Ross prodded him slightly with two fingers and felt the tension in the muscle. "You're still making excuses. Deal with it, instead of running." He turned away and opened the fridge. Kit's gaze never left him as he gulped down mouthful after mouthful of tart cranberry juice. Ross ignored him, focused instead on the explosion upon his taste buds. Neither of them could alter the past. The difference between them was that he'd moved on. Kit hadn't. Kit had lost himself in a cornfield six years ago and never found his way out. The shadow of that golden valley still clung to his skin.

Kit moved so fast, he was on Ross before he'd had a chance to react. "You want me to deal with it?" Kit was right in his face, so close there wasn't room for a whisper to pass between them without it raising hairs. Hard fingers dug into Ross's upper arms. The cold metal of the fridge door buzzed against his back. Nerves across his loins and torso jumped when he felt Kit's hips meet his own.

"What are you doing?" he barked, unintentionally showering Kit in vibrant red drops of juice, which clung to his pale skin and rolled down his cheeks like blood tears.

"Dealing with it. This is what I came back for. You, Ross. Not Flora's legacy, not to apologize, or face their continued suspicions, but to see you. You're right. We left things undone. I don't intend to make that mistake again."

Cold washed up Ross's spine as he stiffened. Heat washed down to his loins just moments later. "I'm with Evie now," he protested, clinging to the juice carton so that the cardboard crumpled beneath his fingertips.

"And I was with Sammie then."

Ross felt his skin drain of warmth and colour at the mention of Kit's ex. Hard enough to hear her name, let alone hear it spoken with the growled note of possession Kit had produced. Ross knew the facts. Told himself he knew the truth, but that didn't mean he hadn't lain awake on numerous nights past, picking over events, and letting the darkest reaches of his soul mount suspicions. Kit's reassurance, his denial, should have been enough. Most of the time it was, just every now and then the demon imp of suspicion roused itself and crowed, "what if?"

"Kit, no," he whispered, but he wasn't sure if his protest was real. It certainly carried no weight with Kit. His friend leaned closer, stretching and pressing his body against Ross's. Ross sensed the hardness of him, smelled the natural scent of his body beneath the lingering trace of aftershave. "Evie—she could come back down."

"One kiss, Ross, that's all I'm asking. I don't intend to break you apart. I like Evie. She suits you."

Ross shook his head, but even as he did so, he tilted forward, bringing his lips closer to Kit's.

One kiss! The tremble in his loins told him he wanted more.

So many shared moments, but this was only the second occasion they'd properly kissed. If they'd resisted the first time would things have turned out differently? If he resisted now, what would happen? Would Kit walk away, go back to Japan and leave him to his cosy, normal life with Evie?

The trouble was, just looking at Kit was tantamount to being teased by the devil. Something about him beckoned you closer, made you want to touch him, and long for him to touch you. It's how it had happened the first time. He'd spent too long looking at Kit, admiring the lines of his wiry body as he fucked. In those days, he always seemed to be watching Kit fuck. More often than not it had been Sammie, but there'd been a host of other faces too. Then Kit's interest seemed to wane. He was suddenly all for stepping back and letting Ross sow his oats.

Kit's lips barely brushed the surface of Ross's own. Whisper light, they dusted the over the sensitive skin, offering the promise of enjoyment, but not yet delivering.

"I love her," said Ross, half-turning his head away. A wave of melancholy besieged his tired mind.

Kit's hard fingers curled around the side of his jaw, and forced them face-to-face again. "This doesn't change that. I don't expect it to."

Kit might say it and believe it, but Ross wasn't so sure. Everything impacted on everything else. He had no idea how Evie would react to even knowing that he'd shared a homoerotic encounter or two with Kit in the past, let alone that Kit seemed intent on picking things up exactly where they left off as if nothing had bloody well happened in-between.

"Ross," Kit sighed. Their lips finally met, Kit leading. Kit pressing him hard up against the humming fridge and not letting up, forcing compliance and taking what he wanted.

Somehow Kit managed to get a hand down between them. He covered Ross's loins, kneaded his already hardening cock through the layer of denim, leaving Ross gasping.

"Kit," he shot out a warning. His friend merely smiled and playfully circled the button fastening of Ross's jeans.

He'd resist, Ross told himself, holding himself rigid, every muscle in his body pulled taut. But he'd fail. He always did where Kit was concerned. He just couldn't say no to the guy. Not ever.

Instead of springing his cock free and going down on his knees to blow him, Kit relinquished his grip and turned away.

"You taste just as good as you ever did," he said. A hint of sadness tinged his voice. "Good night, Ross. We'll talk more tomorrow." And he went upstairs to bed.

Shocked and aroused, Ross remained slumped against the

fridge, his thoughts a raging bag of emotions. That was it? One kiss and then walk away? Damn, Kit! Ross's heart was racing, and his cock begging for some action. He couldn't go upstairs to Evie like this. Chances were she was already asleep, and he didn't even want her suspecting that he was horny over someone other than her.

"Shit!" he cursed and freed his cock. He rested one hand on the corner of the kitchen table, while he quickly pumped his cock. He came quickly, exploding onto a square of kitchen towel. No points for style or stamina for that performance, he thought ruefully as he tidied himself up. A trace scent of sex still clung to him, even once he'd finished washing the dishes, but at least he was no longer standing to attention.

For some reason, despite the yawn stretching her face, Evie couldn't seem to settle. Kit's presence had changed the dynamics of the household, warmed areas that were previously cold and made others less inviting. The main bedroom was freezing after the companionable warmth of the living room. The heat from the radiator stung her palm when she grabbed it to see if it was still on. Shivering, she climbed into bed and lay facing the meter of empty space Ross usually occupied. She'd grown used to his presence, a solid, warm shape beside her.

She thought about the two men downstairs and the easy camaraderie between them. Was she threatened by it? Perhaps. She almost certainly would have been, if it weren't for a certain edge to some of their interactions. Although, some level of wariness was inevitable after so long apart. Six years constituted a lot of catching up, but that prickliness piqued her curiosity too. Perhaps because Ross was the least jumpy person she'd ever met, and yet beneath his sociable calm he'd been agitated this evening, and at times, picking his words ever so carefully.

Then again, Kit did seem to inspire that sort of nervous tension. She felt twitchy herself every time she thought of him. Maybe it's because she'd seen him naked twice having known him only a few hours. Maybe it was the way he held his tumbler in the palm of his hand that screamed of sensuality. He certainly had a way of injecting sexual intent into the smallest of actions. Just asking Kit to pass the pepper grinder seemed like a lesson in flirtation. She'd never known a man whose movements were so fluid and yet unpredictable. Like water racing along a rocky stream, sometimes his actions met with a smash. She'd been unable to take her eyes off him most of the night, despite spending a goodly portion of it curled against Ross's side.

"Still awake?" Ross asked, slipping into the room and out of his clothes in the dark. He climbed into bed naked and cuddled against her.

"I thought you'd be hours," she said, snuggling up to the solid length of him, and seeking a kiss.

"Nah, we don't need to say everything at once. Some of it can wait. He's going to be about a bit." Ross draped one arm around her body and squeezed. "Night, Evie. I'm knackered." He gave her the sought after kiss then rolled over and scooted over to his side of the bed. Ross liked to sleep in his own space. It was one of his quirks. He liked the space to stretch and roll. He didn't like to be touched in case that somehow melded their thoughts. It didn't make sense, but not sleeping spooned together was a minor inconvenience, and one she hardly missed, except tonight. Tonight, she wanted that comfort.

Ross's breathing began to soften almost immediately. She reached out and touched his shoulder. "I take it he's quite well off," she said of Kit.

Ross hunched his shoulders, which she took as a "don't know", although it could just as easily have been him nudging the covers up a little farther to cover his ears, or an attempt to shrug her off.

Evie pulled the bedclothes more tightly about her shoulders. The house was definitely cold tonight. "Ross? I mean, he must be, if he's doing up a house."

Ross turned to face her again and captured her gaze across the white topography of the pillows. "I expect he inherited some money along with the house. Flora might have been madder than a hatter, but she wasn't poor. That, and Kit had a good job over in Tokyo. He's not staying with us 'cause he's broke, Evie. Don't pretend that's not what you're hinting at. He's here because I offered. The pub's a bit grotty."

"Grotty?"

"Yeah." Ross frowned at her narrowed eyes.

"That's not what you said on the phone to your mum about Christmas."

"It's all right for the odd night." He sniffed and pushed his nose into the pillow. "Besides, that's different. I don't want my mum here. She'll just bang on about how successful my brother is and how many gorgeous grandchildren he's spawned."

Evie smiled at his wriggling. It wasn't his mum's heartfelt desire for more babies causing the uncomfortable jig, but the fact that he really did want Kit to stay. Maybe that was simply a function of them being old friends and wanting to catch up. Maybe it was something more. Certainly, there'd been times over dinner when the two men's gazes had locked across the table and additional layers of conversation had passed between them without them exchanging a single word.

Old friends did that.

Lovers did that. She and Ross had shared numerous moments like that back in their former shared flat. They were doing it now. Her questioning. Ross sleepily suggesting she back down.

"What did you say Kit did in Japan?" she said, ignoring his voluble yawn.

"Come off it, Evie. I need to sleep. I've a crack of dawn start tomorrow. One of the mares on Hazel's farm has an ulcer." He gave another yawn and dipped farther below the covers so that only a few tufts of brown hair remained poking out.

Evie poked him beneath the covers, provoking a grunt. "So,

it was dodgy, then?"

"No!"

"Then why not say he was in I.T., or marketing, instead of being so evasive?"

"Because he wasn't."

"Don't split hairs."

"He worked in a bar, all right? Can I sleep now?" He tucked the duvet around him so that it formed a valley-like dip between them.

Evie continued to stare at him in the dark a minute or two longer. Something told her there was more to Kit's job in Japan than him simply serving drinks. In her experience, barmen— and she'd dated a few—didn't look nearly so knockout gorgeous. Sure, some of them looked good, but not in the expensive clothes and haircut way that Kit did. If he'd worked in a bar, and not the highflying business sector, it had been an uber high-class cocktail lounge.

"What was the place called?" she asked.

"Evie!" Ross groaned. "For godsakes, go to sleep. Ask him yourself in the morning. I can't remember. Cloud One, or something like that."

"Okay, I'm asleep."

"Good."

"Good night, Ross."

"Night..."

Chapter Three

When Evie came down the following morning, Ross had already left the house to make his Saturday morning calls. Kit slopped into the kitchen a few minutes later, wearing a loosely tied kimono and a pair of tiny red shorts.

Red for danger, she reminded herself as a high-voltage charge of lust sat her bolt upright. The man was torment incarnate. He had something Ross didn't, no matter how wonderful a boyfriend he was. Kit had the X factor, more than just sex appeal, more than good looks—and to be honest, he didn't look especially good at the moment. Shorts aside, he appeared rather dishevelled and a bit green, but he still oozed dangerous, bad boy vibes in the same way one or two of her exes had oozed slime. He managed a feeble smile, and suddenly the shiver-inducing winter morning seemed a whole lot brighter. Evie uncurled her fingers from the side of her porridge bowl as a hot flush tracked across her skin.

"You're not subtle, are you?" she remarked, her gaze hopping between the shorts and his expression.

"Huh?"

Still, just because he was dangerous and she was attached, didn't mean she couldn't look if he insisted of flaunting his hot, semi-naked self. Coaxingly, she waggled the cereal box at him, hoping he'd come closer. Kit stared blankly at her before taking a hesitant step forward. He ignored the cereal box and squinted longingly at the kettle instead.

"You're not naturally an early riser, are you?"

Kit shoved his fingers through his long fringe and scratched, making his hair appear even more mussed up and adorable. "I'm used to working nights. This is the first time I've seen this side of midday in months." He blinked a bit more, as if trying to clear his vision. "Got any green tea?"

"Just Yorkshire."

"Should have guessed that." He pottered over to the sink, filled the kettle and threw teabags into two mugs. "You want one?"

Evie abandoned her porridge and rose to pass him the milk from the fridge, intensely bemused by the changes morning had wrought. Out went her original assessment, the self-possessed, glitzy bad boy of the previous evening having been replaced by something more like a teddy bear with a hangover. She almost wanted to pet him and tuck him back into bed. Except with fear-inducing certainty, she knew physical contact was a bad idea just from the zing that zipped through her midriff at the very idea.

"Ross said you worked in a bar," she said, venturing into the territory of her unsatisfying conversation with Ross the previous night. Neutral territory, that's what she needed in order to deal with Kit. Jobs were generally a safe topic, far less volatile than religion or politics. Besides it was far too early in the day to be mourning the state of the economy.

"Did he?" Kit took the milk and poured.

"An expensive one, right?"

Kit remained poised over the teacups, his head bowed and his teeth pressed into his lower lip. When he finally looked up his expression remained curiously guarded.

"I just meant that it was obviously a step up from the White Boar over the road." She gave an awkward laugh. "You only have to look at the landlord and yourself to realize the bars were clearly worlds apart."

Kit glanced down at his attire, and so did Evie. The belt of the kimono had come undone and now tickled the floor tiles, and his shorts seemed even more microscopic. "Oh, I see," he said. He fastened the belt again and rested his bum against the sink while he sipped his tea. "It was a place in Kabukicho. It's a kind of entertainment district in Tokyo. Lots of clubs, bars and pachinko parlours, that sort of thing."

"Pachinko whats?" Her mind conjured numerous semi-legal possibilities. "What are they, some sort of massage parlour?"

Kit smiled through a yawn. "High tech slot machines."

"Is that a euphemism for something?"

A second smile stretched his lips, this one lighting up his whole face and crinkling the corners of his eyes. "No, Evie, although there are certainly places that do have those. Both robots and dolls are very popular in Japan, particularly with middle-aged men."

"No way." She reached out, intending to poke him, but changed her mind and swiped ineffectually at the air instead. They were still barely acquainted, and that zing only got stronger the nearer she got to him. Doing her best to seem busy, she started tidying away the breakfast things. Kit showed no signs of eating. "So, what are your plans for the day?"

Having finished his first cup of tea, Kit set about pouring another. "I thought I'd head over and survey my new domain, since I keep hearing it's such a wreck. See what needs doing and whether I need to call in the builders."

"It is a wreck."

Having come alive a little on his diet of tea, Kit watched her flutter about the kitchen emptying porridge into the bin and shaking the various juice cartons. "What about you?" he asked.

"Shopping. Supermarket, for all the stuff we're out of. Ross has finished all the juice again and I think we'll need more teabags."

The remark earned her playful smirk, which shot straight to those magnificent dark eyes of his. "Mind if I join you? I've a few bits and pieces I need to pick up." He rubbed his hand over his chin. "Like a new razor for starters."

"Sure," she said as nonchalantly as she could manage. "You can help push the trolley."

He'd been forgiven, or mostly forgiven, for spying on her and Ross last night, Kit thought as he leaned over the ice cream cabinet trying to decide between mint chocolate chip and cherry spagnola. In the end, he put both in the trolley at which Evie raised her eyebrows. He noticed she'd stuck to the essential five fruit and veg a day sort of shopping his mum would have approved of. The luxuries reduced to a tub of olives and packet of croissants. Still, there were fun things you could do with both ice cream and olives, and not all of them involved adding an inch to your waistline, which he figured was what she was concerned over. Honestly, women. You couldn't get through to them, but at least you could eat 'em. Of course, he hadn't actually seen Evie's stomach, just her back and her wonderfully voluptuous arse, but that didn't stop him envisioning running his tongue over the soft surface as a pleasurable experience. Hell, maybe she had a piercing through her navel he could tease. Not that he had serious designs on her or anything, only little ones... Small, somewhat complicated ones that he couldn't really put into words.

It had been stupid of him to imagine Ross would still be unattached after all this time. The thing was, he hadn't really been thinking all that straight when he'd agreed to come home. If he had, he'd never have stepped onto the plane. Sure, Flora's legacy was a nice bonus, but he'd never been all that enthralled by money. It had its uses, and he did like to look good, but he didn't long for riches in the way some did.

"I'll pay for all this," he said and was pleased to find she didn't argue.

Although Evie's presence in Ross's life had been a surprise, he had to admit she'd been a pleasant one. In truth, he'd have been sorry if he'd come back and found Ross alone. His friend was too nice a guy to deserve that sort of loneliness.

"I'm all done, apart from some wine, if you are?" Evie said.

"Not quite. I still need shaving foam and stuff. I'll catch you up."

Nose down, he strode away, his mind flicking over all the events they already shared and before long he was fantasizing about licking the ice cream from her skin again. A little farther down the same aisle he stopped for a few other little essentials. Leastways, he suspected they'd be essential if his sixth sense was anything to go on.

"Planning on getting lucky?" Evie asked when she caught him waving a bumper pack of condoms.

"Yeah. Maybe I am." Kit glanced from the packaging to her and held her gaze just a fraction longer than was entirely polite. She coloured immediately, a fact she rather endearingly then tried to hide behind her hair. "Let's go," he said and chucked the package into the trolley.

Rose Cottage stood on the very edge of the village, set apart from the other nearby properties by several acres of heath land and a severely overgrown hedge. Once inside its wrought iron gateway, they found the lawn of what had clearly once been a colourful showpiece garden now pitted with molehills, and the flowering borders reduced to a collection of weeds. A huge pile of refuse sacks stood to the left of the front door, filled with decaying vegetation and bits of old carpet the local cats had peed on.

"Apparently they sent a clearing firm in after she died," Kit remarked as he stared absently at the scarred façade of the former manor house. A moment later that half-whimsical expression had turned to horror as he found the remains of a rat tucked amongst the rubbish. "I guess it was pretty bad if this is what they left behind."

Hesitantly, Evie patted his shoulder. If it had been Ross, she'd have taken his hand in order to offer that extra bit of reassurance, but just touching Kit's shoulder seemed decidedly risqué. He turned towards her. "I'm all right. It's just a shock seeing what's happened to the old place." His gaze fastened upon the right wing of the rambling building, where the loft space lay exposed to the elements. Even from this distance the roof beams were clearly rotten and speckled with mould. "That used to be my room."

"You lived here? I take it there was a roof back then."

"Over the summers. My folks travelled a lot whereas I preferred to stay put. Ostensibly, Aunt Flora looked after me, but it was a bit of a two-way thing. She was barking mad. The product of a different era, I suppose."

"Lots of memories for you here, then," Evie observed. The whole garden seemed tinged with melancholy too, and she wasn't sure she liked this solemn, maudlin version of Kit. She crossed her arms protectively across her chest, feeling the winter chill start to nip at her clothing and wondered if there was a non-dangerous way of getting him to smile again.

The rumble of a car passing outside the gate startled them both, forcing a burst of nervous laughter from her throat. "Maybe we should go inside," she said and hurried towards the front steps before he had the chance to lead her by the hand. Something told her that when it came to the physical, Kit remained a consummate flirt, regardless of the downwards swing of his emotions.

She waited by the front door for him to dart up and join her and stood back as he turned the key in the lock. The discomforting stench of mildew and bleach assailed them in the hallway. Evie clasped her hand across her nose, wondering if both her lungs and nostrils would ever forgive her. She even contemplated sitting in the car, but Kit didn't seem ready to give her up. Instead he guided her through the rooms, lovingly describing their former glory. Thankfully, the noxious smell quickly dispersed, or else she simply stopped noticing it. For some time they wandered aimlessly between rooms, poking into corners and peering at what little remained of the furnishings as if they were taking part in some alternate-universe version of

Through the Keyhole.

"It's a big job," she observed. Bits of plaster and wiring littered the upstairs corridor, and fallen leaves carpeted several of the rooms. There were floorboards missing and huge patches of damp crawling up the Hessian wallpaper in the old study room. "Bit different from your place in Japan, I bet?"

Kit turned on the kitchen tap. It sputtered a bit, and then spurted clean water. "That's something, at least. Yes, it's different from Japan, about as far removed from Shinjuku as you can get, but it's better than I'd been led to believe. Sure there are a few big jobs that need doing, but most of this is cosmetic."

Evie turned a full circle in the centre of the room, her arms raised in disbelief. "You're kidding, right? I wouldn't even know where to start on this."

"The roof." Smouldering coals lit in Kit's eyes, the prospect of transforming the place clearly having pressed his buttons. "I'll need to get the place weather tight first, and remove the rest of the rubbish. After that, I'll probably start in here and work up. With any luck the Aga's still functioning and just needs a service."

Prompted by his optimism, Evie opened the lower oven door. Something scuttled within, retreating to the darkness beyond the assortment of blackened pie tins. Just as quickly, Evie slammed the door. "You may have to terminate a few rent agreements first." She scurried back from the oven.

"Evict the squatters, you mean." Kit's face further brightened with laughter. "I can't believe you're scared of mice. How do you cope with Ross? I bet the cat's not the only thing he's brought home."

"That's different. I do like animals. I'm just not keen on wild rodents." She continued to back out of the kitchen, her spine rigidly straight and her toes curled within her boots. Kit followed her into the former lounge, where he flopped onto the decrepit sofa, making the springs whine. It and an ancient iron bed upstairs were the only two real pieces of furniture left in the place.

The way Kit looked, sprawled out before her like a bounteous gift, made her hesitate about taking a seat next to him. Nobody had really turned her head since Ross. She'd taken herself right out of the available market and settled contentedly, feeling neither the need nor desire to even notice other men, but Kit was damn near impossible not to notice. The fact that she'd already been intimately acquainted with his rather spectacular anatomy only exacerbated the effect. There were years worth of erotic fantasies waiting to be constructed around him lying in the guest bed at home, offering himself up to her mercy, but she didn't need that sort of chewed-up emotional guilt. Far better that she continued enjoying sexual escapades with Ross and kicked any images of getting too intimate with Kit out of her head. Truthfully though, that was a lot easier said than done. It took hardly any imagination at all to envisage him slipping his hand down his body and unzipping his fly in order to touch to his cock.

She wondered what he looked like when he came. Quietly restrained? Or did he let his emotions out in a violent explosion? Ross exuded passion like a force of nature. Outwardly, Kit seemed more refined, less earthy somehow, and more teasingly urbane, but that didn't really give her any insight into what he was truly like beneath the surface.

"Penny for them," Kit remarked.

"Eh?"

"You're staring. That or you have some sort of weird zombie eye disorder."

"Zombie what?"

"Nothing, forget it."

Something kept her focus fixed upon him, despite the observation, which in turn made Kit sit up. "What is it?" he asked. "Did that mouse tell you all about my evil deeds?"

"What evil deeds?"

"If you need to ask, I guess not." He slumped back down again, his hands clasped behind his head so that his elbows stuck out to the sides.

"Were you and Ross the village tearaways?" she asked.

Kit's brows furrowed. He turned partially onto his side and curled his legs up towards his body. "We got into all sorts of trouble, just like most teenage boys. Scrumping apples, nicking asparagus, twanging bra straps, all the normal stuff." He counted them off on his fingers, turning one down without remark and leaving the little finger noticeably standing.

"And later you broke hearts," she said, curling the last finger down for him. The contact stoked a shocking fire in her innards, quelled a moment later by the hollow look in Kit's eyes. The realization struck her that he hadn't just drifted away from Kirkley in search of adventure. He'd run, all the way to Japan at a guess, with no intention of ever coming back.

Despite the dark swarm in his eyes and the thickness in her throat, Evie had to ask. She couldn't just ask him straight out why he'd gone though. If she did, judging by his current expression, he'd probably just tell her to go fuck herself. Instead, she twisted the question round, eventually asking, "What was Ross like the last time you saw him? Tell me about the last day you spent together."

"What do you damn well want to know about that for?" His knees got even closer to his chest, until he was virtually hugging them. "Nothing happened. We had a few beers together out by the ruins." The tone of his voice suggested that far from being an unremarkable occasion, it'd been positively influential. She'd have to remember to ask Ross about it later, to see if he clammed up in the same way he had over Kit's job, which was something else she still hadn't had a satisfactory answer over.

"Tell me something else, then. How did you and Ross first meet?"

The hunch vanished from Kit's shoulders, and he uncurled a little from his foetal position. "God knows, Evie. I was probably only five months old. What did I do to suddenly warrant the inquisition?"

"It's not an inquisition." She perched on the sofa arm. "It's called getting to know you. It's what normal people do in place of innuendo and exposing themselves. They ask questions. You are living with us. I have a right to know a bit about you."

The mini rant finally earned her a grin. Kit pushed his fringe back off his face, revealing a thin silvery-white scar just above his right eyebrow, on which her attention honed in, until he let his hair fall back into place. Scars always came with stories, not that she expected him to be very forthcoming over that one given his current record. "You want a story, right? I'll give you one. About Ross and myself and a camping trip."

"You go camping?"

He sniffed and looked rather put out.

"Okay, you go camping. Tell me."

"It was part of what I like to refer to as the summer of sin and seduction, when—"

"The what!" Evie lurched forward, which resulted in Kit's explosive laughter filling the empty room.

"You know, it hardly seems fair to be telling you about this when Ross isn't here. Maybe we should save it for later."

"Oh, no, you're not wriggling out of it." Evie battered his knees until he budged along the sofa far enough for her to sit comfortably without touching him. "Start talking, buster, or you can pack your bags and move into this dump right now."

"Are we agreeing the rent criteria here?" he quipped. "Tales for torment? Your guest bed's lumpy as hell. I reckon this one's good for a month."

"A fortnight."

"Without prying?"

"Prying as part of the flow of conversation is allowed."

The look he gave her—a wickedly calculated glare—suggested he had a more visual form of snooping in mind.

"All right, if you're sure you're ready for this."

She probably wasn't, but without him even having breathed a word of the tale, she was on tenterhooks to hear it. Kit settled himself with his legs crossed and his fingers steepled before him, the tips of his index fingers pressed to his generous lower lip. "Every year we used to escape for a week, fly south a bit, and try and plan a music festival into the jaunt. They were always good times, away from all the gossips in the village. I swear there are people around here who count how many toilet rolls you buy. Anyway, I think you can imagine we were rather like two exuberant puppy dogs let off the leash for the first time. Ross was still living at home, and he never took anyone back to his place, and I was still rooming here for the summers, contending with Flora. My aunt was never the biggest respecter of privacy. She once came into my room and watched the entire EastEnders omnibus while I was in bed with someone. Needless to say, the lady in question and I didn't do much besides look meaningfully at the ceiling for an hour."

"Not at each other?" she asked. "But you were telling me about Ross."

Kit continued. "It was the last night of this particular festival. Really late. We'd both turned in, when this girl starts calling among the tents for Ross. Turns out that we'd been chatting to her earlier on and she'd taken a bit of a shine to Ross, because no sooner had he replied than she was in the tent and crawling up to the head end of his sleeping bag to plant a great big smooch on his lips." He turned his black gaze upon Evie again, looking her over as if he were about to drink her down. "Ross has never understood his attraction to the ladies, and he's even crapper at turning them down. Not that I think he wanted to in this case, and well, you just don't when the lady in question has gone to quite such lengths to find you."

"Nothing to do with him being pinned inside his sleeping bag?"

"He wasn't," Kit clarified. "It was too warm to sleep completely zipped up, and she wasn't a big woman. Nicely curvy, though." He glanced at Evie in a way that suggested a figure not dissimilar to her own. Ross put her at ease about her abundant curves, but not everyone was quite so appreciative and she'd had her fair share of snide remarks over the years. Kit was probably into fine-boned, petite women, much like the Japanese ladies he'd no doubt dated. Only his next remark didn't really tally with her assumption.

"She had this delicious way of shimmying her arse like she was a flamenco dancer or something that just made you want to grab hold and squeeze." His fists tightened so that his knuckles bulged before his tone turned wistful. "Ross wasn't stuck, but I was. Stuck inside a scrap of canvas with two smooching lovebirds, and in danger of becoming a mattress for their antics if they ever rolled over. I'd just figured that I'd better take a stroll and do some stargazing, when Ross happened to catch my eye. His date was whispering frantically into his ear. I couldn't make out what, but that look stopped me dead in my tracks. Stay,' he said."

The moment Kit said the word Evie guessed where the tale was headed, and it wasn't anyplace she'd ever envisioned Ross having been. She knew all about his kinks and turn-ons. They'd shared and acted out more fantasies than she could easily count, so that falling back on old favourites had become second nature when they were both tired. But Ross had never given any hint that he'd ventured along this particular avenue, and the knowledge that he'd kept it secret smarted more than learning he'd shared past lovers with Kit. Though looking at him and remembering the way in which Kit had casually loitered in the doorway watching last night, that wasn't such a surprise.

If she had any sense, she'd stop Kit now and forget the whole issue, but of course she didn't. She sat, riveted, gnawing the skin around her thumbnail.

"I stopped unzipping my sleeping bag, and Ross and I sat and looked at each other for a few seconds, and I looked at the girl, and instead of specifically making a decision, I just didn't move. They fell back into kissing again, and I watched, not really sure if that was all I was supposed to do, or if joining them had been part of that odd request."

"But you did," said Evie, trying to picture the woman with Ross and spectacularly failing to do so. She just kept seeing herself. "What was she like?"

"She had on one of those gypsy tops, the type that's all ruffled around the top, and slips off the shoulders all the time. And a skirt, an itsy bitsy little tie-dyed thing, she'd been wearing with pink spotted Wellies during the day."

The description gave Evie no clearer image of the woman. Instead she imagined herself in the ridiculously flirtatious getup, writhing against Ross's hard body. As Kit's words continued to pull her into the story, she could smell the organic scent of earth, mixed up with a hint or two of aroused male. The inner space of the tent lay in darkness but shadows flickered across the outside of the canvas, bodies moving nearby. A thread of music played somewhere in the distance. It coalesced with the faraway hum of the traffic. Kit's eyes shone like black diamonds, longing scored across their surface. He leaned over and pressed a whisper light kiss to her bare shoulder, causing a zing of electricity to shoot up her spine. Completely immersed in the role, Evie turned, breaking the kiss with Ross in order to meet Kit's gaze. Still holding her lover tight, she opened herself up to Kit, kissing him in a slow, deliberate way, so that warmth and desire swept across her body.

"It was one of the most pleasurable sensations I've ever experienced, having her lie between us like that, all that softness sandwiched between wiry muscle," Kit said, continuing to reel her in. She'd seen pictures of Ross from way back, before they met, when his hair flowed halfway down his back, but she imagined him much as he was now. Kit too appeared as he was, or at least how she'd glimpsed him last night: lean, lightly muscled and perfectly clean-shaven. Currently, a fine shadow covered his jaw.

"You didn't touch each other?" she asked, still submerged, imagining four hands caressing her body.

"No. It was all about her." Kit tapped his steepled fingers to his chin. "It involved a whole lot of wriggling as I recall, negotiating with sleeping bag zips and limbs going everywhere, and Ross and I trying not to inadvertently end up in the middle or put our mitts in the wrong place. I think we might have thrown our rucksacks into the porch if we'd been thinking well enough, just so that we could have stretched out properly, but none of us were demonstrating all that much brain power."

Too much blood flowing elsewhere, Evie thought, picturing the smooth contoured lines of three naked bodies pressed together. There didn't seem much space for rational thinking. Her gaze strayed down Kit's body, following the path his hand had taken just a moment before to where it now lay against his thigh, failing to conceal the swell of his cock. Assuming he was trying to hide it, which given Kit's previous record, she seriously doubted. If she muttered a few magic words, such as "please" and "unzip", he'd probably oblige without missing a single beat of the story.

"Of course, we both wanted her, and neither of us was all that eager to sit back and wait our turn. She'd started with Ross, but then I'd been invited in."

She didn't imagine them arguing, but silently locking horns, in a very underplayed, masculine contest to see who was top dog. Neither man won, exactly.

"She kept pressing against me. Pressing and pressing. Really getting off on my cock being up against her bottom. So, when Ross rolled over and she straddled him, I got on my knees behind her."

"You didn't!" Evie clamped both hands across her mouth. Damn, she hadn't meant to blurt that out loud.

Kit's eyebrows shot upwards. "Didn't what, Evie? Get onto my knees, or are you pre-empting the story?"

"You did?" she said and apprehensively pressed her teeth back into the groove in her already bruised lip. "Oh, my god!"

Kit burst into laughter again. He flopped back against the

arm of the chair and lay howling at the ceiling, until he had her laughing too at her own embarrassment. Awkwardly, she leaned over and tapped him on the stomach, perhaps not the ideal location, because his cock, which was still forming an impressive hump beneath his fly, gave an appreciative little jerk.

Still beaming, he sat up. "God, you're incredible! Do you really think we'd do DP with a complete stranger? I thought you knew Ross."

"You're making this up?" Shock, followed by rage, relief and a bitter hint of disappointment caused her to gape at him.

Kit looked up at her from beneath his brows then slowly shook his head. "Nah, it actually happened. Crazy, I know. But I swear it's the goddamned truth. Bet you didn't know Ross had such a wild past."

In her experience there were only two places Ross got wild: in the bedroom and in a downpour. "Was it raining?" she asked. Although she guessed Ross hadn't really been all that instrumental in the kinkier aspects of this liaison.

"Don't recall," huffed Kit, still wheezing slightly from laughing. "Actually, now that you mention it, it may have been."

The gentle thumping of raindrops against the canvas dome drew Evie back into the scene. Ross lay on his back, almost invisible beneath the naked girl straddling his lap. He remained recognizably Ross, though. His long legs darkly furred, and his blunt-tipped fingers held tight to his lover's hips, in the same way he often held Evie. Kit—Kit straddled Ross's legs, his cock risen and pressed tight to his stomach already shiny with precome. His gaze focused entirely upon the girl's bobbing bottom, over which he ran his hands in repetitive circles, his thumbs delving into the dimpled crease.

"What did you use for lube?" she asked.

Kit's jaw dropped in astonishment. "Good god, woman! Talk about practicalities."

"Well, if I'm going to be spun a tale. I'd like it to be

believable, and I've heard it's painful without."

He was on her immediately, making her realize that had been a titbit of information she'd have been wiser not to impart. "Meaning you don't actually know?"

"No. I don't." Evie sat on her hands, waiting for a follow-up question. At the least she expected him to ask how come. Anal seemed to be all the rage these days, if lifestyle mags and some of her friends were to be believed. Personally, she'd never felt any burning need to have a cock thrust up her bottom. She shook her head. Post *Queer as Folk*, she wondered if women were taking it up the arse as some topsy-turvy measure to be part of something they couldn't.

"They were fucking pretty hard." Kit took up the story from where he'd left off, leaving her to blush, and feel prudish and resentful. "I put my hand on her bottom just to let them know I was there and up for some action too, and they both slowed down, which I took as an invitation to go ahead. Being young, we didn't have any lube, because that's what you normally use when you can't get her excited enough, isn't it, and naturally Ross and I considered ourselves talented enough to not need such aids. Luckily, we did have some cooking oil, which went everywhere and made a god-awful mess of the sleeping bags because the buggers wouldn't keep still while I was pouring. Still, it did the trick."

Evie felt herself in Kit's body at that moment, poised and ready, slippery with oil, the coating of which glistened upon his skin. Simultaneously, hesitancy threatened to cripple her. More rode on this moment than simply the fulfilment of a fantasy. Would he and Ross still be smiling in the morning, or would the aftershocks put dents in their solid friendship?

"I think I was more nervous than she was."

The fantasy continued as she pictured him pressing forward, expecting resistance.

"I think she'd done it before, because I slipped inside without any trouble. Actually, I wondered if she hadn't sought us both out deliberately and that this had been what she was after from the start. Certainly, she was on fire. She pushed back onto me, impaling herself to the hilt, while I was trying to be considerate and taking it slow.

"Fucking arse is not the same as conventional sex. Don't let anyone tell you it is," he mused. "It's hotter, tighter. It's a bit more difficult to keep control, and no matter how many times you do it, there's always that little nagging voice in your head telling you it's taboo, and that you're downright dirty for even thinking about it, let alone doing it. As for doing it while another guy's already fucking her, that just about makes you Satan himself."

The slide into Kit's mindset gave Evie a curiously warm glow. Sex might make him feel guilty, but she'd swear Kit got a kick out of being bad. He wasn't exactly being good now. Spinning yarns of DP sex to your best mate's girlfriend while sitting in a derelict house wasn't your typical Saturday afternoon, after-shopping pursuit. Again, her gaze fell to his loins. Oh, boy, was he hard!

"Ross, god bless him, was whining and thrashing about. I know I was shaking. We had to fight to keep ourselves still and let her control the movement, and meanwhile, the whole experience is intense and novel in a way you can't imagine. I mean, there's this beautiful woman between us, and her arse is so sweet that I'm on a hair trigger, and every time she moves I can feel Ross's cock like it's butting up against my own. Every little jerk, every pulse, even...well, especially, when he came. In fact, that did it for me, feeling the pair of them come. Complete engine shut down. Nirvana. Absolutely fucking incredible."

Kit fell silent and for a moment, Evie patiently waited for him to continue the tale. Only when he turned his head and smiled did she realize she'd gripped his arm tight. Evie slowly uncurled her fingers. Thankfully, his jacket had protected him from nail marks.

"What happened afterwards?" she asked.

Kit shook his head. "Nothing. We hung out for a while the

following day, and then Ross and I packed up and came home."

"You never saw her again?"

"Nope."

Evie brushed down her clothing. Looking at Kit, it was easy to imagine him walking away from an encounter like that, but Ross... Her Ross wasn't the sort to get involved in trysts and walk away without carving a great big scar in his psyche. Ross, despite his brawn and largely down-to-earth character, couldn't let go of anything without mourning its passing. "It only happened that once, didn't it?"

Kit shrugged. "Whether it did or didn't isn't part of the story. If you want to know more, first you have to share. Fair's fair, Evie."

Share? "I thought we agreed this was in lieu of rent."

"Chicken."

"I've nothing to share."

"Sure you do. Everyone does." Kit leaned towards her as if to take her clasped hands, but Evie moved them out of reach. She didn't want him coaxing her, and definitely not if it involved physical contact. No, Kit, was far too dangerous to be allowed that close. She leapt off the sofa and made a performance out of checking the time. Ross would be home by now, having finished his morning surgery. Time she headed home for their typical Saturday afternoon picnic of cheese, crisps and pickles before heading over to the Boar for a few rounds and a late fish and chips supper.

"It needn't be about you and Ross. It could be you and whomever you please," Kit coaxed. "It could even be a secret fantasy. Maybe you could tell me how you discovered your fetish for watching guys jerk off."

"It's not... I don't... Much." *I walked out on you, didn't I?* Evie inwardly justified herself. Just because certain things were prone to pushing her buttons, didn't mean they were at the full on fetish stakes. "I'm going home. Ross'll be home."

"Okay," Kit said, rising. "I'll make my own way back." He

followed her into the hallway and held open the front door while she checked her pockets to make sure she had everything, including the car keys. "You still owe me a story though, Evie. I'll let you run away this time, but don't think I'll forget."

She ticked the engine key towards him. "I don't owe you anything."

He waited until she'd turned around before muttering, "Okay, we'll play dirty."

Evie whirled on the spot. She glared at him, but Kit allowed his gaze to wander to where a robin sat perched upon the sacks of rubbish. "Bye," she snapped. "Don't hurry back."

After Evie pulled out of the drive and chugged off down the lane, Kit deadlocked the front door and wandered upstairs to his old room. Barely a scrape of familiarity remained; just a few patches of wallpaper and a threadbare rug, which he lay down upon and stared up at the hole in the roof. He hadn't been entirely honest with Evie. It hadn't been about the girl at all, only ever about Ross and himself. When their eyes had met in the darkness of the tent, and they'd made that silent pact to have her together, what he'd really been thinking was what it would be like to fuck Ross. No, they hadn't touched one another except by accident on that occasion. Yes, they'd concentrated upon the woman between them, but ultimately, for him, it had been all about Ross.

Ross's hard naked body beneath him, the tickle of his hairy legs, and the scent of him that lingered long after sex. Yes, he'd seen Ross naked before that point, but he'd never seen him naked and hard, or anticipated that he'd look so goddamn magnificent.

The erection that had faded when Evie marched off stiffened again, making his trousers uncomfortably tight. Kit unzipped and wrapped his hand around his cock.

Night after night, they'd slept beside one another in their purple dome, so many nights cocooned in Ross's scent, and he'd never dared act upon his desire. The girl had made everything possible. She'd opened his eyes to the future. Images of later days scrolled across his field of vision. Erotic patterns formed in the clouds beyond the hole in the roof, and in his mind, Kit rewrote the camping trip, removing the girl from the scene. He'd forgotten her name eons back, and the remainder of her faded just as easily. Instead, he bucked into the fiery heat and tight clasping grip of Ross's arse. He held him, stroked his palms across Ross's chest, and pumped his cock until Ross rolled his eyes into his head and came in fountaining spurts over Kit's fingers.

Kit's hand stilled upon his own cock. He focused his efforts around the head, pressing gently into the sensitive spot below the eye. If only everything had gone as smoothly as his make-believe, instead of them pussyfooting around each other for eternity before making a move. That dance of denial had gone on, and on... Shit! It had to be three years.

Three years of rampant fucking denial, pretending they were just mates and nothing more. Of course, every now and then one of them would reach breaking point, and then they'd both go out and get plastered, and end up picking up some poor unsuspecting girl, and bringing her home together, and giving her the time of her life. Not one of those women ever twigged that the reason for all that lavish attention was so he and Ross could vicariously fuck one another, because neither of them had the guts to act upon their feelings. Too afraid of having read things wrong and destroying their friendship. Too scared of being punched in the face.

At least he hadn't wasted time worrying over being gay. Kit knew sexuality wasn't as simple or fixed as that. He knew he could get off looking at another guy's cock, just as easily as he could staring at a pair of tits. Hell, once the whole deal with Ross had blown up, he'd even gone out experimenting. He'd sucked cock and wanked a few guys. Then, when out of the blue everything suddenly fell into place with Ross, it'd promptly fallen apart in a way that hadn't just spoiled their friendship.

It'd kept them apart for six bloody years, on opposite sides of the globe.

Japan had seemed so easy. No connections, nothing familiar. No strings and easy peasy money. Kit hadn't set out to become a host. He hadn't set out with any idea at all other than leaving Kirkley far behind. He'd walked into the airport that day with a suitcase and a credit card, and ended up in a *ryokan* in Tokyo. There he'd met Tsuyoshi, who'd taken him to Cloud One the following evening and found him a job. He'd spent most of the first eighteen months of being a host steaming drunk. He'd blamed the job, but really that was an excuse and a nice easy way to blot out the memories of home. Then one evening he'd woken up and realized he'd be dead within another few years if he didn't start looking after himself. He cut his alcohol consumption down to a reasonable level and learned how to pour drinks sober. The thing with being sober was that he could actually do his job better. The ladies liked him. He started getting laid again, not always in circumstances of his choosing, but he never let himself get too heavily swayed by the size of anyone's purse. He built himself an easy life. No strings, no hassle... No love. Right until the grenade had landed—Flora's death. A summons quickly followed, and he'd come back. But the darkness he'd flown remained. Boy did it remain, and sooner or later it'd all come tumbling out for Evie's benefit, because people never could resist a scandal, or sticking their noses in.

Kit let go of his cock, his erection gone. He didn't know what he was doing here, but now that he was here, he couldn't leave. This time he'd have to weather the inevitable storm. He'd been in Kirkley twenty-four hours; likely, word of his presence had already been passed along.

Not that it mattered since he had only one single-minded goal—to get himself comfortably settled with the girl and guy of his dreams and spend a hell of a lot of time screwing them.

Chapter Four

"What time did he say he'd be back?" Ross asked, looking up from the remains of his recently demolished baguette. He dripped his finger in the remaining crumbs and held it aloft.

"He didn't." Evie leaned over his shoulder and sucked his finger into her mouth. She released it with a pop, cleaned, a moment later. "How come you took Whiskers with you this morning? I had no one to cuddle."

"Whiskers? Evie, you can't name her after a brand of cat food." He glanced towards the kitten, still curled up inside the cat box. "I did mention that she still needed a few more shots and I had Iris to appease."

"Fine, I'll think of something else," she huffed, leaving the table in order to scoop up the sleeping kitten.

Ross scraped his chair back, following her route with his gaze. "I'm sure Kit would have given you a hug if you'd asked."

Evie eyed Ross curiously. He'd pulled his mouth into a somewhat sour expression with his tongue pressed to his teeth. "And why would I want to hug Kit?" The question restored his grin.

"I never said that you wanted to, only that he was available."

So, he did realize his mate was more of an enticement to sin than was wise to leave alone with your girlfriend. Well, assuming said girlfriend had no willpower, which, of course, she did. Although, Kit hadn't really tried anything on, he'd just told her a story—an undoubtedly fictitious story.

Aware that Ross's attention hadn't waned, Evie concentrated on the kitten, afraid that her expression would reveal her inner turmoil. The panther and the pussycat, she thought. They'd both arrived on the same night, and both tugged at her heartstrings, if in entirely different ways. At least the furry addition to the family didn't leave her heart pounding with turmoil every time they touched. She'd been buzzing from the contact with Kit ever since she left Rose Cottage, her mind still burning with his tale. What had he been trying to achieve with that story? She certainly couldn't look at Ross in quite the same way, even if she had decided it was pure invention. Maybe that had been Kit's purpose.

"Something on your mind?" Ross asked. He wrapped his arms around her waist and nuzzled the back of her neck.

"Nah, no, it's nothing."

"Good." He squeezed her shoulder. "As long as you've forgiven me for last night."

Last night! She'd never ever forgive him for bringing Kit home, or for not mentioning that they were being spied upon during sex, although she might be appeased. She smiled winningly at Ross, hoping he'd get the message that after her fraught morning with the nefarious Mr. Scrumptious, she needed a good workout.

"Hey, I'm gonna get changed. Back in a few," Ross said, squashing her fantasy of them getting frisky against the side of the fridge.

Evie listened to the thump of his shoes on the stairs. A few minutes later, he thundered down again, and went out of the front door. Surprised, she strolled into the living room intent upon the window. Halfway there, the phone rang, startling the kitten, who began to squirm. "Hello," she muttered into the mouthpiece, still juggling the yowling fur ball.

"Ah, good afternoon, Ms. Latham." Ross's voice echoed down the line, presumably from his mobile, or else he'd nipped across the green to the call box. "This is *Rent a Fantasy* calling to let you know that your order is just five minutes away." The emphasis on certain words made him sound like a cross between a double-glazing salesman and a cheesy game-show host.

"My what?" She laughed into the receiver. Phone wedged between her shoulder and ear, and now trying to extract the kitten's claws from her shoulder, Evie tweaked back the curtain, but couldn't see any sign of Ross.

"Oh, I am sorry, madam." Ross's voice lost its screech of excitement and turned butler serious. "Do you mean to say you didn't order your free trial from this month's catalogue of mouth-watering man whores?"

"Man whats?"

"Whores, madam. Mouth-watering man whores. They're on special at the moment."

Determined to find out exactly what Ross was up to, Evie returned to the kitchen and dropped the kitten into her box, before checking out of that window too. Ross stood at the bottom of the garden, huddled between their decrepit shed and the line of Norwegian Spruces. He appeared to be wearing his favourite pinstriped business suit.

"Well," she hedged. Maybe he had something better than a kitchen quickie in mind. "Now that I think about it that does sound familiar. Perhaps if you reminded me of the order."

"One man-whore, required for subjugation, extreme tongue gymnastics and repetitive solitary stimulation. Intercourse, verbal and otherwise, optional, but not required." He sounded as if he were reading off a sheet. "You did request an outdoor location, but I'm afraid we only do home visits with our free samples."

Laughing now, Evie opened the back door and made her way down the steps into the garden. "You know, I think I see him coming."

"Oh, no," he assured her. "He'd never do that without your

express permission."

"Ross." She tapped him on the shoulder.

"Evie, you're supposed to stay inside." He hung up and pushed the mobile into his back pocket. "Honestly, woman."

"Shh!" She slid her hand inside his jacket and up around the collar of his shirt, before teasing him with a gentle kiss.

"Evie."

Evie grabbed him by the tie and walked him back towards the house, already planning out what to do to him. That tie would be coming off first and going back on around his wrists. She'd keep his belt fastened and just undo his fly to get out his cock, so she could see how aroused he got from licking her.

She saw Kit's feet first, sporting a pair of black leather winklepickers. He stood at her eye-level at the top of the back door steps, holding the cat. "Both doors are open," he said, his brow crumpled. "Are they supposed to be?" Then quickly followed with, "Oops, sorry! Guess my timing's a bit off again," when he caught sight of Ross. "Maybe I'll just go make myself scarce in the shed, or my room, or something."

"Forget it," Evie snapped, unable to prevent her annoyance from permeating her voice. Sex was off the menu while Kit was in the house. It didn't matter if he wasn't standing over them, he'd still be listening, and he'd still be aware of what they were up to. For a fleeting moment she pictured him on the narrow single bed in the guest room, his leather trousers pushed down and his cock thick in his hand. She wasn't making love to Ross with that image in her head.

"Evie," Ross protested when she let go of his tie.

"It'll save." She gave him a second, sloppier kiss and patted his bum. "Why don't you two go over to the pub and play catch up for awhile." She stormed inside before either of them had the chance to argue.

Damn Kit! Damn him to the infernal pits of hell.

Ross gaped at the toes of Kit's shoes for several minutes

before closing his mouth. Trying to explain why the White Boar on a Saturday afternoon possibly wasn't the best place for him and Kit to be seen would only provoke questions on a topic he had no wish to discuss. "You know your timing sucks. But then, it always did," he said.

Kit glanced sheepishly at him and responded with a meek nod. Ross wasn't fooled.

"You know my spidey sense tingles whenever you get your cock out," Kit joked a minute later as they strode across the green, having first shooed the mewling kitten back into the house.

"Shame you take no notice of it, then."

"Unfortunately, it only works over short distances, and you know I hate to miss out on seeing you in action."

"Back off, Kit," Ross hissed, picking up the pace. The burning prickle of high emotion trickled down his spine and through his nose, making him sneeze. It was crazy how his world could be so ordinary one day and topsy-turvy the next. He wanted to throw his arms around Kit and cling onto him, and at the same time longed to punch him in the guts for all the anguish he'd caused. Of course, he did neither. Although, maybe a muddy wrestle on the green would've diffused some of the rattling tension between them. Problem was, it'd probably turn into the foreplay of a bloody good shag, and that was somewhere they weren't going, especially not with half the village likely to turn up to spectate, Evie included.

"I don't suppose it's changed in here," Kit remarked, pushing open the barroom door.

Ross shook his head. As typical for a Saturday afternoon, the bar smelled of stale beer and wood smoke from the fire in the snug. A group of men were leaning over the pool table, while another set engaged in darts. Footie filled the huge screen along the back wall, and the sounds of the match boomed over the gaggle of voices. Having sidled in expecting the room to fall silent due to Kit's presence, Ross looked around, momentarily bewildered by the lack of response.

"Let's head into the lounge. We'll at least be able to hear ourselves in there," Ross muttered, before leading the way.

Pints procured, they settled at a table by the window. Kit doodled an obscene drawing in the dust on the window ledge, then scrubbed it out when a couple came in with their kids. The difficulty seemed to be in knowing where to start. In the end they mulled over Kit's experiences in Japan and his plans for Rose Cottage, all of which hinged on Kit being mobile, since he planned on doing a lot of the work himself. "There's a big car second-hand dealership out towards Harrogate," Ross said. "We could all go over there tomorrow and see if we can pick something up."

"Is that you, Christopher Skye?" The interruption turned both their heads. Expecting trouble, relief washed through Ross's chest like the first rush of desire when he recognized the old lady hobbling towards them. Her young companion remained by the bar, in embarrassed shock. "It is you, isn't it? Good grief, you need a haircut. Can't see your eyes behind that overgrown frippery."

Kit slid off his chair and stood to greet her. "Yes, Doris. It's me. It's good to see you."

"Hm, well I can't imagine why you'd think that. I seem to recall you scampering off as fast as you could in the past, afraid an old lady might hamper your style. Laura's just the same. She only brings me over here because her mum twists her arm. Amazing what the young folks will do for twenty quid. My great-granddaughter, Laura." She nodded towards the girl at the bar, who winced and dipped her head to concentrate on sucking up the Technicolor fruit and vodka drink she had sat before her, clearly embarrassed at having been caught checking them out.

"Don't you even think about it, my girl. He's far too old for you," Doris bellowed, at which the girl slunk off towards the toilets. In all fairness, Ross could see why she had to be bribed into playing escort. "We don't normally do Saturdays. Sunday's our day," Doris continued, in a hideously loud whisper. "But the boyfriend stood her up. Complete waste of space he is."

Expecting a full blown account of poor Laura's unfortunate choice of companion, Doris's next knocked him for six.

"I didn't think we'd see you back here." Her wizened face fastened intently upon Kit's face. "Flora always believed. It's why she told the cat's home to F off. Wiltshaw kept pestering her for money. He told her that if you had any sense you'd stay in whatever hellhole you'd found yourself in, and Kirkley would be all the better for it. Well, of course, Flora didn't like that one bit."

Nor it seemed did Kit. His smile wavered.

"I stayed with her to the end," Doris continued, oblivious to the strain slowly colouring Kit's face. "Flora was ever so upset you didn't come, but I don't think she'd have recognized you anyway. Poor thing had quite forgotten you'd all grown up. Kept telling us all that you only ever stayed for the summers and that you were with your parents. She kept calling my Laura 'Sammie'."

Ross heard the air stall in Kit's throat. He didn't realize the remark had much the same effect on himself until his lungs began to scream in protest. They inhaled in unison, two volubly loud breaths. Several heads craned in their direction. That was it; within minutes the whole village would know that Kit had returned, assuming they didn't already. Laura still hadn't returned from the toilets. Ross had a sneaking suspicion she was in there texting her mates.

Kit pulled on his jacket. "It's been lovely seeing you again, Doris." He cut her off mid flow and gave her a peck on the cheek. "Ross and I are off now. Things to do, places to be."

"Tea," she blurted, her eyes as sharp as a hawk's. "You must come round, both of you. I still like to have my Thursdays. And Ross, you must bring that lady of yours with you. She's such a dear. Everyone at the big house says how smashing she is. We're all looking forward to the wedding. You're not going to have one of those horrid registry affairs, are you?"

"I'll mention the tea," Ross muttered. Kit's hand locked around his wrist. They didn't speak until they were back outside and several hundred yards from the pub.

"Wedding? Have you got plans you aren't telling me about?" Kit remarked as they strutted across the icy green towards the Post Office cum shop. Years of old habits swung them away from home and in the direction of their old hunting ground out by the ruins.

"Of course not. Although, even if I did I don't see how it'd be any of your business. Whatever you think is going to happen between us, forget it. What you started six years ago, ended then too. You can't walk in and out of people's lives like that and expect everything to fall into place the way you want it."

They paused at they end of the verge and waited for the car approaching to pass. "You have no idea what I want."

"I wouldn't lay money on that."

Having passed them, the car swerved ninety degrees and mounted the curb. Seconds later a crumpled can sailed towards them, founting dregs of lager. It landed woefully short of their position and rolled into the gutter. "Fuck off, Skye. You fucking murdering bastard. You're not welcome here," yelled a duo of voices from within the car.

Kit turned his back on them and started walking back towards the house with his head bent low and his hands stuffed deep into his pockets.

And so it begins, thought Ross as he jogged to catch Kit up. "You all right?"

Although paled by the experience, Kit nodded his head. "Name calling I can weather. It's no more than I expected and no worse than I got every summer I spent here. The local boys never liked me on their turf."

"That's because you nabbed all the girlies." Kit, who haled from beyond Kirkley and its adjacent parishes had, even at the age of fourteen, seemed like an exotic creature from another planet. Ross recalled how his friend's arrival in the village each summer would cause a wave of gossip and an upsurge in the sale of mascara. The intrigue over whom Kit had been with, or had even just been seen talking to would last them all summer. The older Kit grew, the more intensely the hearsay raged. There'd been too many people around with already sharpened staves when the news about Sammie had spread.

"I don't want to discuss it. I don't need to go over it," Kit growled. He kicked open the front gate and barged through. Ross allowed the wrought iron to bang a few times before he followed.

"I've not told Evie," Ross said when he joined Kit by the front door.

"What's there to tell? Nothing happened, Ross, we both know that."

"Yes." More doubt filled his voice than he'd intended. It didn't matter how determinedly Kit tried to brush things off, the past had a way of sneaking up on you, and deliberately hiding it from Evie, when no doubt the whole village would be talking about it within a few days just smacked of guilt. Not that he believed for a second that Kit was guilty.

Evie opened the front door while both he and Kit were fumbling for keys. "You're back quick. Thought you'd be hours. You haven't run out of things to say already, have you?."

"It was just a bit busy," Ross mumbled. He inwardly cursed himself for the lie. Kit offered him a wary smile. "Besides, we can open some wine and spend the evening together."

"A great idea," seconded Kit. He made himself comfortable on the nearby sofa, whereupon, Evie's kitten leapt upon his lap. Kit shooed it away. Ross ruefully found a space on the floor and set about stoking some life into the fire. If they were planning on settling in for the night, they may as well get comfortable. Evie produced wine, chips and dips a moment later, and they fell into a discussion on films. Consequently, despite all his mutterings about keeping things from Evie, Ross pushed the episodes in and outside of the pub, and Kit's past, to the back of his mind.

Afternoon extended into evening, the night descending over Kirkley like a thick, swaddling fog. Kit took charge of the kitchen, leaving Evie and Ross to fight it out for the TV remote. For the second night running, food, alcohol and candlelight smoothed the irritation Evie felt at Kit's presence. If he'd been vexingly flirtatious and charming this morning, by night Kit transformed into a beguiling angel. Candlelight softened his sharp features and made his already deep, dark eyes shine like rain-washed slate. He didn't touch her, his body language towards her was no different to that with Ross, and yet he managed to imply everything and nothing with a few choice words and his glittering gaze. Just the way his words curled around his tongue as he spoke left her feeling wet, so much so, that when she finally fell into bed with Ross, the urgent quickie they shared barely quelled her feelings of rampant lust.

"Evie... Evie..." The sound of her name being called seemed to echo into her dreams, where a strange conglomerate of Ross and Kit had transformed the bottom of the garden into a hermitage with internet access, from which he liked to record podcasts on the nations favourite sexual fantasies, peeping through windows being his personal favourite. He'd stare though various upstairs windows in the village and phone her up to describe the lewd goings on inside, until one or both of them ended up unbearably aroused and desperate to shag. Then only in the absolute dead of night would he come to her as an elusive incubus.

Evie stirred, hot and parched, arousal stripping her body. Vision still hazy with sleep, she rolled onto her back. A streak of light streamed around the edge of the bedroom door. Kit must have left the landing light on when he'd followed them upstairs to bed, and then she guessed the cat had found her way upstairs and nudged the door open. Evie tensed, anticipating an imminent dip in the bed and the delicate press of paws upon her body as the little kitten sought out the ideal spot. Instead, something weightier settled upon her ankles. Groggily, she peered at the foot of the bed. Kit gazed back at her. The pale outline of his body shone with lamp begotten hues—shades of orange, brown and bronze.

"What is it?" she asked, aware that beyond the solid composition of the bed and its tactile reality, the room was drawn with hazy strokes.

Kit didn't answer. Instead, he lifted the foot of the duvet and dipped his head below the cover.

"Kit?"

His hot hand settled upon her shin and slid upwards to her knee. Evie squeaked in alarm. She clamped her legs together tight, even as she felt herself grow moist. Tension screamed within her muscles as Kit's hand moved higher to caress her inner thigh. He ducked under the duvet and crawled over her, until he covered her like a second blanket, bare skin gliding against bare skin as he settled into position. His thighs pressed to her thighs, hips aligned like two neatly stacked blocks. A scream echoed inside her chest, but when she opened her mouth all that emerged was an excited gasp.

Ross lay snuggled up beside her, his breathing even and content, undisturbed by the rustling of the duvet or the significant tilt of the mattress. Kit couldn't be doing this. And she couldn't be excited by just how incredibly wrong and yet right it all felt. *It's a dream. Had to be.* She hardly dared to open her eyes and meet the inky depths of Kit's pupils. His weight above her felt real. The hot brand of his cock against her thigh more so. Kit clasped her wrists and lifted them over her head.

"Open your eyes, Evie."

"No. This isn't real." The words resonated inside her head.

"It's real. Say the word, Evie and I'll give you what you've been thinking about all day."

Pinned, by both his body and his words, Evie kept absolutely still. She had thought of him. Not willingly, but her mind had wandered. Snapshots of him in sultry repose masturbating in the spare room, and of him and Ross in the tent with the girl had troubled her ever since she'd left Rose Cottage that morning.

"He won't wake, Evie," Kit coaxed, his voice whisper soft against her ear.

"We can't. We can't do this," she protested. Fear coupled with anticipation roused every nerve in her body as her denial rang hollow. The tiniest shift in his position sent shivers chasing across her skin. Moisture bathed her skin, and between her thighs the lips of her vulva plumped, ready for his assault. The mere thought of him sliding his cock home only further opened her up to him, and another gush of moisture bathed her opening. Her hips lifted in urgent need, so that his erection nudged between her labia.

"Oh, god! We can't." She glanced warily at Ross again, so blissfully unaware of her duplicity. Everything. Absolutely everything about this moment was wrong. Dreadfully, horribly wrong. If Ross woke now, the hurt and betrayal he'd feel would crush any spark of love he bore for her completely. Kit surely wasn't worth that. So why did she feel so excited by his presence?

His cock pressed tight to her cunt, rubbing against her in an alluring simulation of sex. Not entering her, and not directly stimulating her clit, but arousing her all the same. "Say the word, Evie, and I'm all yours."

"He'll be so hurt."

So why did she feel so excited? Why instead of screaming and fighting Kit off with every available object was she raising her hips in time with the roll of his body? She looked up into his eyes and caught only a glimpse of darkness before a kiss swallowed her remaining whimper of denial. The truth, despite how she felt about Ross, she wanted Kit exactly where he was: poised to enter her, on the verge of fucking her into oblivion.

His tongue traced one puckered nipple, setting her

squirming again. Three fingers struck gold between her legs, pushing into her with embarrassing ease. She was so wet and eager, his fingers met with no resistance and she cried out when he withdrew them. The cry transformed into a whimper as his cock replaced the digits, and their bodies slammed together.

So hot. Too hot.

Evie wanted to squeal. She had to bite down on her tongue to stop herself from screaming out his name. Countless emotions ricocheted inside her head, but she kept all the accompanying sounds she wanted to make locked up tight inside her. Only when he touched her clit as he fucked her with perfect ease did a hiss escape through her teeth. She gripped Kit's bottom hard, digging in her fingertips until he slowed the rhythm of their loving. Then they rocked, so, so, smoothly, gliding, while staying absolutely silent.

It couldn't last. It didn't last.

Slowly, steadily the tempo built again, until the headboard thudded against the wall and Ross stirred beside them, rolling over to paw at her shoulder. "Hush, you're dreaming. Hush, Evie. It's okay. Wake up."

The weight of Kit's body still pressed down upon her. Evie tentatively opened her eyes to find Ross staring at her, not in open-mouthed disgust, but in concern. "You all right?" he asked.

"Huh!" she choked. She pulled her arms down from above her head, where she had them wedged under the bottom of the headboard and patted the duvet, still curiously aware of the fading heat of Kit's presence. "You were dreaming, Evie. I'm not sure if it was good or bad. You were moaning quite a bit and thrashing about."

The lingering trace of Kit's cologne clung to the sheets and her skin. He hadn't been here. It had been just a dream.

"Want to tell me about it?"

"No." She blinked a few times trying to wake up. "No, it was nothing. Bad dream."

"Sure you don't need a hug?" He cast his arm over her stomach and snuggled up, placing a kiss upon her shoulder.

"Kit," she said sleepily. "He didn't actually work in a bar, did he?"

"Didn't you ask him?"

"'Course. He didn't really answer."

She sensed Ross's smile. He continued to nibble at her skin, his lips moving up towards the sensitive skin of her neck. "He worked as a host, Evie."

Suddenly, she was awake. Wide-awake. "You mean like a gigolo?"

"Not exactly. No. Leastways, I haven't asked if he had sex for money. He entertained women in the bar, talked shop and relationships and poured drinks for them. If it went beyond that...well...let's just say it wouldn't surprise me." Ross fell silent.

"It isn't important," Evie provided. Whatever Kit had done in his past didn't affect them now. It sure explained a lot about him though. Like why he'd seemed so at ease with her watching him.

Ross rolled onto his back again and his jaw stretched into a yawn. "Knackered," he mumbled.

"Ross. One other thing, did you ever have a threesome involving Kit?"

The tense jerk of his shoulders answered the question more succinctly than any amount of words. "What has he been telling you?"

"All your dirty secrets, I guess. It's true, then?"

Propped on one elbow, Ross met her gaze. He chewed his lip a moment and his brows furrowed. "I'm not sure I'd call it a threesome as such. That kind of implies we all got it on." His frown deepened. "It just happened sometimes. Kit and I were mates. Sometimes we shared the same girl."

"You mean it happened more than once?"

Ross shiftily glanced at the headboard. "Yeah. More than

once. Jeezus, what the hell have you two been talking about to bring that up anyway? I thought you went grocery shopping."

"We did." Evie sucked her tongue as jealousy stirred inside her stomach again, despite her best efforts to quell such nonsense. What Ross had done before they met hardly mattered and had no bearing on the present. Besides, she wasn't sure what about it rattled her so much. The fact that he'd obviously liked threesomes, that he'd engaged in them with Kit, or hadn't engaged in one with her. "Ever have one that didn't involve Kit?"

"No."

She nearly pressed to see if he was up for involving her. They could creep into Kit's room right now and pin him down on the narrow bed. Then maybe she could straddle him, while Ross watched, although the thought of being watched still unnerved her. Still, the notion of sharing brought back her earlier conversation with Kit, tucked up together on the sofa at Rose Cottage. Nothing he'd said then had been straightforward. There'd been a stonking great subtext to it from the outset. Kit had deliberately flirted with her, and given himself a hard on like a blooming torpedo. Far from sharing a few memories, he'd deliberately opened up a can of worms.

"You know you're really hot," Ross remarked as his lips continued to skim over the pulse point in her neck. His hand drifted down over her stomach and slipped between her thighs to find her dripping wet. "Oh, that sort of dream was it?" He laughed. "Am I not giving you enough?" He rolled onto his back, pulling her on top, so she straddled his thighs.

"I thought you were knackered."

"Only certain bits of me. My elbow." He pointed and she bestowed a kiss there. "My right knee." Another kiss, though that one involved some wriggling. "My nose, my left nipple."

"Let me guess, your cock?"

Laughter rumbled through his chest again. "No, I think that bit's definitely wide awake."

"Then we'd best make sure he stays that way." She closed

her mouth over the head of his erection.

"Oh, god, Evie. You have the mouth of a fucking angel." And he lapsed into a string of sighs.

That's right Ross. Drive away the images of the past by fucking me. He did taste good. The sexual tension remaining from her dream tingled with renewed interest. She left off sucking just as soon as Ross was really hard and meandered up his body until their lips met and their bodies joined.

Still, no matter how hard she rode him, or how powerfully he thrust into her, she never quite dislodged the impish version of Kit sitting on her shoulder.

"Shit!" she cursed as she came, wondering if even now, Kit was lying in bed listening to them and driving his cock through the ring of his fingers.

Chapter Five

The weekend soon passed, Sunday bleeding into Monday and so on. Both Ross and Evie fell into their normal patterns of work and play, while Kit made a start on transforming Rose Cottage. By Friday, he'd started disappearing before dawn and not returning until late in the evening. "Keeping busy and keeping out of the way," he'd told Ross that morning when he'd challenged Kit on the front drive before they went their separate ways. "Figure I came on a bit strong and rattled Evie's cage, so I'm downplaying my presence." Although Ross had accepted the explanation, he suspected there was more to Kit's prolonged absences than lulling Evie into a false sense of security. More likely, he'd been holing himself up in the cottage hoping the village wouldn't notice him. Curiously, the ploy appeared to be working. Despite Doris's less than subtle greeting in the pub, no one else had commented on his friend's return.

A knock on the surgery door disturbed his thoughts. "Are you free? Oh, yes, you're free. Wonderful." The owner of the chirpy voice waddled into the surgery, arm aloft, trailing a small dog on a lead.

"Nice to see you again, Mrs. Hawes, and Hamish, of course. What can I do for you today?"

"Just his nails, please, Ross. I know I could get Margery to do it in her mobile unit, but between you and me, I'm not so sure she does quite as good a job."

"Nails, right," said Ross, his head going down as he looked

around for the clippers. Scratch the lack of gossip. There was one reason behind this impromptu pet pedicure and one only. Sheila Hawes relished gossip in much the same way other folks loved chocolate, and was never more satisfied than when presented with a nice juicy morsel. The bigger the scandal, the greater the delight in her beetle-black eyes, and the more stops on her busy social calendar.

"I saw Doris yesterday. Went to her knitting circle, not that she knits much now with her arthritis crippling her joints, but she does still like to chat."

Yes, here it was, thought Ross. Wait for it... Wait for it.

"She said she'd run into you in the Boar. Think Doris half thought you might show up and surprise us all. Silly bleeder," she added with a cackle.

"Surgery," muttered Ross. He found just the implication of a sick animal on the operating table generally derailed too much digging into his actual doings and whereabouts. Folks didn't like to think too hard about sick pets, and he didn't like to tax himself too hard with the village's peculiar brand of social chess. "Afternoons are never a good time. We've been booked up pretty solid all week."

"I suppose it's the season. Cold affects the poor mites, same as it does us. You wouldn't believe how much my joints ache first thing."

"Bitterly cold this morning," he said, hoping to further sidetrack her digging long enough to finish off Hamish's nails, so he could shoo her out before she got her teeth into anything meaty. As it was the cry of a distinctive baritone proved to be a far more diverting distraction that grilling him.

"Is that... Is that him?" she cried. Her beady eyes lit with excitement.

"Who?"

"Is he here? In the surgery!"

"I'm sure I don't know who you're talking about."

"Don't mock me, Ross Hatton. That fiend you call a friend.

Christopher Skye."

Denying Kit's presence seemed rather pointless since he could clearly hear Kit shouting his name. A devil of a ruckus seemed to have begun in the waiting room. Mrs. Hawes began waggling her finger at him, but Ross released the now yapping Hamish into her arms and swiftly opened the door.

"Well, how rude…" Her words faded as Iris ushered Kit through the open doorway, with a tea towel clamped to his head.

Time froze and then split apart. Ross's heart clenched tight at the sight of his friend's ashen face. Blood coated the cuff of his jacket and had already seeped through the Working Dogs of Great Britain tea towel, turning the Border collie ox-brown. Iris bundled Kit into a seat and nudged the wide-eyed, slack-jawed Mrs. Hawes out of the door, shutting it firmly behind them.

"Lock it." Kit's words burst from his mouth as a snarl. Unquestioningly, Ross turned the bolt.

"What in god's name happened? Kit!"

Kit pulled the cloth away from his face, causing a trickle of blood to roll down the side of his face and drip into the open neck of his jacket. "Get this off me." He switched hands and pressed the cloth back to his brow before shaking his left arm so that his hand disappeared inside the sleeve. Ross grasped the soiled cuff and pulled. Beneath the jacket Kit wore a soot-black T-shirt, the collar of which was slashed open on the same side as his wound.

"Who did this? Jesus, we need to get you to A&E."

"I'm not going. I've already had that out with Iris."

"Is that what the shouting was about?"

"That and she said I was upsetting the animals."

Pleased to find Kit his normal argumentative and masochistic self, Ross slapped him across the back. "Let me." He poked tentatively at the cloth. The blood flow seemed to be slowing. The gash itself lay straight across the top of Kit's eyebrow, virtually parallel to the silvered remains of a previous wound. It was straight and a good few centimetres long. "Come on, I'll drive you."

"I'm not going."

"What, you're just going to sit there? It'll leave a bloody enormous scar."

"It will anyway."

"It needs stitching," he snapped back. Of all the crazy stunts he'd known Kit to pull, this had to be the most stupid and annoying. "Hospital. Police station. In that order." He wasn't being fobbed off over this. They could tell Evie later that he'd whipped himself with a yard of electricity cable to stop her worrying, meanwhile the bastard who was actually responsible wasn't getting away with it.

"No." Two big unblinking, dark eyes bored into him. Hell, the heat in that gaze. It was as if he were being sucked in, tempted, offered hell knows what if he'd just back down.

"You're not—" He meant to say *pulling your Mephistopheles act on me today*, but the hot sparks had already started running up and down his neck, making the underside of his chin prickle. Kit was far too accustomed to being in control and manipulating moods to suit his purpose. Though how he could turn on the old sexual fire while sporting a head wound was utterly perplexing.

"You fix it." Kit's voice dropped to a husky whisper as he made the suggestion. For a moment, it even sounded reasonable. More than that, it felt like a blooming caress. Ross pulled back. He let the reality of their location sink in, cut Kit out of the picture and acknowledged the turmoil still raging in the waiting room. Snatches of the speculative conversation leeched through the walls, Mrs. Hawes loudest of all.

"Shit in hell, Kit!" Ross swore, snapping back to reality. "I'm a vet not a fucking doctor. Who was it? Tony? One of the Bryant boys?"

"Didn't see," he said, succumbing to an obvious snit. "If you won't do it, give me some glue and I'll fix it myself. You know that's all they're going to do at A&E."

Ross got right up close and growled in his face. "I'll do it, if you report it."

"It's not happening, Ross. It wouldn't do any good anyway. Probably just make things worse." Kit gave him an angry grin and kissed him, the shock of which sent Ross scuttling away again, so that he backed into the examination table. "Shit!" He rubbed frantically at his violated lips. "Shit! Don't do that."

Kit rose somewhat shakily and took a step forward, his intent written clear in his expression. Hot sparks flared within the depths of his eyes. The slender high curve of his cheekbones along with those sexy hooded eyes and the streaks of blood across his cheek made him a hundred percent drop-dead irresistible.

"Shit!" Ross snarled again. He half turned, not taking his eyes off Kit and tugged a pair of latex gloves out of box. "I'll do it, all right, I'll do it."

Kit shrugged and sagged back into the chair. He pulled his hair back off his forehead and waited patiently as Ross cleaned up the wound and applied a layer of Vetbond. "Don't come crying to me when it starts itching like hell, okay."

"Whatever you say, honey." Kit released his hair so that it flopped back over his forehead and shrouded his eyes. He leaned into Ross, pressing his face to the hard plane of his stomach. "Mind if I engage in a sniffle or two now? It bloody hurts."

It wasn't quite so easy to shrug away the intimacy when he put it like that. Ross cupped the back of Kit's head and tried not to react to the rasp of Kit's breath against his stomach. "Really, Kit, who was it? What happened?"

Kit simply pressed his face more firmly to Ross's stomach. He wound his arms around Ross's hips and squeezed him tight. Next minute he was kneading Ross's arse and his lips were drawing shifting circles across Ross's abs.

Ross stopped stroking his hair and tried to back step, but

Kit clung on tight. He should have known this was coming from his experiences of old. Kit only had one avenue of expression—sex. It didn't matter if he was miserable, in pain or delirious, everything sparked the same reaction. "Kit." Ross wedged a hand between them and pushed. "I'm at work. We can't do this."

What he should have said was, "I'm not ever doing this". He wasn't. He had Evie. His relationship with Kit was remaining completely platonic. Unfortunately, his body didn't agree with his brain. Just as they had that first night in the kitchen, Ross's senses reeled and reared. His loins grew heavy and arousal danced up and down the length of his stiffening cock.

"No one's going to come in," Kit coaxed as he mouthed along the obvious swell in Ross's trousers. "You've already bolted the door and I need the comfort."

Comfort! He needed a lesson in propriety. Hadn't this sort of behaviour led to all the trouble six years back? "You need to get a grip."

"Excellent suggestion." He pressed a hand between Ross's legs and cupped his balls. Ross's cock jerked and swelled, and Kit mouthed the very tip of it through the trouser fabric.

"I've appointments, Kit."

The plea fell on deaf ears. Kit's lips continued to move. His hand gently squeezed, causing shivers to run from the base of Ross's spine down to his toes and then shoot right up his spine. Blood began to pool in his groin. His cock stiffened seeking further stimulation.

"Kit!"

"It's fine, Ross. I'll make you feel better. I know you were worried." Kit's nimble fingers worked open the belt. He gently peeled back Ross's underwear and sucked the tip of his cock.

It didn't matter how many times Ross said no, that intimate kiss bulldozed aside his reservations. Kit had the skills of a whore, only with more passion and extra guilt. Ross clung to him, guiding Kit's head, as his hips picked up the rhythm.

"Fuck, this is wrong. Oh, that's good, oh, so good." Evie would kill him. She'd wrap her fingers around his throat and throttle him. Even that thought didn't stop the explosion of lust in his guts.

"Oh, Kit," he sighed, lacing his fingers through the other man's dark hair. Why wasn't anything simple? The truth was, he did still want this. Their one brief time together in the past had been just that, too brief. They hadn't had time to explore more than the basics. There'd been so much more he'd had planned out for them, when it'd all been cut so tragically short. He loved Evie. Loved her to bits, in fact, but this was different, separate to that. Fucking Kit was different, but perhaps not worth the risk of sacrificing something equally precious, especially when Kit could take off again at any moment. A flight back to Japan had to look more appealing than whatever had gone on this morning. Superglue aside, that cut was nasty.

"Stop it!" He pushed at Kit's shoulder again. He needed to get a hold of himself. He wasn't some randy irresponsible boy anymore. "Stop it! I don't want an affair, Kit." The force behind the push was enough to persuade Kit to release him. Ross zipped his fly before Kit launched another attack. "We can talk things over later, but we're not falling into this. I know you're hurt, but…"

Kit continued to gaze up at him from his knees, while sucking his thumbnail. He rose, looked as if he were about to say something, then retreated and undid the bolt on the door.

"Where are you going?" Guilt pangs tightened the muscles in Ross's chest, making it hard to breathe without sounding as if he'd just run a four-minute mile. "I mean—maybe you shouldn't go back to the cottage just yet. Not alone. You're supposed to stay with somebody after a head injury."

"Are you suggesting I sit in on your dog grooming?"

"I'm not sure that'd work."

"It definitely wouldn't work."

Genuinely concerned, Ross reached out a hand to stop

him.

Kit blinked ever so slowly at the gentle pull upon his wrist, then the corners of his lips turned up and the inky depths of his eyes lit with mischievous sparkles. "Maybe I'll stop by and take Evie out for lunch."

The words were barely out before Ross's heart thudded hard against his chest. Jealousy curled his lip, but he forced himself to be calm and rational. Kit knew how to play him, and that's all he was doing. He wouldn't follow through with his implied wickedness, and Evie wouldn't stand for his nonsense anyway. There was nothing to fear, despite the rapid pitter-patter of his pulse.

"There's not a problem with that, is there?"

"No." Ross spoke too fast. "I'm sure she'll be delighted. She commented last night that you hadn't been around much for her to get to know you."

Kit's malevolent smile broadened. "Then I'll be sure to spill all my dirtiest deeds and yours too. All except the one about us, of course. Whereabouts up at the big house is she?"

"Um, Fridays she's normally in the tearoom."

"Wonderful. I could do with a cupper."

"Don't do anything stupid, Kit."

"You mean stupider than I have already."

"Don't—"

"Like falling in love with you?" Kit said, cutting Ross off.

Ross's mouth dropped open. He closed it, only for it to fall open again. "You're not."

Kit looked him right in the eyes and let his expression convey his emotions. Not simple desire, but whole-sale longing, of the type that bordered on full scale obsession. Ross found it hard to look at him and keep a neutral visage. Fuck! Kit had been pushing for picking things up from where they'd left off, but he'd never realized his feelings ran that deep.

Sweat began to pepper his brow, his temperature spiralling out of control more fiercely now than it had while Kit had been sucking him.

Maybe, he had known it all along, but confronting that sort of thing head on—Fuck, he didn't know what to say. He gulped. "Fuck, Kit! Are you serious?"

"Of course... I'm not." Kit gave a little burst of laughter, just enough to clear the worst of the tension between them, but not enough to entirely dispel the notion that what he'd said might actually be true. Of course it was true. It was bloody obvious. The bond between them ran far deeper than simple friendship, always had, and physically, it was hard sometimes not to just give in and stuff the consequences. Just because they'd never mentioned love before didn't mean it wasn't there.

It was there. Shit, if he didn't feel it writhing about like a maggot in his guts, making every interaction between them a challenge in self restraint. He wasn't about to make a confession though. "You know I'm with Evie," he said instead.

Kit saluted him. "I know it, and I won't screw it up for you."

Nevertheless, something about that promise niggled.

Ross sat down and pressed his thumbs into his eye sockets once Kit had left the consultation room. Shit! Today really wasn't shaping up so well. Nervous jitters were playing havoc with his insides, and he had to trust that whoever had taken that pot shot at Kit didn't try anything else, particularly while he was with Evie. To top that, he'd swear Kit had something major up his sleeve, as if that confession hadn't been movement enough on the Richter scale.

Iris came in, her face crumpled into a sour expression. "I can't believe you're sending him over to Evie. Is that safe?" she asked in a fashion that plainly said she didn't think it was. "You know what happened before."

"Nothing—nothing happened before. Kit never did a thing."

The fact that he'd been with Kit at the time in question made that obvious, but even without that, he trusted his guts on this one, and they said Kit was clean. He was no killer.

"Evie Latham! What's this about you and a houseguest?"

"Huh?" Evie looked up from the chart she'd been doodling on for the last two hours as she tried to predict what would sell over the coming month, to find Lillianna Stainbrook stretching over the counter towards her with one pencil-thin eyebrow raised. Once a dedicated goth chic, Lillianna had recently thrown out the porcelain-white and boxes of black hair dye in favour of a flame-haired temptress look. The result was a clash between Bette Midler and an orangutan as frizzy red curls stuck out from her head at alarming angles.

"Spill!" she demanded, slapping her palm down on top of Evie's order form, which successfully prevented Evie from resuming her naughty stick figure drawing of a girl going at it with two guys. Evie dropped a napkin over the sketch and smiled sweetly at Lillianna.

"They're nice." She grabbed her friend's outstretched hand in order to examine her new acrylic fingernails. Truthfully, the gold and red looked rather grotesque against the black base, rather like someone had had a nosebleed over her nails, but humouring Lillianna was the easiest way to distract her from latching onto the subject of Kit. Evie didn't want to discuss Kit. She'd hardly mentioned him to Ross all week, and it had been a relief to find he wasn't constantly around cramping their style. Mostly he came home to eat and sleep, and sometimes he skipped the food part.

"Ooh! Do you think so?" Lillianna cooed, now waggling her fingers as if she was showing off a fifty carat diamond, not a few bits of airbrushed plastic. "Molly did them. She's set herself up in her conservatory, and in exchange for being her practice dummy, she's going to do them for me once a week for the bargain price of a tenner. These babies would normally cost me fifty."

"Wow."

Lillianna's brows both shot into her hairline. "Not just wow,

Evie. It's an absolute steal, especially as she lives right next door to Kirkley's most eligible bachelors, Jason and Saul." She swooned a little and rested her head in her palm.

"Aren't they gay?"

"No." She perked up again immediately, staring Evie straight in the eyes, before adding in a breathless, rather childish voice. "You can see right into their place from the manicure chair. Wednesday nights, six o'clock prompt. It's wild, I tell ya." She clapped her hands. "But see, we're getting sidetracked. You were going to tell me all about your new lodger, before I tell you what the boys get up to."

Evie nonchalantly tapped the end of her biro to her lip. "How many scones do you think we need for next week?"

"Hot is he?" Lillianna shrewdly remarked. "You wouldn't clam up if he wasn't. So give me a rating. Ross being a six and Jason and Saul, nines."

"Um, twelve," muttered Evie. Six wasn't a very fair score for Ross, but they'd been over her boyfriend's merits in the past, and actually it was a relief to know Lilli's interests didn't stray too far in that direction. Kit was a different matter, being neither Evie's to defend, or anything less than pure raw sexiness. The fact was, rather than dim her interest, Kit's long absences during the week had made her increasingly aware of him, so that she'd actually started looking forward to and anticipating his appearances. Annoyingly, the kitten had taken to him in much the same way, only the cat got to curl up on Kit's lap and purr in a smugly contented fashion. More irritating still, she'd started to respond to Kit's name for her—Mimmy.

"Evie." Lillianna poked a fingernail into the back of Evie's hand, making her squawk. "Seriously, you need to qualify a twelve. Nobody rates a twelve. Not even Bauhaus's Pete Murphy."

"Kit does," she said absently and immediately regretted imparting his name when Lilli's face filled with wonderment.

"Kit!" she bellowed. "Oh. My. God! Are we talking about

Christopher Skye, Ross's mate from way back? You've got Christopher Skye staying with you. You bitch!"

Shocked by the outburst, which had even raised the heads of some of the tearoom's perpetual grazers, Evie pushed Lillianna off the counter, and ushered her towards the store closet. She pushed her inside and closed the door on them.

"Keep it down, will you, or I'll be dealing with complaints for the next fortnight. You know the tearoom regulars bring in most of the revenue for the house."

"Yeah, suppose."

Melton Manor, the Big House, as the locals liked to call it, was a crumbling Jacobean pile, set in ninety acres of gardens and grazing land. Too small to market itself as a conference venue, it survived primarily on guided tours, goodwill and the occasional private party. The Tearoom, more formally known as The Satyr's Horn, due to a curious bronze statue set outside, was housed in the Victorian extensions that had once been an icehouse and launderette.

"But holy shit, Evie! Prince Lucifer himself comes strutting home and you don't even mention it to me. Bugger this mess." She pulled at the coils of frizzy auburn hair in dismay. "I'm going black again and digging out the hair straighteners. Don't you think couples always look best when they're nicely matched?"

Far from it. Evie found the whole concept of his and hers clothing, hair-dos and even bath towels completely revolting. However, she let the remark go, in the wake of her friend's hyperbolic reaction to Kit's name. "You know him?" she ventured, backing into the corner that housed the locally made jars of pickles, in order to avoid the worst of any further spitting explosions.

"Know him! I spent every summer between the ages of eight and eighteen chasing him. 'Course, I bloody know him. And he's not a twelve, he's a fifteen, unless he's gone bald or something."

Evie shook her head.

"Only stopped chasing him 'cause he absconded after all that trouble with Sammie Dean."

"Trouble?" Her second attempt at nonchalance drew a quizzical look from Lillianna, who twirled an auburn ringlet around her finger and popped it into her mouth to suck.

"Hasn't Ross told you about it?" she eventually replied, releasing the now wet strand of hair. "I'd have thought he would. I guess you're cool with it, which in itself is cool. I don't know if I would be. I mean there's sexy bad, and there's bad bad, and none of us ever quite worked out what side of the fence Mr. Skye is truly on."

Caught between the desire to press Lillianna for every minute detail of what she knew and yet somehow not reveal her apparent ignorance on a seemingly important topic, Evie wallowed for a moment in confused silence.

Bad boy? Yes, she agreed that Kit certainly deserved that description, but to suggest his badness actually went as far as making him downright evil, seemed unjustified to say the least. What the hell had he done? Dealt drugs on the corner, nicked a car, maybe spray painted a few walls? Hardly clever stuff, but not exactly things to make him legendary, even in a pokey village like Kirkley. In her home town of Leeds, Kit's antics wouldn't have raised more than an eyebrow. She was just about to carefully prod Lillianna into spilling a few more details, when the service bell on the tearoom counter rang.

"I have to get that."

"I bet it's just one of the old biddies demanding another free cupper. They don't like to think you're idling."

"Well, it is as many refills as you like for two quid," Evie muttered. Her eyebrows pulled low into a frown as she emerged from the cupboard. The waiting customer, rather surprisingly, didn't have grey hair. Rather, he had on a leather jacket, with a Maltese cross and pattern of roses painted across the back. "Kit." Her half-strangled gasp caused him to turn and Lillianna to whip out of the cupboard, still holding the cigarette she'd obviously just been about to take a stealthy puff upon. Evie scowled and she immediately stubbed it out, grinning sheepishly at the numerous no smoking signs. Two seconds later she was the other side of the counter, right in Kit's face.

"You're back." She jabbed him in the chest with her cigarette butt. "You've a nerve. Has Tony seen you yet?"

"Tony who?"

It was only as Kit back stepped that Evie noticed he had a dressing on the right side of his forehead. Concerned, she leapt forward, shoving Lillianna out of the way. "What happened? I've been saying to Ross all week that you shouldn't be working alone in that house. It's dangerous, and lo' and behold you've had an accident."

Kit despite the odd wary glance at Lillianna, smiled. "I'll live, Evie. It's just a scratch. Though, it's nice to know you care." He pouted slightly, an expression that prompted a mew of appreciation from Lillianna.

"Of course I care." She raised her hand to his brow, in order to sweep back his hair to better see the wound. "What happened? Have you been up to the hospital?"

He gave a quick shake of his head. "It's nothing, really."

About to say more, Evie noticed that his gaze kept flicking back and forth between herself and Lillianna. Curious, she turned to her friend, thinking introductions were probably out of place since they clearly knew one another. Lilli was gaping at them as if she'd just discovered the crown jewels in her coalhouse.

"What? What!"

"Are you two shagging?" Lilli's words burst from her in a near incomprehensible gush.

"No."

"Does Ross know?"

"We're not," said Kit, although there was a distinctly implied "yet" in his tone.

"Oh my god!" Lillianna continued unabashed, clearly not

persuaded by their denials. "I bet he joins in. God, that's it, isn't it? You're all screwing each other. Aw!" She clapped her hands, unfortunately snapping the forgotten cigarette in two, so it added to the small pile of litter already accumulated on the floor. "Just wait 'til I tell Molly about this. She's gonna freak." Without another remark, not even a goodbye, she snatched her handbag from the counter and zoomed out of the door, flicking the remainder of her cigarette butt at George the Satyr.

"Nice seeing you too," muttered Kit.

"Bother!" Evie cursed at Lillianna's retreating back, although a much stronger expletive rang in her head. "Now the whole village is going to think we're having an affair, threesome or both."

"Let 'em," said Kit. "Who cares what they think?"

"What about Ross? What's he going to think when people start spreading rumours about us?"

"That his neighbours are inveterate gossips and that they should mind their own goddamn business. He sent me over here, by the way. Thought you might like taking out for lunch. Obviously he can't do it himself, so I'm the substitute."

"I'm at work."

"Um, don't you finish at two?" He lifted his wrist and glanced between his watch and the clock on the wall counting down the last forty seconds of the hour. "There, you're finished. So, name your location, lady, and I'll chauffeur you over there."

"Home," she muttered, dubious about being seen in public with Kit considering the rumours Lillianna was probably spreading even as they spoke. Lilli knew everyone and she was the gossip queen, particularly if it was a nice fat juicy bit of scandal or involved an attractive bloke. By the end of the day, once the Chinese Whispers had gone around the village a few times, it'd probably be widely regarded that she was carrying twins with two fathers and that she and Ross regularly hosted orgies in their shed, or worse, although, she couldn't actually envisage much worse. Having it put about that they had a live-in lover seemed bad enough.

"I'm not taking you home. Pick somewhere else. Somewhere that actually serves food and has a wine menu."

"There's the Black Bull," she muttered dubiously.

"At Thirl?'

"Yeah." The next village over seemed like a safe enough choice. Although only five miles down the road, there wasn't much to-ing and fro-ing between the two communities, so hopefully them being out for dinner sans Ross would pass un-remarked upon. It was unlikely she'd even be recognized. "I just need to get Josie to take over serving." She stripped off her frilly Edwardian style apron and hung it on a peg inside the store cupboard. "She's probably parked in front of the fire in the morning room. And I can't be long. I'm not actually finished. There's a planning meeting for the Spring Bazaar at four."

"Two hours should be plenty," Kit said with a worrying glint in his eyes.

Chapter Six

Kit pulled off the dressing on his brow on the way over to Thirl in the car. To be fair, he did look better without it, and the wound itself didn't look too bad, just as if someone had drawn a second brow above the first with a crimson lip-liner. It might even look sexy once it was no longer matted with glue and had turned silver.

The Black Bull was boarded up when they got there with a large "Rent this Pub" sign prominently displayed on the roadside. They parked up regardless and strolled into the centre of the cobbled village planning to resort to fish and chips. In the end the only place open was a specialty coffee and ice-cream parlour with a selection of cast iron furniture in a sheltered courtyard out back. The place was deserted. Evie sat under an ivy-strung arbour shivering with her hands stuffed inside her pockets. "I bet you have to fight for a seat in the summer."

"What'll you have?" Kit asked, glancing at the menu. He wasn't shivering, but the tips of his fingers did look cold. "I was thinking hot chocolate and marshmallows. Ice cream might be a bit hard on the stomach."

"Was that snow?" Evie rubbed at a cold droplet that had just hit her nose and glanced suspiciously up at heavily clouded sky. "I think it was. I'm not sure this is a good choice. Let's get some drinks and go back to the car with them. I'm not bothered about lunch. I normally skip it anyway."

"Okay, I can go with that." Kit pushed himself up again.

"Although, I have to say, I've never known taking a woman out for lunch to be so difficult."

Laden with steaming beverages, and several bags of tortilla chips, they traipsed back to the car. Evie, content to be inside with the heating on, was happy to stay in the car park, but Kit was having none of it. He drove them back along the narrow winding lane with its parallel dry-stone walls on either side and parked up in a lay-by overlooking a vast rolling swell of the moors that reminded Evie of a beloved threadbare rug.

The sky above was white, with only the faintest hint of blue on the very edge of the horizon. As the last purr of the engine died away, the first flurry of snow softly pattered against the windscreen and stuck, obscuring the view with a crystalline lattice work.

Evie cradled her drink, warming her hands through the corrugated cardboard as she watched Kit flip the lid off his chocolate and fish the marshmallows out with his fingers. He held one between his forefinger and thumb, and curled his tongue around the sticky white blob, before popping it into his mouth to savour. A dribble of chocolate ran down his chin.

"I guess you know Lillianna," she said, offering him a tissue.

Kit looked nonplussed at the tissue, and wiped the drip away with the back of his hand. "Not really. No more than anyone else in Kirkley."

"Oh! I just thought from her reaction that you must have known one another pretty well. Like you'd gone out or something."

That earned a hurried shake of the head and a scowl of distaste. "Not my type. I don't do smokers."

"Right." Evie sagged a little deeper into the passenger seat, wishing now that she'd pressed Lillianna a little harder for information. Obviously, she knew something about Kit's past life in Kirkley, before he'd trotted off to Japan to work in whatever dubious trade he'd been part of, and she felt she could use a bit of insight into how his mind worked. Something told her there was more to him being here than Ross suggesting they get better acquainted. Actually, she wasn't sure Ross would have made that suggestion at all. He'd been slightly twitchy all week about her interest in Kit. But curiosity was natural, and the guy was staying in their house. She dug out her phone and started tapping out a message.

"What are you doing? Put that away."

"I thought I'd warn Ross about what's coming."

"Why?"

Evie frowned. Wasn't that obvious? "'Cause he might get a bit upset if people start hinting that we're having an affair behind his back."

"But we're not," Kit said bluntly, leaving her with the distinct impression that his words didn't mean precisely what they seemed at first glance.

He undid his seatbelt and took the phone off her, slipping it into the glove compartment. "Don't waste your time on theatrics. I think Ross'll manage to handle any chaff that gets thrown his way."

Evie remained unconvinced. If their situations were reversed, she'd be livid if she caught wind of rumours about Ross having an affair, particularly with one of her oldest friends. Then again, she was far more easily wound up than Ross, who mostly let things blow past him like autumn leaves in the wind. Maybe he'd trust them and ignore the circulating nonsense.

"Kit, why did you leave Kirkley? I've been wondering, and Lillianna said…"

"Surprised it's taken you all week to ask." He tilted his head to one side in order to look at her, and his dark fringe fell over his face so that it shrouded his left eye. "I had to. Didn't have any choice. I wasn't welcome anymore, and my presence wasn't doing Ross any favours. I didn't want to get him tarnished by association."

"Not welcome? In what sense?"

"In every sense, Evie." His dark eyes bore into her and yet revealed nothing beside a hint of cold lingering anger over the injustice of it all.

"I don't get it. Tarnished him how?"

Kit shrugged and drained his cup, which he crushed within his hand and chucked into the back. "Just stuff. It happens and people form opinions, and then it doesn't matter what the truth is, because you're already damned."

"Hence the implications that you're the devil incarnate?"

"Is that the current consensus?"

Evie shook her head. "Lillianna's description, no one else's. She said you were a bad, bad boy."

Suddenly a spark lit in his devil's eyes and he glanced at her from under his brows and long fringe. "No, Evie. I'm a bad, bad man. Not a boy." He placed his hand upon her thigh. "Want to find out how bad? It'll make your toes curl."

Her toes were already curled, a combination of the rapidly drifting snow outside and the heat suddenly surging through her midriff in response to his touch. Shit! This wasn't happening. It couldn't be. It wasn't allowed to be happening, and yet his palm print seemed to be seared into her thigh. What the hell was going on? Where had this come from? One minute they were talking and agreeing that nothing was going on that Ross needed to worry about, and the next he was getting all touchy-feely and husky voiced.

Kit fanned out his fingers and then dipped them down between her legs.

Terrified and squeamishly aroused, she jumped as much as the belt and the back support would allow, which was only a matter of centimetres and clamped her legs together, unwittingly trapping his fingers.

"Nice and warm in here," he mused, wiggling his fingers. His grin stretched, seductively broad. "We're getting a bit steamed up."

Condensation now coated the inside of the windows while snow flakes peppered the outer. Evie's skin felt similarly dotted with perspiration as hot need sent prickles running up and down her throat. It made her breasts tingle and her abdomen swell with the rush of blood. Don't move that hand, don't move it, she repeated, mantra-like in her head, while a second devil's voice coaxed in a sultry whisper for him to do exactly that, and more, to press his thumb up against her willing slit.

Damn him. Damn everything. He made her want to do the wildest, craziest things. She fancied him. Okay, she admitted it. Had from that first moment she'd seen him in the shower, but that didn't excuse her behaviour. It wasn't as if she wasn't getting any, nor that her relationship with Ross sucked in any other way. At least if that had been true playing away from home might have been justifiable. But it wasn't, and she wasn't going to. She was going to stop this rampant nonsense, right now. She wasn't sacrificing happy ever after with a mortgage and a houseful of pets for a stealthy grope from Mr. Bad Man.

"Kit!" she croaked, intending to sound commanding, not like a frog with a sore throat.

To her dismay, instead of being put off by her warning, he made an ungainly exit out of the driver's seat and clambered over the gear stick to straddle her lap. "Yes-ss."

"What are you doing? Get off me. You're not proving anything besides how irresponsible you are."

Kit grasped her hands, folding his fingers around hers so that their palms lay pressed together at her shoulder height.

"May as well be damned as a sinner than as a saint." He leaned a little closer, so that their loins slid closer together.

Pinned by his weight, the seat belt and the clasp of his palms, Evie stared at him unblinking, unable to turn away from the intensity of his gaze, or the seductive promise of his parted lips. Ever since that night when she'd dreamed about Kit fucking her while Ross lay beside them asleep, her libido had been haywire. She and Ross had been going at it like bunnies every night, until they collapsed into exhausted, dreamless sleep. The dream hadn't recurred, but she'd re-imagined it during idle moments at work, reworking the scenario so that Ross was awake and watching them, and another time an active participant in their lovemaking, taking her as he and Kit had taken that girl in the tent years ago.

"Kit. Don't," she bleated, their lips almost touching.

His breath caressed her face as he spoke. "Is that your best defence?" He raised an eyebrow and winced as the movement tugged at his wound. "That's hardly an encouragement to stop. It's barely protest enough to stop you feeling guilty."

"I love him."

The soft whisper of his breaths tickled. "So do I." There wasn't enough time to think about that. He pecked her upon the cheek, in the quickest, most chaste manner she'd experienced since kissing the vicar on Christmas Eve, his lips barely brushing her skin. Then he opened the car door and got out.

Relief flooded Evie's chest, followed immediately by a wave of regret. She starred numbly at his retreating back as he strode away from the car, head down, facing the wind. Fighting with the belt, her sex still liquid with arousal, she leaned out of the door. "Hey! Where are you going?"

"Home," he called, not turning. Having reached the dry-stone wall, he nimbly leapt over.

"What? Get in the car, Kit." Face screwed up against the biting wind and the patter of wet snow, Evie pitched after him. "What the fuck has got into you? Is this some sort of bollocks game? 'Cause if it is, quit pratting about, it's bloody freezing."

He stopped and slowly turned to face her, his shaggy hair blowing around him and his hands stuffed deep into his pockets. "Here, take the keys." He threw them so that they landed forming an indent in the settling snow. "Drive back to work. I can walk home from here."

"You can drive back from here." Leaving the keys where

they'd landed, she slowly approached. "I'm not leaving you out here in the snow. Ross would never forgive me." Cautiously, she straddled the wall.

Kit remained stock still, watching her, his face in shadow. "He might not appreciate you being in the car with me either."

"Don't play games, Kit. This is a game, isn't it?"

"Maybe," he said darkly.

"So, what's the purpose of it?"

"To see what makes you tick. To turn you on."

"Freezing doesn't turn me on." She scooped a handful of wet snow from the wall and chucked it at him. The crude snowball splattered across the front of his jacket. Kit's smile merely thinned, becoming tightly pursed and brooding, if not quite menacing.

"So, what does?"

Her gaze flickered down to his loins.

Kit laughed. "Oh, right, that. You really get off on that, don't you?"

"Yeah. So, what if I do?" Humouring him seemed the best way to get him back in the car. Not that he showed any signs of moving in that direction. Evie tentatively lowered herself down from the wall. The drop was considerably farther on this side of the boundary, and the grass sloped downwards at a steep incline. One wrong foot and she'd go skiing into him on her bum.

"I once fucked a snowman," he said.

"The hell you did."

"It's true." His gaze rose heavenwards. "Fucking cold. Fucking stupid."

Evie reached him and placed her hand gently upon his arm, not convinced his curses were linked to his confession. There was something going on here that she couldn't quite figure. His lip quivered slightly as he glanced down at her before turning his head to the sky again. "Fucking Kirkley," he muttered. The low sloped roofs of the village cottages could just be seen from here, huddled together in the valley basin.

"Kit, what happened?" She wasn't sure if she was asking about the injury to his brow, or some event from the distant past; either way, he trembled when she wrapped her arms around him and drew him into her embrace.

He remained curiously stiff as she embraced him, not the hot, sensual creature she'd grown used to.

"I couldn't stay away any longer," he said, speaking as if to some invisible onlooker. "I realized I'd been running for too long. That people had a right to closure."

"Running from what? From Ross?"

"We're fucking lovers, Evie. There's no running from him anymore."

That was another smart arse wisecrack, the twitch of his cheek, which formed into a dimple proved it. Evie dug a finger into his ribs. "That's not funny, Kit."

"Isn't it?" His eyes were dancing again with warmth and humour. Too late, she realized just how close they were standing, and how their embrace was not simply comforting, but downright intimate. Kit's leg brushed between her thighs. His palms lay spread across her rump. "Tell me 'no' again," he whispered. "And I have had him. He's got a really cute strawberry birthmark at the base of his spine."

Having spent hours kissing that mark, she knew it existed, but that didn't prove that the rest of what Kit was saying was true. There were plenty of ways to know that mark was there without them having been physically intimate. For that matter she remained unconvinced about the snowman too.

"I like running my tongue over it. Biting it. Do you like being bitten, Evie? You know it's the one thing Lillianna and I have in common."

"You do know her?"

"If giving her a hickey or two as a teen counts as knowing her, then yeah, I suppose I do."

Could she believe a thing he said? He seemed to talk in

circles, never sticking on one topic long enough for her to draw any conclusions.

"Evie," he sighed, dragging her thoughts off in yet another direction. "I take it you realize where your hand is?"

"Hm." *Clamped around his truly delectable butt.*

"Like, inside my underwear."

"Oh! Right... Yeah." She hadn't been concentrating on that, only on what he was doing. He'd turned up the collar of her coat, and still had hold of the edges, which he was using to draw her inexorably closer. Just one kiss, said his expression. You know you want to, and it won't hurt anyone.

Maybe it would. Maybe it wouldn't. What if it were true that he and Ross were lovers? Nah, it wasn't. How could it be? Ross had never shown any signs of being homo-curious. Her fingers curled into the bare flesh of Kit's arse, where she'd unconsciously sought the feel of his skin and had pushed her hand under the hems of his T-shirt and jacket and inside the back of his trousers.

"Evie." She heard him call her name as clearly as if he'd said it aloud, but his lips never moved. Instead he continued to look at her, his gaze intently focused, and his lips ever so slightly parted, so that they invited her to stretch up and taste him.

Kit had such incredibly sensual lips, slim but mobile and so expressive. Her lips tingled with the prospect of savouring him, of kissing him slowly while she raked her nails across his back. Her next breath seemed to stall in her chest. Kit continued to hold her, his touch barely there and yet curiously supportive. An image of them sat side by side in the car swam in her field of vision, her hand upon his cock, stroking him, then her leaning over and tasting him, blowing him as if it were the most natural thing in the world and not a good way to get done for public indecency.

But the montage of eroticism didn't stop there, more images bombarded her sense, snapshots of them naked and fucking, and of Ross entwined around them.

Stop it, she thought. Take a deep breath and step back.

The trouble was...her feet didn't want to move. Instead, the tension between them built until it virtually crackled in the air, and creeping lines of fire flowed across her skin, making her breasts tingle with the need to be touched. Still she didn't move, and nor did Kit. Instead, he just looked at her with his deep dark eyes, right at her as if he could see into her soul and there was a light there drawing him closer.

"Evie." This time the whisper was real. It rippled across her senses, a gentle breeze across her lips as he leaned forward. Yet it whipped tornado-like at her insides, throwing everything into disarray. Nothing made sense anymore. With a single action he'd destroyed her inner peace and wreaked abject chaos. Even so, she didn't want to undo the kiss. No, she wanted more than that simple intimate brushing of lips. She wanted a real, all out, tongue-clashing tango.

She leaned into his body. Let the warmth of him seep into her skin. The second kiss wasn't cautious. He struck boldly, pulling her to him, one hand upon her shoulder, the other splayed possessively across her lower back. He kissed as she imagined he would. Giving all, taking only what she willingly offered. Demanding nothing and everything. His tongue stroked hers, coaxed her further into submission.

Evie wrapped her arms around his broad back and clung to him, her fingers sliding over the contoured planes of wiry muscle beneath his clothing. Kit reciprocated, startling her with the coldness of his fingertips as they stroked upwards beneath her clothing to cup one breast.

His fingers closed upon the nipple, gently rolled it.

"Come back to the car," she gasped.

"Best not," he whispered. Before she could ask why, he grasped her hand and turned it so that he could press it to the swell of his cock. "If we go anywhere warm I might get ideas." As if fondling her breasts and driving himself up against her palm weren't already building to that. "I want you, Evie. Why do you think I got out of the car? You weren't supposed to follow."

"I'm still not letting you walk home in this."

"Then what are you doing? What are *we* doing?"

He kissed her again, hard. Bruising her lips. Kit walked her backwards towards the wall. He unfastened the fly of her tailored trousers and pushed his hand inside, found the edge of her panties and pushed inside those too, so that two long fingers speared through her curls and into the dripping heat of her slit.

Evie hissed as he touched her clit. The snow-covered wall was cold against her back. Thicker flakes hung in the air around them and caught in Kit's hair and eyelashes. She couldn't take her eyes off him as his fingers moved, sliding back and forth in her heat and wetness, and touching her clit. She drowned in the coal-dark pools of his eyes as streamers of pleasure ran through her body. "Kit. Kit," she sang out, clinging to him for support.

She was buzzing, steadily climbing that vertigo-inducing slope towards orgasm. Tighter... Faster... Her broad hips swaying to the dancing rhythm of his fingers. God, the heat and smell of him were too much. She wanted to rub up against him like her bloody cat.

"Oh, yes. That's it. Ride it. Give in to it." Just the sound of his voice growling in her ear pushed her higher.

So close now. So close. The climb was so swift. There was no time for thoughts or comprehension, only for sensation. Her thighs trembled. Her fingers curled into the toned muscles of his back, nails digging into the flesh, her hands inside his clothing. Hell, she was almost there. Just a touch farther to the right...

Kit responded as if they were psychically bound, stroking quickly and lightly, then slowing down for a few heartbeats before picking up the pace again and making her whimper.

She was going to come.

As if the realization was the requisite spark, her muscles pulled tight, and a long whimper of pleasure tore through her chest.

Kit's fingers slowed. He pressed hard on her clit, extending the moment of pleasure into a series of crests, each satisfyingly sweet, until the last pulse died away and she collapsed against him, thoroughly spent.

"Your eyes are turquoise when you come," he said.

The moment the endorphins and adrenaline surge passed, guilt hit her in a nausea-inducing wave. "Oh god!" Evie pulled back from him, breathing hard. What the hell had she been thinking? Was she out of her bleeding mind?

She hitched her trousers up fast.

All she could think of was Ross, his hurt. The awful sense of betrayal he'd feel. It'd be easy to lay the blame at his feet, saying he'd brought Kit into their home, and almost encouraged a close relationship between them, but Evie wasn't so conceited that she couldn't recognize when something was her fault. And hers entirely. She was a grown woman. She'd made her own decision, and there'd been no point at which she couldn't have said stop.

The threat of tears stung her eyes. Evie hurriedly blinked them away.

"Say something." Kit leant towards her, concern softening his features. "Anything. Tell me I'm a bastard if you like."

"Why? Why are you doing this?"

"Because like everyone, I want what I can't have. The only difference is that I'm not afraid of tumbling a few obstacles in pursuit of my goal."

"I'm your best friend's girlfriend."

"So you both keep reminding me, as if that's the most important hurdle." Without being asked, he lifted her back over the wall, before hopping over himself and leading the trek back to the car.

Evie followed him up the slope, her mind in confusion and

her heart racing. What had she done? What was going on?

"What do you want?" she asked as he fished the car keys out of the slowly thickening layer of snow.

Kit shrugged, his head still at her hip height. "Do you want taking back to work?"

"Yes, yes, I do." She watched him straighten, broad shoulders squaring up to her and his expression setting into blank concentration. "But don't ignore me. I asked what you wanted."

"And I heard." He got into the car and revved the engine.

Evie crossed her arms, her guilt transforming into anger at him. She hated the way he'd studiously withdrawn from her questions. Her mum was a pro at the tactical silence. It wasn't a trait she looked for in her friends.

Getting back into the car with him without having received an answer felt like defeat, but she didn't put it past him to drive off and leave her if she prodded too much. Well, maybe not leave her exactly, but she reckoned he'd think nothing of driving down the road a bit and making her jog after him.

They drove back to Melton Manor in silence. Kit pulled into the staff car park and she opened the door to get out without them having exchanged a single word, having reclaimed her phone from the glove compartment.

"Evie, wait." Kit leant over and grabbed her wrist. "I didn't... I wasn't deliberately ignoring you. It's just I don't have a straight answer to give you. It's complicated. I guess I want more than friendship between us."

"That's too bad," she replied as she jerked her wrist free of his grasp. "Because that's all that's on offer."

Having slammed the car door, she walked away with the words "fuck you" echoing inside her skull. She did want more than simple friendship. She did desire him and would savour every delicious moment of their encounter on the hilltop over and over during the coming days. It's just that it wasn't possible to have him and Ross without someone, perhaps all of them, getting hurt. She had to write off what had just happened as an anomaly and focus on ensuring it never happened again. Besides, she sure as hell didn't want anyone as mutable and secretive as Kit occupying space in her heart. She couldn't deal with anything other than openness in her relationships, which was another reason why that the line about him and Ross was obviously bollocks. Ross would have told her if anything like that had gone on, especially after she'd brought up the incident of the threesome in the tent.

Chapter Seven

Kit went straight home to Ross and Evie's place from Melton Manor and set about clearing the drive of snow. With a spade in his hand, it was easy not to think. He could thrust, shovel and sweep on autopilot in much the same way he'd helped keep the bar clean in Tokyo. The less glamorous side of working as a host was the unfortunate cleaning chores, hours of sweeping and swilling floors, and polishing brass plaques according to the weekly rote. No one escaped it. Not even the top earners who were raking in enough to hire maids to clean their own apartments.

He hadn't really thought about Japan since he'd got here. Maybe he was actually starting to miss the busy social whirl and easy routine of his life there. It had been the right time to come home though. He knew it in his bones, and despite endless complications he kept making for himself, it was going to work out somehow.

The phone rang, and Kit dashed inside to answer it. "Moshi-moshi," he said out of habit. When the greeting was met with no response he added a more dubious, "Er, hello." The silence stretched out for several more seconds, although Kit could hear the caller breathing on the other end of the line. A sense of unease rippled across his shoulder muscles making them feel tight and achy. "Who is this?" Not expecting a reply, he was just about to cut the sinister caller off, when the disconcerting breathing transformed into a sanctimonious purr.

"Christopher Skye. I know what you are. I know what you did. Don't think you can get away with it. Justice is coming. An eye for an eye, a tooth for tooth. We're watching you."

Click. Kit slammed the phone back into the cradle, then pressed random buttons in order to end the call. "Damn. Damn. Fuck!" He kicked the edge of the sofa, startling Mimmy, who darted out from behind it and ran up the curtain.

The kitten looked down on him, eyes full of curiosity and scorn. "Sorry," Kit mumbled, reaching for her. For the first time ever, the tortoiseshell moggy shied away and dug her claws into the curtain when he tried to pick her up.

Kit raised his hands in frustration and scrunched up his hair. "Okay. Okay, you think I'm a bastard too. I get it." Overwhelmed, he turned on the spot, seeking an escape route that didn't exist, and never would as long as he stayed in Kirkley. There were no convenient magic portals and no diversion that would neatly bypass his former life here. "Sammie, why?" He stumbled forward to the fireplace until his head hit the mirror above, skin connecting to the silvered glass.

What he needed was a convenient rewind, a method of exploiting Einstein's relativity theory so he could make different choices and say different things. Not that he was sure any changes he made would make a difference. People believed what they wanted to believe, and they'd decided long ago that he was the devil incarnate.

Sometimes he almost believed it of himself.

Kit raised his head and focused on his reflection, humourlessly checking for horns. Of course, there were none. He sighed. He wasn't looking quite so polished anymore. The last week and certainly today had both taken their toll. Dark smudges ringed his eyes, courtesy of his screwed up sleep pattern. Adjusting to a different time zone and to daylight hours combined with more generalized fretting meant he was awake most nights until five a.m. He'd been taking afternoon naps over at Rose Cottage, but really that had to stop. It was only exacerbating the situation.

Mimmy jumped down from the curtain and settled in the basket full of logs. Kit bent to scratch her ears and this time the kitten accepted the caress.

He wasn't going to dwell on the past, or the horrid call. Hopefully, it'd be a one off, and whatever prick it was, wouldn't go upsetting Ross and Evie.

It wasn't Tony. He'd seen Tony earlier. The meeting had been brief and ended in a rather inevitable fashion. He reached up and ran his fingertips over the uneven line of glue. That whack had been a long time coming.

The phone rang again. Kit snatched it up. "Fuck off, will you?" he snapped this time, letting his frustration get the better of him.

"Your phone manner sucks," Ross remarked dryly. "Didn't they teach you how to be polite in Japan?"

Ross. Relief relaxed Kit's straining muscles. "Sorry. I've just had a wanker on the phone."

"Salesman?"

Kit made a noncommittal grunt.

"I phoned to make sure everything had gone fine between you and Evie."

Fine? Well, that depended entirely on your definition. He sat down and pulled his booted foot up on his knee. "'Course."

"Really?" The question in Ross's voice highlighted his disbelief. "That's not quite her version of it. I'd say you'd pissed her off."

"You've spoken to her?"

A snort of mirth echoed along the line. "Hardly a shocker. We are an item. She sent a text a while ago."

"What did she say?" The fact that Ross was laughing rather than yelling suggested she hadn't said anything too bad.

Throaty laughter still rumbled with his words as Ross replied. "She said that you're a prize dick, whose idea of lunch is a cup of cocoa in a polystyrene mug and a bag of crisps in a lay-by. Real classy. I can only assume you left all that sophisticated charm of yours back in Kabukicho."

"The place she wanted to go was closed, and it's nicer up on the moors looking at a bit of scenery than it is sitting in a car park." Heavens knows why he felt he had to justify himself. She'd been the one calling the location shots.

"I'm teasing you, Kit. How's the head?"

Kit ran his fingers over the seam of glue again. "Aching."

"Don't suppose you've taken anything."

"You know I don't do drugs."

An exasperated sigh bled into his ear. "I'm talking about a couple of frickin aspirin, not suggesting you start snorting coke. Painkillers. Headache. They work. I'm not surprised Evie thought you were a prick."

"I'll make some green tea."

"'Cause that's known for its analgesic properties."

"It is actually."

"Okay, okay, you win. I'll see you in a couple of hours, take it easy. See if you can get some shut eye."

Ross ended the call. Kit flopped against the back of the sofa still cradling the handset. After a moment or two of indecisive fidgeting, he hit recall. There were better ways to deal with stuff than swallowing a handful of pills, like using positive associations to replace the negative ones before they properly took hold.

Ross picked up on the fourth ring.

"Are you alone?" Kit asked, deliberately making his voice sound low and husky.

"Kit?" The question in Ross's voice rang out. "I'm in the staff room. I was just getting a coffee before my next appointment. But there's no one about. What's up?"

"Switch the phone to your left hand."

"What?" He wondered if Ross could detect his smile, even as he grumblingly followed the command.

"Comfortable?"

"Look, what's this about? I've only got a few minutes."

Kit deliberately didn't answer, although maybe the pause in itself said volumes. It certainly said plenty to him about the images in his head. "Undo your fly."

"Kit." Ross's voice sank to a choked whisper. The guy was no doubt surreptitiously looking around to make sure none of the veterinary assistants were going to interrupt. "Bleedin' hell. I can't do this right now."

Ignoring the protest, Kit cleared his throat. "Slowly now, Ross, so that I can hear the bite of the metal teeth as you unzip."

Tense prickles rode up his thighs as he waited for the crucial decision. Relief washed the sensation higher, into his balls, when he heard the corresponding scratch of the steel teeth parting. He grinned at the mouthpiece, his teeth clamped together. This was going well. Better than he'd anticipated.

"Ready?"

"No."

"My head hurts for more than one reason. You should've let me finish this earlier."

"Shit!"

"Now wrap that big hand of yours around that equally big boner, and let's hear you pumping it."

The only response he got was a grunt. Comfortably reassured by that, Kit sank back against the leather cushions and closed his eyes. Ross's image formed crisp and whole in his brain. Dark tailored trousers, worn with a charcoal sweater that accentuated the breadth of his shoulders and narrowness of his hips, and topped by a standard issue white lab coat. He was standing, bottom to the worktop in the narrow windowless kitchen at the surgery, his mobile pressed to his left ear and his hand just covering the gash formed by his open fly. Overhead, the electric strip light made a constant, bleating whine.

"Are you doing it?"

"Yes."

Kit's arousal climbed a fraction higher at the affirmative. One handed, he unfastened his belt buckle and released his own fly. Beneath, his shaft had already begun to fill with blood and lay diagonally inside his underwear. His balls were pulled up tight against his body, already heavily loaded after a series of frustrating encounters. Hell, he liked to ratchet up the tension, but today hadn't seen much relief. "Are you hard?" he asked.

"Yes." The admission was more exciting than the touch he bestowed on himself.

"Imagine it's my hand. Now, wrap your fist around the shaft and stroke it. Up and down, real slow, so the head peeps out between the ring of your forefinger and thumb."

"Shit!" Ross hissed, clearly obeying.

"That's right," said Kit, now circling his thumb over the tip of his own cock. Concentrating became a little harder as blood surged towards his loins and shivers began to run down his now fully hard shaft.

"Are you wanking too?" asked Ross.

"Do you want me to be?"

"Yes."

"I'm touching myself, Ross. I'm leaking a little and I'm rubbing it into the head and I'm thinking of you, and how much I want to be there with you, touching you."

"Christ!" The exclamation sounded rough in Ross's throat, all croaky and exhilarating. In response, Kit squeezed his cock, his fingers curling, muscles working of their own accord. Gradually, his hips started to rock too. He gripped the phone more tightly than his flesh and tried to rein himself in a little. Ross's breathing had become light and rapid.

"I know what you taste like," Kit continued. "And I want you to come in my mouth again, so I can drink you down. But there's other stuff I want us to do too. Things I've thought about. Things I've got off thinking about all the time we've been apart. Have you still got that chair, Ross? You know the one I mean, the leather wingback. It's not here in the living room. Is it upstairs in your bedroom?"

"It's here in my office."

"I want to lie naked in that chair, my arse up on the arm, and my legs up over my head and I want you to fuck me, Ross. It's not something I'm prepared to do with anyone else. Do you understand me? I won't let anyone but you take me like that."

"Oh, god!"

"We have to do that soon."

"Are you trying to make a bleedin' date with me?"

"I'll let you know a time. I guess we know the place."

"Fuck!"

"Oh, yes. Just imagine it, Ross. Your cock swelling against my arse. Going in deep. I'm pretty tight back there and hot. And you needn't worry about Evie, 'cause she can be right there with us, engaging that voyeuristic streak of hers."

"Uh!" Whatever Ross was trying to say lapsed into a serious of indecipherable grunts.

"Are you going to come for me, Ross? I need you to come for me."

Already there, Ross gave an orgasmic "huh" and a series of airless gulps as his cock gave up its load. Kit talked him through it, staying with him, embracing him with words and endearments until he'd wrung every last drop of pleasure from his friend. A loud clatter spoiled the concluding moment of post-orgasmic closeness.

"Sorry, I dropped the phone," said Ross. "Hell, Kit, I'd better go. I need to get cleaned up. My next appointment is in forty seconds."

Kit nodded at the phone. Despite the clipped manner of Ross's voice, he could hear the desire still rattling around in his chest.

"We'll talk about stuff when I get home," said Ross.

"I can talk real dirty."

"I know. Do I ever know."

Kit let the phone fall from his hand, and it dropped onto the carpet. Despite the fact that his cock still lay hard in his hand, he gave a contented stretch, hands spread over the cushions with his fingers splayed. Save it, he thought, looking down at his cock, which lay flat against his belly in a small puddle of precome. A bit more self-denial would keep him stoked until Ross got his arse home. Shit! Maybe the guy would be peeling him off the ceiling after a single touch by then. His nerves were certainly pulled taut enough to strum, and his cock was just begging for a kiss or two, or better still Ross's solid male palm wrapped around it.

Of course, there remained the issue of Evie too.

Game plan loosely in place, and having tucked his stiffy back in his pants, Kit wandered back through to the kitchen. He made a cup of tea and swallowed it while it was still scalding, before heading back outside to contend with the remaining snow on the driveway. Only, there were four large sacks of newly delivered coal sat in the way.

"I guess I'll be shifting them first," he said to the back-end of the coalman's truck. "Gee thanks, mate."

Sodding coal fires! Great for a seduction, bugger all good for anything else besides making a mess. The fuck with that! He was installing state of the art central heating and a clean burning, real-flame gas fire in Rose Cottage. And he intended to crank up the thermostat every time Ross or Evie came round.

It really was time they upped the stakes.

Evie got home at half past five to find Kit out on the driveway splitting logs with an axe. She parked on the roadside and hung back near the gateway to watch him. He'd thrown his jacket over the top of the wheelie bin so that he had on only a black, long-sleeved T-shirt. Two oriental dragons entwined the sleeves and faced each other across his chest, mouths open, forked tongues flicking forth with intent. The shirt lifted every time he raised his arms, displaying a good five inches of his ripped torso, flesh she'd felt beneath her fingertips only a short time ago, and based on the liquefying action it had on her cunt, skin she longed to feel again.

Her anger had subsided a little since they'd parted, largely because the planning meeting for Melton Manor had turned to the subject of a slave auction, and since she had no intention of letting anyone get their hands on Ross, Kit was her prime candidate for volunteering his services.

"Frightened I bite?" he asked, raising an eyebrow and prompting her to shuffle forward up the driveway to prove she wasn't.

"I know you bite. You told me so."

"Actually, I said I like being bitten."

She noticed he had gloves on, leather ones with the fingertips cut off, and his hand sat in a disconcertingly comfortable manner around the axe haft. He'd probably spent a good portion of his former life in Kirkley cutting firewood, if that swing of his was anything to go by.

Kit brought the weapon down hard on another unfortunate log and the splintered pieces shot off his improvised breezeblock stand in three different directions.

Another pace closer—she couldn't help it. It felt as though something was dragging her. When she tried to blindside herself with visions of Ross's imminent arrival, she found she couldn't actually form his image properly in her head. Instead, her gaze just kept swaying between Kit's tight arse and his wiry shoulders. Maybe it'd be better if they properly smoothed things out between them before they had to face Ross, and got their story straight, so to speak. She didn't want to start the weekend with a row, but how did you tell your boyfriend you'd snogged— actually, considerably more than snogged—his best mate without causing a cosmic outburst?

"What happened earlier can't happen again," she told Kit.

No amount of deciphering could translate the look she got in return. "I heard you spoke to Ross."

"So what if I did?" She circled around behind him, and Kit's gaze followed her the whole route. Even when she stopped before the coalhouse door his gaze remained unblinkingly fastened upon her.

"Feeling guilty?" he asked.

"Aren't you?"

Evie pursed her lips together and defensively folded her arms. That look of his was deep as the ocean and as sweet as sin. Worse, this close to him she could tell he'd worked up a sweat. The scent of it, musky and male, shot with a harsh dash of testosterone wrenched at her insides. She wanted to sink into that smell and get herself all coated in it. Maybe even shove her nose right into his armpit and take a good sniff. She pictured the scene, but with her tongue darting out to lick the salt from his skin too.

Kit gave a humourless chuckle. "Hey now, guilt's my middle name. Don'tcha know anything?"

"I know you're bad, Mr. Christopher 'Guilty' Skye."

He smacked down the axe and left it sticking out of the newest log. "You'd better believe it."

Left without an escape route, as it was still several meters to the back doorstep, and he could move a darn sight faster than she could, Evie took an expectant gulp. However, instead of grabbing her, Kit stretched past her and tugged open the coalhouse door. "Delivery came, if you're interested. Four sacks. I take it that's right?"

"Four?" She glanced at the interior and at his nod, wandered inside. Sure enough there were four new sacks lined up against the wall along with the three that were already there. "Goddamnit! I told him to drop it down to two the last time he came. We'll never use all that."

The coalhouse door closed behind her, blown by the wind, leaving the tiny store in semi-darkness. Only a small amount of gloomy light filtered through the soot-filmed window. Evie swung round to push open the door again, only to find her palm in contact with Kit's chest.

"Hey now," he said when she jerked away. "I didn't realize my efforts sucked that much."

She could only see him as a silhouette against the door, all that black clothing and black hair blended in, but she understood the slow shake of his head. There was no escaping, leastways not until he'd said whatever it was he wanted to say.

"It shouldn't have happened. More than that, it can't happen again," she said. "Forget about it."

Kit smacked his lips together. "I can't do that."

"Can't or won't?"

Evie shuffled up against the amassed store of coal as Kit took a pace towards her. His hand snaked out and brushed lightly over the gentle waves of her hair. "There are things you don't understand." His voice took on a low, husky tone, a pitch that made her heartstrings vibrate and threatened to completely undo her. But there was too much at stake here to give in to such a tawdry feeling as lust. For god's sake, it wasn't as if he cared about her, he just knew how to work women to get what he wanted.

"You're playing havoc with my relationship. I don't want to lose Ross. I love him. This is too much stupid risk. I'm sorry if you got the wrong idea. I should have thought before flirting, but it's going no further."

He gave a huff of disbelief. "Do you expect me to just back off?" He clasped her shoulders and stroked his thumbs back and forth over her collarbones. "This isn't as simple as not acting on attraction. Evie—us being together doesn't have to impact badly on Ross. I've told you, things have been unusual between us in the past."

"Fucking some girl together in a tent eight years ago doesn't make this right, Kit. Don't you think he's going to feel betrayed? You're his best mate. I'm his girlfriend."

"That wasn't what I was talking about." Kit's thumb nicked the underside of her chin. He stood close enough to her now that she could see the dark glint of his pupils and just about make out the even contours of his face. "Evie, Ross isn't going to get hurt. Not by us being together at any rate. The parameters of what we both consider permissible are different to what other people accept."

"I don't know, Kit. You're still talking about years ago."

"No—I'm talking about right now." His thumb slid across her parted lips.

Damn! It was hard to think clearly when he touched her like that, and the enveloping darkness concealed so much. Evie's breathing hastened, her chest rising and falling with the urgency of her desire for his touch, and just to make it worse, something about the wrongness of them being together like this, made everything tingle all the more—her nose, her limbs, her nipples...and lower, the same prickle tormented her clit.

What if it were true, what if Ross truly wouldn't mind? He certainly hadn't batted an eyelid over her seeing his mate buck-naked, and he'd kind of involved Kit in their sex life that first night when he let Kit stand and watch.

Surely, Ross realized that she'd been reliving that scene over and over, replaying it with different endings. Maybe, he'd been doing the same. Maybe all this was building towards Ross asking her if Kit could join them.

"Evie," Kit whispered again.

The sound of his voice reminded her of the sweet taste of his kisses. Fact was, she wanted him, plain and simple. She longed to feel the warmth of his body again, his length and hardness in her hand, as it had been earlier out upon the hillside, when he'd rubbed her towards bliss. Even now, her body hadn't forgotten the explosion. How could it? He'd made her feel so high, she'd virtually been floating. There were few enough men in her life who'd made her feel good, let alone afforded her that much pleasure for so little short term reward.

She'd phoned Ross out of guilt and then sat through the meeting at Melton, flushed and aroused, desperately craving Kit's touch again. When they'd paused for a break, she'd slipped away and frigged herself to orgasm in the store cupboard among the buckets and brooms, her supporting hand wrapped around the haft of the decrepit carpet sweeper for support.

"It's okay," Kit soothed. "It's okay. I swear it. You'll see." His lips touched hers, simultaneously blotting out reality and flooding her body with hot expectation. "Trust me. It's not going to be a problem."

With that, his softness departed. Kit's mouth crushed hers, his teeth bruising her lip. He slid his tongue into her mouth and she opened to him, letting him delve and tease until her senses were alight and she clung to his form. Kit kissed her with every inch of his body, not just his lips. His hips swayed against hers, his fingertips caressed her throat, the lengths of her arms, and her bottom. He took charge, but without forcing his will upon her. Kissing Kit reminded her of dancing, sometimes subtle, others raucous, but always in time with the beat.

His kiss changed everything and nothing.

"Kit, I can't do this," she protested as his tongue-tip dipped into the hollow at the base of her throat.

"Part your legs a bit," he said in response as if she'd said, "Fuck me now," instead of a pathetic attempt at "stop".

His hand snaked across her thigh and pushed between her parted legs. His mouth covered hers again, if indeed they'd ever really parted. Evie hissed in her next breath as his fingers inched inside her underwear and made contact with her clit. He rubbed and she sagged against him for the second time that day, her knees once more ready to buckle.

Evie clung to the thick leather belt around his waist as she rode his hand. Two fingers slid inside her, while his thumb circled. It felt so good, so perfect. She couldn't seem to stop herself, no matter how many bad images ran through her head.

There was no fighting the chemistry.

She dropped to her knees, startling a gasp from Kit's throat. On her knees, she unfastened his belt and drew down the zip of his trousers, leaving her with just a pair of skimpy black briefs to tease away from his skin.

She'd seen him before. Knew he didn't have a speck of hair down below, but was shaved bare instead, all silky smooth and exposed. Evie traced her fingers over the smooth expanse of skin, before wrapping her palm around his cock and angling him down towards her mouth. The taste of him, musky and slightly tart upon her tongue pushed her libido higher. Leisurely, he fucked her mouth, his strong hands mussing her hair. Evie sucked, frantic with fear and desire. Ross was due home. Any minute they'd hear the thrum of the car engine turning into the frost covered drive. Still, she couldn't back away. She couldn't let go.

Scared, she pushed against Kit's hips, forcing him up against the door and launched herself backwards away from him, only to land in an ungainly heap on top of the sacks of coal.

Her vision having finally adjusted to the dark, she could now make out Kit's expression—shocked, aroused and angry. He held back a moment, breathing raggedly, his lips pursed and his eyes hooded, before launching himself towards her.

"No, you have to let me go." The words formed a thick lump in her throat, before gushing free.

"I'm not stopping you." He took a pace to the side so that she had free passage to the door, but Evie never made it off the sacks.

Kit stood with his back pressed to the stonework, his trousers hugging his narrow hips, with the fly undone so he was displayed in all his masculine glory. His cock stood erect, virtually flat against his muscular stomach, and he'd wrapped his fist around the length. "I bet you'd like to watch us both doing this... maybe sat side-by-side?"

Foxed, she gaped at him, unable to deny the lust that wound tight around her body and threatened to consume her. Kit's hand action that first night was what had started all this off. She deeply regretted not sticking around to watch him toss himself off. Now, her gaze fastened upon the motion of his fingers around his shaft, and the way his thumb playfully brushed the tip.

Suddenly, his hands stopped moving.

Kit raised his brows. "Wanking's a solitary pleasure," he said with a grin. "It's not what I do when I've a willing woman to hand."

"I'm not willing, and you offered before."

He squeezed his pursed lips between his forefinger and thumb at her statement, and then smacked his lips. "That was different. I owed you. We've already settled that score."

Evie leaned towards him. "Are you saying you only masturbate if you're bound by obligation?"

"I'm saying," he said as he stretched towards her, "that I'd much rather entertain you with it properly, than just show you the warm-up act." His hands landed either side of her body among the coals.

"Have you had women pay you to do it?"

His soul dark eyes turned blacker than the coal.

"How much?"

Kit nervously licked his lips. "Doesn't matter. You're not ever paying me."

The thought hadn't actually occurred to her.

"If you really want to see me toss myself that much, come to my room tonight, because I can guarantee that's what I'll be doing, considering what I have to listen to most evenings. Right now, though, we're doing something else."

He grabbed her wrists and pressed her down into the Hessian sacking. Evie wriggled, not really feeling the discomfort of the lumpy coal beneath her, only the pleasant ache caused by his loins pressing against the tops of her thighs.

"Let go."

"No, not until you admit you want it every bit as much as I do."

"I dreamt you did this," she blurted. The admission burned all the way up her throat. "You held me down on the bed while Ross slept beside us."

Kit's eyes subtly narrowed. "I can do that."

"No!"

"No—really, or no—yes, please?"

"No."

"When did you dream it? The first night? I thought of you too, while I was stuck in that unfeasibly narrow guest bed of yours, all about how good you looked astride Ross's lap and how I really wanted to take what he'd been offering me."

Evie groaned, as Kit moved over her, and pressed kiss after exquisite little kiss, after sharp little bite to her neck and chin.

"Come to me tonight, Evie. I want to make love to you while I can still smell his scent on your skin. I want to make love to you knowing he's just spent himself inside you."

Her breath forced its way from her chest as a gasp. What he was saying ought to revolt her. Instead, it was turning her on. She'd never been with two men in the same month before, let alone while the sweat of one encounter still lay fresh upon her skin.

Kit clasped both wrists in one of his large hands and used his other to shove up her top and bra. Her breasts spilled heavily, the nipples pointedly erect. "I love that you're so responsive." He blew across the steepled peak, prompting a groan. Then he yanked down her trousers and panties. He ran his fingers through her curls and dabbed them into the slick wet heat of her cunt. Finally, he pressed his cock where his fingers had explored so that he coated himself in her arousal.

Evie lifted her hips, wanting him, aching for him. Her muscles protested over the position, but regardless, she pushed her hips up, high on the feel of his hard heat between her thighs.

"You know we can't do this, right?" he purred into her ear, provoking a desperate "huh". "We wouldn't want to go getting that intimate on a first date without some additional wrapping now, would we?"

God, how could he think so rationally?

Condoms! What she wouldn't give for a pack of them to pop into existence and land at his fingertips.

"So this has just been one long tease," she moaned.

Kit touched her clit again. "Come on, Evie. You know you don't really want me to do this naked. Who knows where I've been."

"I don't." What he said made absolute sense, but they were so—oo close.

"Don't you carry one in your wallet?"

"It's in the house." A look of pure wickedness crept across his face. "Do you want me to run and get one?"

"Fuck, no." Never mind Ross being due home; she wasn't having him give the neighbours an eyeful.

"A good fuck is exactly what I'm offering." The sound of a thrumming engine filtered in from outside. "Ah, I think that's the decision made."

Evie groaned as the headlights of Ross's car briefly lit up the interior of the shed as he pulled onto the drive. "Get off me." For a good forty seconds that seemed to stretch into eternity, Kit didn't move. He stared down at her, while Evie struggled, convinced that Ross would throw open the door and find them strewn across the coal sacks as close to penetration as it was physically possible to get without actually doing the deed. "Please." Finally, he uncurled his fingers from around her wrists.

Evie leapt up and warily righted her clothes. Coal dust streaked her trousers and coat, and black fingerprints dotted various bits of her skin. Not sure what else to do, she flung open the door and fled.

Ross called to her as she ran towards the back steps, but she didn't turn or stop. She kept on running until she reached the bathroom. There, behind the frosted screen of glass bricks, she stripped off her clothes and stepped under the shower. Icy water pounded her skin like thousands of stinging needles. What had she just done? More importantly, what sort of message had she just given Ross? Guilt sat ill on Evie's shoulders. *I've got to tell him.* That was assuming Kit didn't simply out them both by strolling out of the coalhouse with his tackle hanging out.

Any minute...any minute, Ross would be hammering on the door, telling her it was over.

"You idiot," she cursed herself, banging her head against the tiles. "You bloody fool."

Slowly, sickeningly, the water temperature rose. The rivulets trickled down her face, mixing with the scalding tears. Be honest, she counselled herself as she sniffled into a flannel. Face Ross like an adult and tell him what you've done and how you feel. Find out if Kit's being remotely honest, and if he's not, tell him to take a hike and find somewhere else to stay.

Chapter Eight

Rather than chasing Evie, Ross hung back on the driveway, his arm looped over the top of the open driver's side door. Sure enough the cause of her flight appeared, as anticipated, a moment later. "Do I want to know the reason she's just run upstairs?" he asked Kit. There were several possibilities trundling around his brain already. In his experience women only ran for a handful of reasons a) they were masochistic Olympians, b) they were being chased and didn't actually want to get caught, and c) they felt guilty and wanted to avoid blurting out whatever sin currently consumed them.

His friend gave him a troubled smile. Troubled, Ross noted, rather than guilty. Kit reserved his guilt for one topic in particular. Still, as Ross's gaze wandered over Kit's wiry form there were certain giveaway signs to what he'd intruded upon. Kit's fingernails were full of coal dust. No surprise, since he'd just come out of the shed. Obviously, the fuel delivery had arrived. But not even Kit could get turned on by a few bags of coal. No, clearly the hard-on the size of the Eiffel Tower he was sporting came courtesy of Evie.

"Have you been warming that up for me, or getting frisky with my lady?" he asked.

Kit crossed his arms and slumped back against the wall. His gaze turned skyward, chin up in the air. The pose was pure feigned nonchalance. Ross got right up in his face and wrapped a hand around Kit's balls. That got his attention.

"It's bad enough when you fuck with me, Kit. Don't start screwing with Evie's head, or I'll start screwing with you."

"Promises, promises…" Kit mused.

This close, the scent of Kit's skin hit Ross hard. "Jesus, you reek of her. Kit…?" He left the question at that. It wasn't as if it needed any further qualification, they both knew what he was asking, and Kit didn't try to conceal the truth. Maintaining eye contact with Ross, Kit held out two fingers of his right hand.

"That's all, I swear. Maybe we should all be together the first time."

Unlike the others, the nails of the fore and index fingers were clean. Ross sniffed at them and then sucked them into his mouth. The unmistakable taste of his girlfriend's body flooded his taste buds. Part of him felt consumed with rage, the rest sank into the mire of…arousal. While he hadn't actually invited Kit to make a move on Evie, he hadn't specifically forbidden it either. He could rationalize it to himself as an unnecessary act. Normal people respected relationship boundaries. The thing was, his relationship with Kit had never been remotely normal. It had been voyeuristic and obsessive, painful, incredible, and in the final moments before he'd left for Japan, blissfully intense.

Ross tightened his grip on Kit's balls, so that his thumb dug into the skin between them at their base, making Kit gasp and hop up onto his toes. Shit—if his squirming didn't turn Ross on. Heat rushed to his groin, and he experienced a burning urge to thrust his hands inside his pants and squeeze his cock. He squeezed Kit's instead, causing another gasp to escape his friend's lips.

Ross stared at those sensual lips, and the five o' clock shadow above, and craved the kiss he'd tried so hard to reject a week ago. He pressed himself up against Kit's body and breathed in the stink of him. He'd been labouring, and there'd been their little phone tryst earlier coupled with whatever he'd been getting up to with Evie to make him sweat, so that his pheromones clung to him like aftershave. "In there, right now."

He let go of Kit long enough to open the coalhouse door and back him inside. He let the wind blow the door shut behind them. "I've had just as much as I can take from you. What is it you want, Kit?"

"You know what I want. I want you, and I want Evie."

"You hardly know her."

"I don't need to know her. I know you. I can see she's the right one."

"You tried this before, remember?"

"That was different: different woman, different time, different expectations. Besides, I wasn't the outsider that time."

"And if I don't want you involved?"

"Just say the word, Ross." Kit reached out a hand towards him and briefly brushed Ross's jaw line before clasping his shoulder. "You know I'll back off."

"Damn you!" Ross grabbed Kit's collar and yanked his head forward. Such a fine, fine line was drawn between what he wanted to do next. His fingers curled tighter on the fabric, until his knuckles ached. Kit's lips were enticingly parted. Ross fell to his knees.

The scent of Kit was even stronger now. Ross rubbed his face up against the V at the top of Kit's thighs and licked at his clean-shaven balls. He wondered if he could persuade him to let the hair grow in again. He liked a bit of camouflage down there.

Kit laced his fingers through Ross's hair. "Is this your decision, or just a torment, because I'd rather not stand here freezing my nuts off if..." His words faltered as Ross wrapped his palm around Kit's cock and swirled his tongue around the head. "Fuck!" Kit closed his eyes and gritted his teeth.

"Not today," said Ross. He teased his tongue over the sensitive slitted-eye again.

"Oh, fuck," swore Kit, pushing forward from the hips, his voice an agitated purr.

"Easy, tiger."

Kit pulled his hair, trying to draw him closer, which made

Ross laugh.

"I ought to get up and leave you like this."

Kit's eyes flickered open, beneath his long, dark eyelashes, his pupils widely dilated.

"But you know what? I can't. I can't do it, Kit. As much as I want to walk away, I want to taste you too much." He caught a bead of precome on his tongue and rolled the taste around his mouth. "Beg me. I want to hear it."

"Pissing hell!" Kit gulped. "I've waited six fucking years for this and you want me to prostrate myself?"

Ross ran his hands up and down the tightly clenched muscles of Kit's thighs, unable to stop himself touching but holding out for a little politeness. When it didn't immediately come, he forced himself to stop and breathe.

Kit's teeth chattered.

"Okay. Please," he hissed when he realized Ross was genuinely going to leave him hanging.

The taste of Kit soon covered Ross's lips and tongue. He sucked, relishing the hint of aggression behind each thrust. This felt so right, he could hardly keep focused enough to keep his teeth out of the way. But while sucking was good, it wasn't going to be enough long term. He wanted more intimacy than that.

His thoughts quickly turned to Kit's earlier suggestion. They'd never actually ventured as far as penetration before. In truth, they'd barely ventured along the path of touching one another without a woman present to make it okay. This was pushing things in a very different direction—one he found scarily attractive. He might not have fucked a guy before, but he could imagine exactly how it would feel—hot and tight and thrillingly taboo.

The idea of having Evie with them, watching them together like that was like adding a sprinkle of rocket fuel to an already roaring blaze, and sent his libido sky high.

Ross let Kit's cock slap against his cheek a few times, then he worked his hand inside his trousers and wrapped it around his own cock, which lay trapped inside his shorts, fit for bursting. He jerked himself to the same rhythm as he sucked Kit, so that everything worked together like a well-greased piston. The taste of salt grew heavy on his tongue, and Kit's moans filled the air. Hell, if anyone happened to be walking past outside there'd be no mistaking what was going on. There'd been times in the past when the thought of being caught inflagrante would have left him mortified. Now, he didn't care.

Kit began to claw at him, and Ross upped the motion of his wrist.

Okay, maybe he balked a little at the possibility of Evie finding them. He'd rather address the situation in a less direct manner.

Kit's knees buckled as he came. He leaned heavily on Ross's shoulders, squashing him against his swaying hips, so that Ross's nose was glued to the base of Kit's cock. Ross relaxed his throat and as best he could for the last few breathless moments, as Kit came. Prior to that moment Ross had been intending to spit. As it was, he swallowed and shot his own load over the floor.

Winded, Ross stayed on his knees until Kit offered him a hand up. They stood facing one another, not quite making eye contact, neither of them managing to speak. Shiftily, they cleaned up and buttoned up. Then Ross went outside and locked up the car. Finally, Kit spoke as they mounted the steps to the kitchen door. "Beer," he croaked.

"There's some draught Guinness in the fridge."

"I'll get them."

Kit set about the task, while Ross went upstairs and changed out of his work clothes. He pulled on his oldest jumper and a pair of ill-fitting jeans that were ripped across both knees. They might have seen better days, but they made him feel comfortable inside his skin. He hadn't meant everything that had happened today to occur, but well...events had rather overtaken him. He grimaced slightly, hearing the shower running next door, and his vexation at Kit over whatever he'd tried on with Evie reasserted itself. He hung outside the bathroom door a moment, wondering if he ought to knock and see if she was okay. Then again, perhaps it was better to let her emerge in her own time.

Back downstairs, Kit had lit the fire and turned on the Playstation. "Punch up, driving, or other." Kit fanned three games out in front of Ross.

"Fighting," said Ross. It'd be less bloody this way. Games to work out their frustrations with one another.

Kit cocked an eyebrow at him underneath his long fringe. He'd brushed his hair forward so that it masked the line of dried blood and glue upon his brow. "I don't know," he said, holding Ross's gaze. "I think I'd rather you just split my lip, if that's what's in your thoughts."

"That—" said Ross, "—is because you're all about the physical. Which is cracked, by the way, considering what an expert at mental torture you are." He slumped onto the sofa. "Sit your butt down and press some mechanical buttons instead of mine for a while."

"Do you want to talk about Evie?"

Ross shrugged. "Let me work out how to approach her."

"You're ready to share?"

"I'm ready to goddamn kill you." Ross began hammering the controller buttons, sending his onscreen sprite into a ninja waltz. "Fuck, Kit! This is mental."

Kit smacked his thigh hard enough to make it sting. "It'll be fucking hot. And she's up for it, don't doubt that. God, is she up for it."

"Not now," said Ross. "I'm not ready for this now."

Chapter Nine

Evie strung out her shower for as long as possible, letting the water cascade over her shoulders and wash away all traces of Kit's scent upon her skin. Then, huddled in a bath sheet and dressing gown, she spent another forty minutes filing and painting her toenails, and smothering every inch of her skin in coconut body butter. In the end, there was no trace of male pheromones anywhere upon her and precious little of her own scent. Instead, she wafted into the living room in a cloud of honey and vanilla, smelling rather like an exotic fruit.

Confessions were best made properly armed, and the sweet fragrance gave her confidence.

It still surprised her that Ross hadn't been upstairs to seek her out. Expecting a confrontation, Evie ironed out the creases in her brow as best she could and tried to look repentant, not that either of the two men hunched upon the sofa noticed.

Having pulled the sofa away from its normal position below the window, they'd aligned it, bachelor style, right across the centre of the living room, facing the TV. A metal soundtrack blared from the surround sound speakers, while onscreen an extremely busty blonde was pounding it out with some sort of ninja wraith.

Ross turned from the screen and gave her a friendly grin. Evie inwardly winced at the warmth and love evident in his gaze.

"K.O.," announced the onscreen commentator.

"Yes," snarled Kit.

Ross swapped the Playstation controller to his off hand and extended his right towards her. "Coming to join us?"

Guilt further chewed at her insides as Evie perched beside him. Even as a child, deceit had never come easy to her. She still remembered with vivid horror the time, aged seven, when she'd taken the chocolate bar from her dad's bait box without asking. "Can we talk?" she asked.

Ross squeezed her around the middle and rested his head in the crook of her shoulder. "In a bit."

Maybe she ought to admit the infidelity now, while Kit was present and they could all say their bits, assuming it didn't immediately devolve into a god awful row. Who knew if Kit's version of reality bore any relation to the truth, or whether Ross would see it as an ultimate betrayal on the part of both of them. No, best she waited and lured him away from Kit first. Kit, who made her blood boil, sitting there without a care for the trouble he'd caused. Interestingly, the shadowy line of stubble that covered his jaw suited him. It made him look less metrosexual and more testosterone-infused hunk, an image only exacerbated by his mussed up hair and activity-creased clothes. He had his legs folded up in front of him and the controller perched on top of his knees. His bare toes curled around the edge of the sofa cushion. Actually, both of them were barefoot, and sitting curiously close. Ross hadn't had to shuffle up to make space for her.

Clearly, they were at peace, which begged the question of whether Ross had cottoned on to what had been going on in the coal shed.

"What's the full on pamper in aid of?" Ross asked, pulling her thoughts back from the fit of speculation.

"Nothing."

He took a good look at her face. "I might get jealous if you keep dressing up for him." His gaze slid towards Kit then back to her and grinned.

"I'm not...I didn't!"

"Sure about that?"

"Ross?" God, did he know? Had Kit said something? Was he genuinely okay with it? Did that mean the offer of a threesome was real too? The fact that he slipped his arm around her waist, and under her top, seemed to suggest it was.

Ever so slowly, Ross's palm moved up her body, until his fingertips knotted under the wire of her bra, and lifted it away from her ribs. Evie hardly dared breathe. The possibility that this was some sort of test kept tumbling around her brain in an endless cycle. Fact was, Evie hated being overheard having sex, let alone being watched. She'd never been the sort to play embarrassing lip hockey, even in a room full of mates. He'd seen her freak the previous time he'd got frisky with her with Kit as an audience.

Unnerved, she bit her lip, while Ross, whose hand now cupped her whole right breast, captured the nipple between his index finger and thumb.

Having abandoned all pretence of playing the video game, Kit's gaze lay fastened upon her, his coal-dark eyes merrily glinting. Desire churned in her stomach, and shot poisonous arrows down towards her cunt. Could she sit here and let Ross make love to her with Kit watching? What if he actually joined in and touched her? The mere thought of it sent another spear of arousal through her innards. Hell, what if Ross realized how much the notion turned her on and got jealous? What would happen to their relationship then? Were a few moments of fun worth the risk of making that discovery?

They weren't. She knew it in her heart, and for once her head was actually in agreement.

Uneasily, she tried to squirm free of Ross's grasp.

He wasn't having it. He surprised her by straddling her lap and ripping her top up over her head.

Goosebumps peppered Evie's skin. Kit put down his game controller and turned sideways on the sofa. He slowly wetted his upper lip as his gaze fixed upon her breasts. Fire streamed into Evie's cheeks. She longed for the audacity to stick her hand in the air and stop this long enough to ask what the hell was going on.

Ross leaned closer, sandwiching their loins together. Like Kit, he bore the faint shadow of stubble around his jaw, only his whiskers were the pale golden brown of malt whisky in a glass. Deep down he had the same sort of burn too. I know what you've been up to and you're a bad, bad, girl, said his eyes. But did he really know?

Evie allowed herself to wallow in their azure depths a moment, pretending Kit didn't exist, but considering he had the sort of presence that made you sit up and pay attention, she couldn't maintain the ruse for long.

"Now the bra." Ross made minimum effort of the catch. He drew the shell-pink silk down her arms and then threw it over the sofa back. Evie clamped her folded arms across her breasts, the large nipples of which were puckered up tight. "Aw, Eve. Don't go hiding 'em from me. You know how much I like to feast upon them." In two easy actions, Ross had uncrossed her arms, and sucked one dark pink peak into his mouth.

A groan erupted from her throat.

Ross roughly crushed her other breast within his palm. Then his hands were moulding both breasts and his lips were tight to her ear. "Don't look at him," he whispered.

This of course, made her stare directly at Kit, and once trapped, there was no helping herself. There was just something about his make up—the sooty lashes that framed those dark eyes, the curve of his cheekbones, and that overindulgent pout, that held her completely captive.

Oh, God, please make this happen.

She could hear the harsh rasp of Kit's breathing, an only marginally less steamy purr than the one that currently rumbled in Ross's throat.

Please, God—she closed her eyes tight—please!

The sofa springs squeaked as Kit shifted his weight, in order to edge a fraction closer to the necking couple. He'd seen the confusion in Evie's eyes, mixed up with her blatant desire for what she imagined was happening. Kit wasn't so sure that Ross had the same thing in mind. His lover's jaw was locked so tight his chin jutted out.

Kit didn't crowd the pair, but he settled close enough to feel the heat radiating off them and to smell the heady musk of their bodies replace the sweet scent of Evie's pamper products.

Evie looked terrific post-coalhouse tryst and invigorating shower. Good enough to eat. He wanted to lick her like he would an ice-cream. Her skin had a slight shimmer to it, giving it a golden glow that added a more tactile quality to her soft curves. Her breasts especially, he wanted to touch. Two nipples, two men... But, it still wasn't happening tonight, not unless he'd completely forgotten how to read Ross. Still, he admired the sight of her. Kit liked that she was shapely and rounded, all soft curves, a real exemplification of pagan sexiness. Androgyny, in either sex, had never appealed to him. He liked opposites, soft femininity in women and hard brawn in men.

Already braced for rejection, he stretched his hand towards Ross's back. For several blissful seconds he enjoyed the feel of Ross's muscles working under the skin, as he pressed his palm flat to the bare band of flesh visible below the hem of Ross's decrepit jumper, then the rejection came. Even expected, it jarred. There were no words, Ross didn't even turn. He simple lifted Kit's hand from where it rested and laid it upon the sofa cushion instead.

If a more eloquent way of saying "no" existed, Kit had yet to experience it. He didn't wait for a verbal reiteration, knowing it would only chafe an already open wound. Ross understood that he wanted to be part of their relationship, not a bleedin' voyeur. Fuck that! If Ross thought that he was going to sit here like a good boy and watch, he was sadly mistaken.

Hoping to prompt a reaction, Kit scooped Mimmy from her

basket and left the room. He sat on the stairs, nursing the squirming kitten and an outrageous hard-on.

How mental was this? Still he held off from charging back in and making demands. He wanted this to work, which called for the softly-softly approach to certain aspects of it. Anyway, they'd made it over several hurdles today; best he didn't risk another quite yet.

He noticed they'd begun talking the moment he left. The two voices tumbled over one another in what he presumed were strings of adjectives and excuses. He didn't want them to admit to what was going on to one another yet. Too much remained at stake. He wasn't convinced Evie was ready to entertain the idea of an intimate relationship between himself and Ross. When he'd hinted at it, she'd exhibited classic signs of denial. So far, her concept of a threesome consisted of a whole lot of male attention lavished upon her, and no straying into gay. They needed to address that, really needed to, because he had no intention of keeping his hands off Ross, as he loved the sandy-haired powerhouse far too much.

The hum of voices abruptly ceased. Judging by the grunts and gasps, Ross had taken charge and Evie was now blowing him.

Kit closed his eyes and recalled the taste of Ross's cock upon his tongue, and then the sensations of both Ross and Evie giving him head. Curious that they'd both lavished that particular pleasure on him today. Evie definitely won on technique, although he admired Ross for his teasing and enthusiasm.

Absentminded of the cat, Kit hugged himself. Mimmy objected by sinking her claws into his arm. Talk about a passion killer. He released her and rubbed at the wounds, and watched her bolt back into the living room, presumably intent upon taking up her favourite radiator perch.

He couldn't resist. Down he followed as far as the door, which sat slightly ajar thanks to Mimmy's entry. Kit lurked in the shadows, his fly undone and his waistband slung low on his hips. He could see Evie's face over the back of the sofa. Her head thrown back, chin up, as Ross noisily sucked upon her nipples. He had her breasts squeezed together, forming an incredible cleavage that he was lavishing attention upon, while she frigged herself and stroked his cock.

Nice, he thought, supplanting himself from his outpost to a central position behind Evie, facing Ross in his fantasy recreation of the scene. He plastered himself to her naked back, roughly jostled with Ross for possession of her breasts, then while rolling her huge nipples between his fingers, he nuzzled closer and sucked hard upon her neck, leaving a vivid mark.

"That's right, Evie, suck it down. God, you're loving this."

Ross certainly was. He reckoned he could probably get off on just the image of her on her knees, half-naked with her head bobbing. The fact that she happened to be doing exactly that was a major bonus. The only thing he'd change in an ideal world was that they'd be doing this in the shower or outdoors in a thunderstorm. Although, it'd have to be a nice monsoon-type thunderstorm so the rain wasn't too cold.

One of these days he really was going to have her do this outside in the rain in some nice romantic location, maybe even on their honeymoon, if she ever let him get that old-fashioned. For now, he wanted to hold her. Coming in her mouth, while nice, lacked the same intimacy as lying pressed together, bare skin moving against bare skin.

Ross clasped the base of his cock and coaxed Evie to release him with a gentle push upon her shoulder. She gazed up at him from her knees, her pale-blue eyes full of glamour.

"Upstairs," he said. "Go."

She shot off as though it was a race.

Ross scooped her clothes off the floor and threw them into the kitchen so that they landed before the washing machine, then turned off all the lights, the games machine, and the TV.

Evie sat on her side of the bed facing the window, a black

silhouette against the cream curtains, when Ross entered the room. She turned her head to eye him across the expanse of the duvet.

Ross gently shut the door. For a moment, he simply drank down the image of her, with her soft curves and lovely, oval-shaped face. Even in the semi-dark, he could make out the dimple in her cheek that formed when she smiled.

"Get on the bed. On your hands and knees," he said quietly. He didn't want it to be a command, even though that's what it was.

Unhesitant, she obeyed.

Ross stood for a moment, his hand wrapped around his stiff cock, trying to make sense of what he was doing. He wanted her, and yet he had an image of Kit in that damn leather wingback chair he had at work, all curled up and desperate to fuck. The same thirty second video loop had been playing in his head all afternoon.

But he'd sent Kit away. Wordlessly banished him. Okay, he hadn't intentionally done so, but he should have realized that Kit wouldn't tolerate being relegated to the side-lines. Nope, he liked running the show too much.

The thing was, everything was changing, and he wanted tonight—now—to be about Evie and him. They both needed to wise up to the risks they were taking, and realize exactly how much was at stake if they let Kit have his way. And yet as he climbed onto the bed, still fully clothed, all thoughts of making things perfect between them vanished.

"You want him don't you?" he said ever so quietly—a sharp contrast to his more violent action as he ripped the flimsy lace thong she wore from her body.

Evie gave a small gasp, but didn't offer a denial.

"Maybe you wish it was him here now, with his cock out ready to fuck you, rather than me. Maybe he already has."

"Uh!" she said, reduced to making inarticulate grunts as he pushed his cock into her wet, hot sheath, and she welcomed him with unprecedented eagerness. Damn, if all this talk of Kit wasn't turning him on as much as it was Evie.

That was a good thing, he reminded himself. Leastways, it ought to be.

"How would you like it if I called him in here right now? I could sit back here stroking myself as I watched you and him fuck." Ross rocked his hips, enjoying the easy slide that made his balls slap against her skin. "You'd like it, wouldn't you, Evie? Jeez, you're so fucking hot for it I can barely keep a grip on you. You're not even denying it." To be fair, she wasn't actually saying anything, but Ross knew arousal when he saw it, and currently, forget cloud nine, Evie was up on cloud ninety-nine.

"I want you." She gave a mangled gasp.

"You don't want Kit?"

She began to shake her head and then stopped. Lying had never been Evie's forte.

Evie tried to say more, really she did, but couldn't seem to get her vocal chords to cooperate. She'd never seen this side of Ross before, so rough and possessive, but in a screwed up, back to front sort of way. She understood that what he was really asking was, "Do you like him better?" and "Evie, are you still in love with me?" But she didn't have any simple answers to give him.

What she had with Ross she never wanted to end, but at the same time, it was safe, familiar and comfortable. There were no big shocks and no nasty surprises. Kit appealed to her in a fundamentally different way. She didn't expect him to stick around, wasn't even sure if she wanted him too. Kit was one hundred percent prime fling material, a bad boy with a spectacularly good ass. She found him sexy and curiously addictive. That he could turn her on so easily she found both enthralling and terrifying.

But he wasn't partner material. He wasn't the sort of man you settled down and started making baby plans with.

Baby plans!

That's why they'd moved here, because she wanted to settle down and get serious. Mucking around with her boyfriend's best mate and hankering after a threesome were hardly the acts of a woman looking for commitment.

Ross shuffled over a bit and stretched towards the bedside cabinet, although his grip remained firm upon her backside. He yanked open her bottom drawer. Heat flooded Evie's cheeks as he raked amongst her ancient collection of hair curlers and odd socks to find her vibrator. Somehow, when Ross lifted it, it seemed twice as huge and far more realistic looking. It actually pre-dated their relationship. He only knew she had it because she'd used it as an impromptu back massager one time when he'd got a crick in his shoulder.

"Ross," she croaked. "What are you doing?"

He squirted the latex cock with lube and rubbed his hand up and down the flesh-pink shaft, making it shiny.

"Ross?"

He pulled out of her in response, leaving her feeling bereft. A moment later, he pushed the squirming vibe into her cunt instead and revved it up a bit.

"I know you're curious, Evie. So, why don't I give you a taste? You can't get that camping story he told you out of your head, can you? I'll bet you've been frigging yourself in the toilets at work imagining having us do you together."

"Tents make me horny."

"Cocks make you horny. I know how much you like playing with mine. The prospect of two must leave you sopping."

"Personality," she whispered under her breath. It wasn't just about exposure. Cocks could be works of art, but it wasn't them, but rather the whole mental mind-fuck thing that she really got off on. It wasn't the motion of his hand upon his shaft that left her breathless when she watched him masturbate. It was the knowledge that he was engaging in a taboo act for her entertainment. Right now though, Ross seemed intent upon exploring another taboo act. Even before he drew his thumb along the channel between her cheeks and circled around the puckered ring of muscle, she'd understood his intention.

They'd been dancing around this act for so long now... She guessed the time was ripe.

The very tip of his finger teased its way inside her arse.

The new sensation combined with the buzz of the vibrator set her hips in motion. Ross drew another item from the drawer, this one an ancient unused Christmas present. He tied the multi-coloured scarf over her eyes, causing another shiver of excitement to roll down her spine.

"I'm going to let Kit fuck you, Evie. You know that I'm in your cunt right now, well, I'm going to let Kit take you in the arse. We're going to have you together. Do you understand? We're going to have you together."

Blinded, Evie became completely submerged in the fantasy. She squirmed over the intrusion of Ross's fingers into her arse, even when her nerve-endings lit like sparklers. Sensations assaulted her from her front and back. Ross's cock felt huge. Huge and hot. He slid into her really slowly. She wasn't sure if that didn't serve to make it worse. It didn't hurt precisely, but it was raw. The sensations involved right on the edge of what she thought she could tolerate. "Ross," she gasped, squeezing her eyes together beneath the blindfold. "Oh, God! Ross."

"I know. I know." The low rumble of his voice soothed some of the tension from her body, as did the slow reassuring stroke of his hands. "Slowly, that does it." He started to rock, sliding into her and withdrawing slowly. "That feels so good. You feel so good, Evie. Shall we pick the speed up a bit?"

He swirled the dial on the vibe up a bit. Ross jerked into her, gasping, and immediately twitched the dial back down again.

"That's a little too good," he squeaked. "Oh, boy!"

Evie wished she could see his face, so she could gauge how close to the edge the sudden buzz had taken him. He wouldn't let her turn though and smacked her arse when she tugged at the blindfold. His strokes quickened, and he began jerking the vibe in time with his motion so that it became easy to fall into the fantasy that both Ross and Kit were filling her.

Ross continued to murmur into her ear, painting fantastic pictures of the three-way coupling, until Evie stopped hearing the words. Her thoughts collapsed inwards as the sensations in her cunt and in her rear overwhelmed her completely. She gave herself up to motion and the rippling stream of pleasure that swirled around her clit and flowed outwards. She came hard, screaming and bucking like a thing possessed, and hugging the pillow as if it truly were Kit.

Ross held her through the waves and stayed with her even when vibe slipped free. He licked the sweat from her back, drawing his tongue up to her shoulder blades, so that he lay so deep inside her, his balls pressed against her swollen, sensitive skin. "I love you," he whispered and squeezed her tight.

The hug dissipated a second later. Instead, he clamped onto her hips and rode her so that their bodies repeatedly slapped together, and only released her once he'd come deep inside her.

"God, you're fucking amazing." Ross held her until his erection faded, then rolled off the bed and padded away. Evie tentatively eased her muscles out of their stiffened positions. She was still rubbing the kinks out of her knees when Ross returned with a warm flannel to help clean her up.

"Ross, I don't want us to fall apart," she said.

He caught her gaze, but couldn't hold it. Ross plumped the pillows up and settled on his back. He tugged Evie into the crux of his shoulder. "You do fancy him, though?"

"Yes," she admitted. "It's hard not to."

"I know," he soothed. "I know. He's hard to resist."

"I'm sorry, Ross."

"Don't be sorry. You know I'll give you whatever you want."

Now was the time when she really ought to make her confession, tell him exactly what had happened in the coal shed and out on the hillside, but a quick glance at Ross confirmed that he was already sliding into post-coital exhaustion. Maybe now wasn't the time. Then again, when would there ever be a good time to confess?

"Hypothetically," she began and bit her lip.

"It's fine." Ross sleepily patted her shoulder. "If you want to fuck him, that's okay as long as you don't mind me humping him too."

Her initial shock—she would never have dreamed of asking him that—transformed into surprise. Mirth spread across her face. "Oh, yeah, I can just see you and him giving each other a knuckle shuffle." It didn't matter how hot she found the thought. It wasn't ever going to happen. She laughed, but her merriment soon died away, and she settled against Ross's shoulder. "Were you serious?" she asked a moment later, afraid of how excited the almost permission made her.

Ross yawned making a braying sound reminiscent of a donkey. "Damnit, Evie, if you want any more action tonight it's going to have to be with him. The only loving I'm fit for now is a date with my pillow."

"So, you were serious?"

He looked at her, but his eyes soon slid closed again, and he gave another terrific yawn.

"It'd be okay?"

Ross mumbled something which might have been a yes and she thought he nodded. The question was, how compos mentis had he actually been? Could she actually interpret his sleepy mumblings as permission to act on her attraction to Kit, or would Ross wake up and think they'd been talking about frogs?

"Really, it's okay?"

In response he curled his big body around her, so that she lay tucked tight to his side. Since Ross wasn't normally one for snuggling she took that as a reassurance, but it still didn't entirely eliminate her guilt.

Chapter Ten

Evie sat up and folded her legs before her. She watched the gentle rise and fall of Ross's chest, even bestowed a few kisses upon it where his hair formed a diamond-shape over his heart. She couldn't settle though, she kept thinking of Kit, and how he was probably stretched out next door, pleasuring himself having eavesdropped on the entirety of her and Ross's lovemaking. In a way that seemed fair, considering they'd made him part of the scenario.

When she crept to the bathroom over an hour later, a faint gleam of light showed beneath the bottom of the guest room door. Evie hurried passed, afraid he was waiting up for her. She hadn't forgotten his request that she come to him with Ross's sweat fresh upon her skin, and though the idea left her curiously excited, she wasn't about to act it out. Instead she waddled across the landing, intending to soak way the cricks in her limbs and the ache in her heart with half a bottle of Radox.

She left the main light off in the bathroom opting for the dim shaving light over the mirror instead. Evie looked at her reflection, barely recognizing herself. Oh, outwardly she remained the same, slightly overweight, blue eyes, streaked mousy brown hair, but inside something had changed. Her vision of domestic goddesshood had been blasted to smithereens by a black-eyed rogue, with snaky hips and a silver-tongue. A man who claimed that being with him wouldn't upset the balance of her current relationship, and whom she truly wanted to believe, only he'd already upset the balance, and surely a threesome wouldn't be more than a one off. What happened afterwards?

She jumped at the knock on the door. Kit let himself in. "Is everything okay?" he asked.

Evie didn't grace him with an answer. If everything had been okay, she wouldn't have been lurking in the bathroom at one a.m.

"Evie?" He padded barefoot over the tiles to reach her, a black silk kimono covering his nakedness. "I could hear you. I heard what Ross was saying. What did he do to you?" His image swam in the mirror beside hers, dark hair swept across his brow to mask his eyes.

"None of your business." She dropped her gaze to the mug holding their toothbrushes, three of them, squashed together where there'd recently only been two.

"Is it not?" Kit spun her around. He held her facing him with his hands upon her shoulders. "Seems to me that I was involved, considering how many times my name got mentioned." He leaned closer, as if he was about to kiss her. The dark line of stubble above his lip had grown thicker. There was a shadow to his jaw line too. "What sort of make believe did you play?"

"Did you tell him?" she asked, seeking out the truth in the dark depths of his eyes. "Have you had a nice chat about me, discussed what's allowed?"

Kit's brow furrowed into numerous tiny lines. He eased back a little and pressed a finger to his lips in quiet deliberation. "What are you suggesting? That we've been debating access rights?" He brushed a stray lock of hair away from where it clung to her cheek, and tried to lift her gaze. Evie stubbornly resisted. "You're your own person. Only you can say who you're with."

Below the hem of Kit's kimono his knees were battered and scarred. Evie concentrated on them in an attempt to push everything else aside. "What happened?"

"That's right, change the topic." Kit began to laugh. "Hell, I know my knees are ugly, but I'd hate to think they were a deciding factor in all this."

"Why did you come here?" she asked.

"Bathroom, here, or Kirkley?" he asked as he hooked the side of his fingers under her chin, in order to lift her gaze.

Evie found it hard to look at him. She was still psyched up after the fantasy she'd just shared with Ross, a fantasy in which Kit had been far more than a friend, or just their house guest. It was a good fantasy, but she needed to remember that's all it was. Three people would always equate to a crowd, one person in the middle, one person always left out. She knew how she'd feel if Ross became involved with one of her close friends, and it wasn't a pleasant emotion. Jealousy—everything about it implied heartache.

Kit brushed his thumb over her lips and slowly began to circle them. "I had unfinished business here. That's why I came. There are some things you just can't leave hanging forever."

"How—will you finish them?"

"Oh, I don't know. Like this maybe?" He tugged the belt of her dressing gown so that the knot gave and unravelled, causing the edges of the robe to part. Evie quickly drew the towelling around herself, hiding the flash of creamy skin and the shadowy hint of curls over her mound.

"This is crazy," she gasped.

He squinted at her, but didn't prevent her hiding. "No, it's honest." A smile lighting his expression, Kit feathered his fingers over the front of his kimono, so that he traced the plane of his stomach through the silk. A tingle of excitement grew inside her at the display. Her fingers twitched with the urge to reach out and trace the wiry slabs of muscle that graced his torso, to explore each hollow and ridge, and make his nipples pucker into two sharp points. She wanted to caress his balls with her fingers and tongue, fall upon his cock again, wrap her fist around the shaft as it stood tall, and watch the resulting erotic meltdown occur in the depths of his eyes.

Kit shrugged off the mantle, and let it drop to the floor behind him, where it formed a puddle like an oil slick, full of rainbow hues.

"Kit..." She couldn't take her eyes off him. Evie loved Ross's rugged physique, the smattering of hair upon his chest, and the way his veins popped out and ran across his biceps, but Kit naked... Words really didn't do him justice. Ripped and smooth, all long limbs and snaky hipped, he oozed the sort of magnetism that made you want to reach out and not only touch, but rub yourself against him. Bloody gorgeous didn't come close to describing him.

Teetering, she stretched out her hand towards him, wanting the contact of skin against skin. Kit took hold and pressed her palm flat against his stomach, just shy of his erection.

If only she was as certain as he was that Ross wouldn't object.

It wasn't about making a choice in the end. Kit held her and he kissed her. She couldn't avoid it, nor could she get him to release her once their lips met. He held her fast against the tiles, his naked body pressed to hers, a hot contrast to the wall behind, as he coaxed her with his tongue.

His hands slid inside her robe to rove lightly over her skin. He pinched her nipples, while his lips traced the pulse point in her neck. He sucked hard, making her whimper and cling to him, as sparks fired and joined together to zip between all of her pleasure points. Edging down onto his knees, he cupped her pussy and pushed his fingers into her cunt, to the welcoming slick sounds of her arousal.

"Do you remember earlier I said I wanted to smell where he had been? Well, I can smell him on you now. I'll bet I can taste him too." Naked before her, he crouched and drove his tongue between the wet lips of her sex.

Evie clung to the towel rail, unable to do much beside

groan and support herself. That boy was downright wicked with his tongue and downright cheeky too, since he kept slipping it places he really shouldn't. Not that he was going to taste Ross there, since he'd been fucking her bottom.

"Let's do this right, this time, shall we?" Kit flopped back onto his haunches in order to rifle through the pockets of his kimono, from which he drew a tiny foil packet. Evie watched in mesmerized silence as he rolled the condom down his shaft. When he got to his feet again, reality struck like a bitch slap.

"Kit—I don't know."

"Come to bed with me." Lie amongst the jumble in the spare room and let him make love to her, he meant.

"I've just...with Ross. Still smell of him...need shower."

"The shower's fine by me."

"Huh!"

Kit scrambled to his feet and turned on the spray. He stood under the silver shower head and let the water cascade down his body in sinewy rivulets.

"I'd like to, but—"

"Forget the but in that sentence, and get your arse in here."

"What if I can't?" She clung to the edges of her robe, but failed to find any comfort in the soft loops of towelling.

Kit flashed her a devilish grin. "Then maybe I'll go climb into bed with Ross, instead. It was 50/50 which way I went when I heard you cross the landing. He's pretty hot stuff."

More doubts and questions leapt through her mind. "He's asleep, and he's not into guys."

A black hole opened in her reality when Kit began to howl with laughter. He flipped his wet hair out of his eyes and held his hand out towards her. "Keep telling yourself that, Evie."

"He's not gay," she reiterated.

Merrily splashing about under the water now, Kit squirted a large dollop of Ross's shower gel into his hand. "Never said he was. He's bi. I'm bi. Likely we all swing that way a little bit, even you. Have you ever kissed another woman?"

Evie shook her head. "And I'm not about to."

"Good, 'cause the only person I want you to be thinking about right now, is me."

"Is this actually about us, then?" she asked, fanning her hands out to indicate them both. "Or simply some weird fucked-up way of you making a play for Ross?"

Kit gave another chuckle. "Did that years ago. No—" he stepped out of the shower in order to take her hand, "—this is about you and me, and how desperate I am to see you come. You look bloody fantastic when you come, did you know that? You get this glow about you, and there's this light in your eyes." His lips traced her knuckles, and his tongue dabbed between the join of her index and middle fingers. "Make a decision, Evie." He glanced at the shower and then at the bathroom door. "And make it quickly, or I'm going to do it for you."

Although she couldn't exactly pinpoint what it was, Evie sensed a switch in him. Maybe it was down to stance, or the hardening of his expression, there was certainly a flare of the dramatic burning behind that ultimatum.

It would be so easy to step forward, wrap her arms around him and forget everything, but loyalty to Ross kept her rooted to the spot. Before today, she'd never cheated. Not once. Ever.

"Okay, answer me this? What's it going to take?"

"I need to talk to Ross."

Kit grabbed a towel. "Okay, we'll go talk to him now. Then we can both fuck him after."

"No!" Horrified at the thought of waking Ross to have Kit ask him if it was okay for them to have sex, she snatched the towel away from Kit. "Don't you dare!"

"Why not, what are you frightened of?"

"I'd rather be crucified for actual crimes than the suggestion of them."

Kit stopped struggling with her for the towel. "That settles it then." He grasped her upper arms and somehow manoeuvred her into the shower, while simultaneously stripping the dressing gown from her back. He backed her up against the glass bricks, lifted one of her legs up against the top of his thigh, then clasped her wrists together high above her head. His cock nuzzled against her body. She jerked and bit her lip as he pushed inside. His lips ravaged hers. He lifted her off the floor, drove into her over and over, fucking her until he jerked in a quick urgent climax.

Still inside her, he rubbed her clit. Rubbed until she tore shreds in the skin of his back, and her climax broke. She cried into his shoulder as its torrent washed through her, and the shower spray turned icy cold.

As they sat cuddled together in the bottom of the shower, Evie realized she understood something about Kit, and how he dealt with the world. Sex was his comfort zone. She retreated into chocolate; Ross went walking in the rain, but Kit... When Kit sought an answer, he looked to the comfort he could find in another's body. She wondered how many one-night stands he'd had as a result. Had he actually been a host, or just a full on whore?

Evie eventually spent the night alone on the sofa. Kit tried to coax her into bed with him, but she was having none of it. Bad enough what she'd done already, she'd been weak, and had given in to her lust when she should have held her love for Ross in higher regard and stayed faithful. It's just that Kit had a way of moving, of looking at her that left her feeling intoxicated. When she closed her eyes, she found she could still sense the scent and shape of his body pressed against hers, like a psychic impression upon her skin. And despite her guilt, she still wanted him again.

That was the really sickening part.

Once hadn't put the flames out, it had merely fanned them to new heights.

Sitting shivering in the dark was her penance. Initially, she'd tried to climb back into bed with Ross, but guilt wouldn't let her keep still, especially when he'd tried to snuggle against her back. She didn't deserve to curl up with Ross or Kit, or even both of them together.

Yes, both of them together... Kit had firmly planted that image of him and Ross in the tent with that girl in her head. Every time she saw them together, it's what she pictured. And she kept thinking that's what Kit was driving at when he said Ross wouldn't have a problem with them getting it on.

It's just, if there wasn't a problem... Why hadn't it happened tonight? Ross's actions on the sofa could easily have built to a fun time for all three of them. Instead, they'd hidden themselves in the bedroom and he'd tortured her with the fantasy of Kit.

"What's going on, Ross?" she silently asked the darkness in the living room. "Won't you talk and explain it to me?"

Chapter Eleven

Evie woke stiff and cold. Ross had thrown a blanket over her on his way out to work, and Mimmy lay curled upon her feet. She scampered upstairs, afraid of facing Kit in the daylight without Ross around, although really she ought to face him and reiterate that what had happened last night wasn't occurring again, unless Ross specifically said it was okay. Though how exactly they were supposed to broach that topic, she wasn't entirely sure.

To her surprise, the spare bedroom was empty. Kit, too, had slipped out, leaving her to sleep off the night's excesses. Having dressed, Evie pottered back downstairs. She tried to eat breakfast, but only managed a spoonful before she pushed it away.

She had to be brave about this. She'd go over to the surgery and see Ross, explain what had happened with Kit and see if they couldn't make sense of it. It meant risking her relationship, if he didn't react how Kit anticipated, but if she said nothing, her own guilt would gnaw away at all that was good between them and destroy the relationship anyway.

They had to be able to trust one another.

Evie phoned ahead to Ross's mobile; unfortunately, his phone had been switched off and the call transferred to voicemail. She hung up and tried the surgery reception desk instead. "He's done for today," said Iris. "Came in at seven and left at eleven. Bob's covering the walk-in clinic."

They chatted a moment, then Evie hung up and glanced at the clock. Ten past twelve. Even if the traffic was bad or he'd stopped at the shops on the way back he should have been home by now. She tried his mobile again, but it was still switched off.

Evie stared thoughtfully at Mimmy, then grabbed her coat and keys and left the house. She headed across the muddy green and down the lane. Rose Cottage was only couple of minutes walk away, and she needed the fresh air to clear her head. If she couldn't talk to Ross, then she'd talk to Kit, assuming—and she had a deep suspicion—that she didn't find her boyfriend over there too.

Sure enough, Ross's car sat on the drive beside Kit's.

Evie climbed the step to the front door and knocked, but there was no reply. She tried again, and met with the same response, so she went around the back and tried the kitchen door, which swung open on squeaky hinges.

"Ross...Kit..." Maybe Ross had agreed to help out with some of the work. They'd probably made the arrangement while they were playing video games last night, and he hadn't exactly had the opportunity to mention it to her.

"Anyone home?"

Strange that he hadn't come home to get changed first.

The kitchen stood empty, stripped to the stonework of everything save the Belfast sink and the Aga in the hearth, but Ross's work bag stood by the door to the lounge, and a faint thread of music hung in the crisp spring air. "Ross?" She lifted the latch and let herself in.

Bright daylight streamed through the huge bay window. Dazzled, Evie squinted and took a few baby paces forward as she waited for her eyes to adjust.

Ross stood a little to the right, with his back to her, completely naked. She squawked in shock at seeing the golden light illuminate his skin. Pleasing shadows cast interesting shapes across his bottom and highlighted the breadth of his shoulders. Confused, she took a step towards him, only to realize as her vision cleared, that Kit lay equally naked, stretched sidewards across the wingback chair from Ross's office, with his legs aloft and his bottom resting upon the chair arm. The old patchwork cushion she'd inherited from her Gran sat supporting his lower back. They were fucking, Ross's pale glutes tightening and relaxing with each stroke, Kit grunting slightly at the penetration, his palm pressed flat to Ross's stomach as if to stop him going too deep.

"Fuck!" she said in disbelief. All this time she'd spent fretting over her infidelity and thinking she was being selfish for wanting the threesome he seemed to be constantly offering, and here they were, screwing one another in broad daylight.

"Evie..." Ross paused mid-stroke, his buttocks clenched tight. He turned his head towards her, and his already flushed cheeks blazed a livid scarlet. "Oh, my god!"

"Bugger!" said Kit.

Ross tried to withdraw, but Kit was having none of it. He clung to Ross, clamping his hand over his hip and digging his fingers into the flesh until Ross stopped squirming.

"Shit!" her boyfriend cursed again for good measure. "Just, shit! Get off me, Kit." Again, he tried to shake Kit's hold.

"She's not angry, Ross. She's intrigued. Aren't you?" He shot a glance at Evie.

Still gobsmacked, Evie met his rather aggressive gaze, and felt her shock give way to the rising heat in her groin. All this time, Kit had been telling her everything was okay, and that Ross wasn't going to mind them getting it on, and she'd never suspected them of this. He'd even told her outright that he and Ross got down and dirty together, and she hadn't believed him.

She thought she knew Ross, and before Kit, before now, he'd never shown any interest in other guys.

"Oh, Eve...I'm sorry." Ross started mumbling, but she wasn't really listening. Instead, she continued to stare at them in stupefied silence, while various interconnecting events reslotted themselves together in her head. Sweat started to bead across Ross's upper lip at her silence, although she noticed his erection didn't flag. "I swear I didn't want you to find out like this. I wanted to tell you, but I didn't know how you'd take it."

"How do you think I'm taking it?"

Lordy, she sounded so calm and reasonable. If only she remotely felt it.

Uncertainty swam in the azure glow of Ross's eyes. "I don't know, Evie. Just don't run, okay?" He stretched his arm out towards her.

Run! She had jelly legs, she wasn't going anywhere, and what would be the point. If she left, surely that was it— relationship over, and that wasn't what she wanted at all.

No, she wanted to stay here, because—damn, they looked good together. Far too good, in fact. The flames in her innards licked a little higher at the sight of so much lean male muscle spread before her, locked together. She couldn't stop staring at the point where their bodies joined, and how comfortable Ross seemed wedged between Kit's spread cheeks.

"She's not angry. She's loving this," remarked Kit. He lifted his hips so Ross slid a little deeper.

Evie shot him a wary glance, only to find Kit's black eyes ablaze and eager. "I told you, she's been up for this from the start. Haven't you, Evie?" He stretched out his hand to her. "Now, come closer where I can reach you."

She instinctively reached out, but pulled back before they touched. "What are you going to do?"

Kit's grin stretched from ear to ear. "I thought maybe you could hold my hand while Ross finishes fucking me. Of course, if you're up for a little more than that..."

"Evie...only if you want to," Ross rasped. His attention zoomed in on her nipples, which were pushing against the thin wool of her jumper, all peaked up and aroused. "Don't do anything you're not comfortable with."

His concern made her want to laugh. "Do you want me to join in?"

Cheeks still burning red, Ross broke into an awkward smile. "Yeah," he huffed. "Yeah, I do."

Evie nervously moistened her lips. Their relationship wouldn't be the same after this, not after they'd let Kit into their lives so completely. There'd be no pretending he was an ordinary houseguest after this, and no avoiding the potent lure of his sexuality. She wanted to touch him, but she kept her attention firmly focused on Ross. She leaned into him and whispered into his ear. "I want to suck him, are you okay with that?" Her fingers tightened upon his disk-like nipples as she spoke, squeezed a little so they hardened into points. Before he had a chance to answer she slid her tongue deep into his open mouth and kissed him harder than she'd ever done before. There'd never been the same urgency, the same need to prove her love. When she drew back, they were both breathless and her lips tingled from the pressure.

Kit lifted his half-hard cock and began to stroke himself. Evie's gaze immediately locked onto the motion. Although he lay with his eyes closed and his head tilted back, he was definitely aware of her watching. "Take your jumper off," he whispered. "And come a little closer."

For a moment, she ignored the demand, content to stand and watch. Ross had begun to move his hips again, and his cock dipped smoothly in and out of Kit's body. She'd never expected to find watching her boyfriend fuck another guy to be so thrilling. It was also one of the most incredibly sensual acts she'd ever witnessed, so intensely focused that even though she'd imagined gay sex to be more raw and concerned with swift fulfilment, she still found this softer version overwhelmingly heady.

"Harder." For several minutes Kit held himself braced, sharing the moment with Ross, whose breathless pace left them both coated with a delicate sheen of sweat. Maybe raw was what they were building too.

"Off!" The phrase was directed at her.

Both sets of male eyes locked onto her as she sent her woolly top sailing across the room. Despite the familiar prickle of embarrassment at being looked at, Evie smoothed her hands over the satin cups of her black and purple bra and found a smidgen of confidence. "Do you want me to take this off too?"

"Come here," Kit beckoned.

When she got close enough, he stroked a hand over her bottom.

Evie walked her fingers over the smooth plane of his chest, down to his stomach, where her hand replaced his upon his cock.

"Easy now," he cautioned.

Flashes of silver chased across the inky surface of his eyes. Evie leaned closer and kissed him. She kissed him until his breath came out as sobs, and his hands trembled over her back, eager to unfasten the hooks of her bra. Off it came, the weight of her breasts falling into the warmth of his waiting hands.

"Yeah," he sighed. Kit lowered her fly and pushed his hand between the V of the open zip. Two long fingers speared through her curls inside her knickers and slid over the wet lips of her cunt. Evie rocked her hips against his rigid fingers, wanting the real thing even as she watched him take his cock in hand again and begin to stroke in earnest.

"Hurry it up," moaned Ross. "I can't hold out much longer." His movements were growing more erratic.

"Just come," said Kit. "The day's young."

"Come over him." Evie's hand flew up to cover her mouth the moment she'd blurted the words. Ross's eyes flew open too. He pinpointed her with his gaze.

"Jeez, Evie! Are you serious?" He was riding really close to the edge, his body already trembling with the rising need to come.

"Please." Why she found the idea of him jerking over Kit so arousing she couldn't identify. It seemed unimportant in the heat of the moment. All that matter was that she did. She'd barely formed a picture of the fantasy in her head, before Ross had pulled out, and having torn off the condom began furiously masturbating himself.

His hand moved slickly, smoothly up and down, leaving his shaft glistening. His balls swung high beneath. For several seconds all three rhythms of their strange triumvirate matched, Ross and Evie's hands working over cocks and Kit's fingers massaging her clit, before Ross outstripped them both, his knees bucked and he came, leaving a streamer of pearlescent come over Kit's stomach.

Curiously, Kit immediately pushed her away, leaving her dangling by an uncomfortable erotic thread, close enough to want to finish, but not close enough to bring herself with just the squeeze of her thighs.

He tugged a T-shirt out from behind him and wryly mopped his skin, then rolled out of the chair and onto his feet facing her. Evie back stepped uncertainly. His lip curled and his predatory grin made clear his intent. He meant to couple with her, fuck her fully while Ross watched.

"Um, can we talk about this?" She wanted to establish the boundaries of what was fine and what comprised a big no-no with Ross first, ask him what the hell was going on. When the fuck he'd turned gay, but Kit didn't seem to be in the mood for talk. Not even dirty talk, and Ross was staring at them like he was about to start shouting encouragements rather than objections. Not that he had a right to many objections after what he'd just done.

Kit followed her, until her back hit the wall. Then his fingers found the slick heat of her sex again. "You're not running away from me, Evie."

"Ross?" she gasped as Kit rubbed his naked body against her semi-naked one. His erection prodded against the inner seam of her jeans, seeking the heat of her body, and the fizz in her insides cranked up to a full on buzz.

Evie's nipples further crinkled as they made contact with Kit's torso. His hand fastened in her hair, pulled a little, forcing her to bend to the side, whereupon, his mouth closed over her pulse point and she felt the nip of his teeth before he began to suck hard. Hard enough to leave a mark. Hard enough that her toes curled inside her shoes, and she felt frozen in position by the intensity of the act. Fiery arrows shot downwards through her chest and seemed to lodge in her womb, so that she bucked against his already coaxing fingers. Her orgasm sparked like flash paper, burned bright and hot. She gasped into Kit's shoulder still aware of Ross watching them, from where he stood slumped against the chair back.

"That's better," said Kit. "You're more relaxed now. Don't think about him watching."

The fact that he'd drawn attention to Ross only made things worse. Guilt and embarrassment coupled with desire as Kit urged her down onto her knees. Still, she shut her eyes and breathed in his heady scent. Considering how his cock butted up against her cheek, it took no instructions to understand his intention. She took the initiative, pushing every last bit of reserve she had to the back of her mind. She'd caught Ross fucking him. There was no reason why she couldn't do the same. And she wanted Kit. She'd wanted him from the moment she'd seen him spread out for the taking on their guest bed. She stuck out her tongue and tasted him, then let him slide inside.

Ross didn't keep his distance long. Recovered, he nuzzled up against Kit's back and splayed his hands possessively across Kit's hip bones so that he controlled their rhythm. "Open wide, Evie. You know you can take a little more than that."

She imagined Ross pushing into Kit again even as she fellated him, and how it would alter his movements, perhaps make them jerky and sharp. Evie slipped her hand between her legs and began rubbing her clit again. Only when Ross stilled Kit's movement completely did she realize they were both watching her with hungry eyes.

"Get undressed." Ross nodded at her jeans. "I know what you really want. Shall I let you have it?"

Evie sagged backwards onto her bottom and kicked her way out of her shoes and the denim. Ross eyed the scrap of black and purple satin covering her mons, but shook his head when she hooked her fingers under the elastic. "Keep them on."

Ross didn't know—her skin burned with the guilty realization—he didn't know that it had already happened between her and Kit. She'd come here to tell him, instead her best intentions had been sidetracked.

"Do you want him, Evie?" He squatted down beside her. "I know Kit wants you. He was talking about you before you got here, saying how much he wants to finger that tight little arse of yours. Shall I let him fuck you there? I don't know if I can let him share your cunt. I might have to keep that just for me."

Kit dropped to his knees and stretched over her with panther-like grace. His long limbs held above her, not touching her in anyway, but holding her hostage nonetheless, so that the space between them became charged with potential.

Ross lifted her arms over her head and straddled her arms. He held them fast at the elbows, leaving Kit free to trail his cock up and down her body in erotic patterns.

Her nipples ached as Kit sucked them into his mouth,

Evie looked into his eyes as his hips dropped and his cock tried to nuzzle its way between her legs. He trailed a wet line down her body as far as her naval, which he teased with the very tip of his tongue. Evie's hips bucked upwards at the invasion of the sensitive hollow, seeking the penetration her body craved. When his tongue delved farther down she whimpered, crying out wordlessly for more, even as she resisted Kit's attempt to push her thighs wide apart. "The thing with threesomes," he coaxed, "is that you've got to keep things even. I've seen you and Ross fucking, and now you've seen us. It's only fair Ross gets a turn at observation. I'm going to take you slowly, Evie. I'm going to slide into you an inch at a time and

I'm going to have Ross hold you down while I do it so he doesn't miss a single detail."

Evie closed her legs. Having Ross watch while she had sex with his best friend seemed taboo enough, without the added stipulation of him taking her in the arse.

"Come on, Evie, don't be coy."

He lifted her knees and pulled off her panties, so he could look at the dusky pink folds of her slit without obstruction. He chucked the scrap of satin at Ross, before applying his tongue. Then he sucked, making her buck up off the floor.

Ross held her steady.

Kit's mouth worked its magic, just as it had done the night before. Her arousal flowed thickly onto his tongue, but then when his touch started drifting down towards her rear, she genuinely began to struggle.

"Easy, relax." Ross covered her face with kisses. "Remember last night. I know you want it, really."

Last night had been with him. They'd worked up to it. She'd been horny and far more certain of where she stood. Their relationship had been solid and trusting. She wanted Kit, but things were moving fast. Was Ross going to take her too? Were they going to pleasure her like the girl in the tent?

The very tip of Kit's tongue gently dabbed against her anus, and then he favoured it with a longer firmer lick.

Evie's hips bucked off the floor again, the sensation walking the line between pleasure and ticklish oversensitivity. It made her squeal and wriggle. It lit every nerve-ending between her bottom and the top of her spine. Soon a warm fuzzy glow swept down through her thighs. His tongue focused on the sensitive puckered entrance, dabbing repetitively against it. He slipped the tip of his finger inside her, then the whole digit, and then two.

"Ross—together," Kit said. They exchanged meaningful glances over the length of her body. "You know that's what we all really want."

"Can you hold out a little while?"

Kit's breath blew hot against her anus. "Maybe Evie could help wake you up a little."

Evie hardly dared look up at Ross, who was so close that when in a second of bravery she did look up, she found they were only kiss distance apart. Evie blinked, hopelessly unnerved. Ross seemed calm, but what if deep down this was a deal breaker for him? What if after a week or two of fun, he decided that he wanted someone who wanted him alone, not him and his best mate?

"Hang in there," he whispered to her, stealing a kiss.

Ross leapt up and darted into the kitchen, from whence came the sound of water spluttering into the sink. He'd left her to Kit's tender mercy.

Kit stretched over her again, this time resting his weight against her body. His cock dipped straight into her cunt. "Shhh!" He pressed a finger to her lips. "Sometimes it's good to have a little secret or two."

She didn't want him to pull out, but he did, just as Ross crossed the threshold smelling of Pears soap.

"Evie first." He knelt down, this time straddling her head, and used his flaccid cock to paint her lips.

"I'm not so good at waiting." Kit cupped Ross's balls from behind and gently rolled them in his hand as he plastered a very wet lick between Ross's cheeks, an act that had Ross bucking eagerly forward into her mouth, even though his cock was still soft. Evie gently sucked him, drawing heat into his shaft, where it had been cold from the wash.

It took mere moments to get him hard.

Ross crawled away to the sofa. Evie straddled his lap.

It was like that first night again as she lowered herself over Ross's cock and he dipped into her where Kit had just been. Only this time, she knew Kit was watching. She turned her head looking for him and their eyes met.

"Still hung up about being watched?"

She half-nodded, half-shook her head.

Kit produced Ross's shirt, which he'd rolled into a blindfold. "Close your eyes, Evie and you might just get a surprise."

"I'll still know you're watching."

"Not watching...doing. And you won't know who's doing what to whom."

She batted him away, but, he pressed forward with the blindfold again. Had Ross told him about last night? Had he mentioned the blindfold he'd used to help build the fantasy then? She had no intention of being blinded now. She wanted to be able to see their faces and what was going on.

"Gimme." Ross took the blindfold and fastened it over his own eyes. He experimentally rocked his hips, and rubbed his face up against Evie's breasts. "Yeah! Kit where are you?"

"Right here." Kit stroked the side of his face, a gesture of such affection it made Evie feel odd for being between them. "Two ticks and I'm all yours."

Unable to help herself, Evie watched him roll on a condom. At least they were mostly playing safe. He squashed her buttocks in her hands and thrust his erection up and down the resulting channel a few times. "Kit!" she gasped.

"I know, babe. You've never done this before. Nor has Ross. We'll take it slow."

That made her pause, which perhaps was Kit's intention.

Ross made an odd noise deep in his throat, obviously confused too. He'd admitted to having done DP before with Kit so there was no need to pretend otherwise, so what did Kit mean to say he'd never done this before?

The answer became clear as he slid his cock downward until it kissed Ross's shaft. He held them together, so that the tip of his cock nuzzled against her opening every time Ross moved. Evie squirmed as he slipped in alongside Ross.

"Oh god!" It felt so tight...so good. She couldn't stop calling out as the twined cocks stretched her pussy, working in perfect unison.

Ross clung to her, his own cries buried in her breasts, but just as incoherent as her own.

"Really, now. You didn't honestly think I was going to start taking orders," said Kit. He held her shoulder, guiding them, moving them. There were no barriers separating them in that moment. Kit had staked his claim and made it clear it was an equal one. They weren't a couple plus one anymore. They were in this equally.

Curiously, the realization made her happy, before the intensity of her pleasure washed away any further clarity of thoughts. Stretched full, Evie felt tears wet her cheeks. Pleasure washed through her in hot bursts as Kit licked the sweat from the back of her neck and Ross sucked upon her tender nipples.

The buzz started in her belly and licked over her skin in fiery lines. She screamed, screamed so damn loud that if there'd been any neighbours they'd have phoned the police. She never, ever wanted it to end.

Ross came inside her, but Kit pulled out. Evie strained her neck attempting to see him finish off. She didn't want to miss out on seeing him come.

His hand moved with agile speed, pumping quickly, but when he saw her watching, he closed in again and rubbed up against her cunt. He held her close, his stomach and chest pressed tight to her back, taking her so vigorously the sofa beneath them creaked alarmingly. "Can you come again?" he asked, his fingers petting her clit. Still on edge, Evie climaxed again almost immediately at the rough contact. Kit bit her shoulder, as he panted hard trying to hold on to some semblance of control as his body finally gave up its reward.

He held on to her until the last pulse of his climax faded.

Only in the aftermath did they look at one another awkwardly.

"What now?" Ross asked.

Kit chucked the condom into the fire and found his

trousers. He shimmied into them, but left the top button of his fly undone. "That's up to you and Evie. Make yourselves at home. We'll talk it over tonight." He pulled on a pair of boots, and then chucked a set of keys at them. "I'll catch you back at your place."

"Wait! Where are you going?" Ross lifted her off his knee and charged into the hallway after Kit. "Damnit!" he swore when the front door slammed.

"Gone?" she asked

Ross nodded. "I don't know what the hell he's playing at."

"We can make him pay for it later," she said, trying to sound jovial, while feeling anything but. She extended a hand towards Ross, who stood anxiously raking his fingers through his hair.

"Yeah, yeah that's right. Good thought, Evie." Clearly, Ross was even twitchier than she felt. Kit rushing off like that had made everything rather anti-climactic. They should have been sitting sharing post-orgasmic drinks and cuddles.

"Does he always run away after sex?" she asked, not actually sure if she could brave a relationship in which he scarpered the moment the deed was done, like sex were a criminal activity.

Ross's features contorted into an uneasy scowl. "Not exactly. I mean he does...or rather he has after pretty much every threesome, but that's normally so they don't get ideas... This is different," he hastily added. Leastways judging by his expression he hoped it was. "He's probably trying to give us some space. I guess we do have a few things to talk over." He squeezed her hand, then sat down beside her, so they were facing. Evie wanted to snuggle, but Ross seemed keen on maintaining eye contact. In the end, she straddled his knees again.

"When were you going to tell me?"

Ross shook his head. "It wasn't supposed to be happening. When I invited him to say, I was just pleased to see him again; I never thought he'd still be interested after all this time."

"And you didn't think to mention that you'd invited a former lover to live with us."

"He wasn't...not really. We were mates, Evie, except for one time just before he left."

"Is that why he left?" She found the notion hard to believe. With the exception of his recent exodus, Kit seemed pretty on top of his sexuality. If he had issues, they weren't with his orientation.

"No, of course not." Trouble briefly clouded Ross's eyes. He seemed about to say something, then shook his head and grinned. "Just as well, he ran off to Japan, else I might never have met you."

They rubbed noses together and exchanged a delicate kiss.

"How come you never even mentioned you were bi? I mean, you haven't exactly held back over what you like." She had a sudden vision of all three of them cosied up in the shower together, only half undressed, shirts and underwear clinging with the flow of water and turning transparent.

Ross shrugged, his brow still wrinkled. "I don't think of myself in that way. It's not like I've ever had a boyfriend. I told you, it was just the one occasion with Kit before he left, and it didn't go all that far, certainly not as far as doing one another."

"Yeah, and how many times has it been over the last week?"

Ross's shoulders crumpled. "How many times has it been for you?"

Evie opened her mouth. Then closed it again.

Ross buffeted the underside of her chin with his knuckles. "Be honest."

"Actual sex, just now and last night, but he brought me off on another occasion too. You?"

"About the same."

They sat uncomfortably, failing to make eye contact for a moment or two.

"Likes to keep busy, doesn't he?"

"Sex is the one thing he's sure of. To Kit, at least, it's straightforward. He sets boundaries and he never crosses them. Shame the rest of life can't be boxed up in the same way."

Evie was still trying to figure out where the hell Kit's sexual boundaries were supposed to lie exactly when Ross teasingly pinched her nose.

"Ow! What was that for?"

"Want to head home and limber up a bit for tonight?"

Actually, considering how much they both stunk of sex and just how wet they'd got her, she was in more of a hurry to get home and shower. "We need practice?" She rolled her eyes and ended the expression with a mocking tilt of her head.

Ross blew a warm zephyr across her nipples. "Absolutely."

"You're positive he's going to come back."

"Seven-thirty, prompt. I guarantee it."

She missed him maniacally texting, while she hunted down their clothes.

Kit got halfway to the ruins before he realized that he was without a T-shirt or jacket, and by then he didn't care to go back, regardless of the blossoming gooseflesh. Best he left them to work things out a bit. Besides, he knew that while he should feel ecstatic over what had just occurred—it was what he'd been trying to engineer—he didn't really know what do to next.

Seduction came naturally to him, and he'd had his skills honed by years as a host. It was hanging on to them after the third or fourth shag that proved difficult. Inevitably his lovers seemed to have different expectations of the future than he did, and off they slipped like phantoms into the fog of life.

Of course, the fact that they'd always had to share space in his heart with Ross perhaps hadn't helped. And *they* had stood the test of time. The pull between him and Ross was just as potent now as it had been that day six years ago when a snap decision had turned his life upside down.

Ross and Evie seemed stable too, which boded well. There weren't many women who stuck around after they walked in on their boyfriend having sex with another man. Most of them probably screamed or stood gaping in horrified silence.

The ruins were more overgrown than he remembered, particularly given the season. Kit guessed they'd seen little love over the years, what with folks associating the place with him. Brambles littered the base of the rocks along with an assortment of beer cans and fag ends. Kit fought his way up and between the jagged teeth that formed the remains of the ancient lookout tower. In the crawlspace beyond, he perched and rubbed the goose bumps from his arms. It might not be entirely comfortable up here anymore, but at least it was out of the wind, and he'd always done his best thinking here. That and it was in this spot that he'd first kissed Ross. Okay, he'd more than kissed him. He'd given him a darned superb blowjob. The memory made him smile, along with others, of trysts with several of the village girls.

Kit bowed his head and hugged his thighs. He hoped his absence was giving Ross and Evie time to work out any awkwardness. That way, hopefully they could have fun tonight instead of getting hung up on the seriousness of what they were doing.

Yes, he wanted a permanent place in their lives, but he didn't want anyone to get too obsessed with that detail just yet. It was more important to have things seem to flow in that direction naturally.

The sound of someone struggling up the hill made him hold his breath. Hopefully, it'd be a rambler, and they'd pass by without intruding upon him. However, the footsteps came right up to the wall and stopped level with him on the other side.

"Coat...ciggy?" the intruder offered.

He guessed thinking time wasn't on the agenda.

"And are you coming out or am I coming in?" She didn't

give him the chance to make a decision, a pair of snow-leopard skin boots swung over the wall, followed by two black satin clad legs and a frilly black smock. Lillianna beamed at him, swinging a jacket from her fingertip, an already lit rollup clamped between her teeth.

Kit accepted the jacket, which turned out to be far too narrow across the back, so he draped it around his shoulders like an old fashioned pelisse. He pulled a face at the noxious puffs of smoke.

"Sorry, forgot." Lillianna stubbed the cigarette out against the rocks. "I saw you head up here, and figured you might appreciate a coat. Probably about time we had a little catch up too."

I'm not having sex with you. He squinted uneasily at her. "Do we have anything to catch up upon?"

"Well, you know." She edged a fraction closer. "We used to get on so well in the past. Where've you been off to all these years? Evie said something about Japan."

He doubted Evie had said anything, but there were plenty of rumours about his exploits circulating the village. What seemed more miraculous was that Evie hadn't cottoned on to any of them. Wary, he glanced at Lillianna from beneath his eyelashes, and then with a sigh, closed his eyes. She hadn't changed. Still the same bitchy vampire bat of old, although her bust had filled out a bit, and her makeup was somewhat less garish.

Lillianna seized the opportunity offered by his apparent repose to straddle the rock behind him and casually start working out the knots in his shoulders, immediately dislodging the jacket she'd just provided. "It must be frustrating for you, coming home and finding Ross shacked up with Evie, especially seeing how determined she is to get settled and start replicating."

He remembered Lillianna's loathing of old of anything small and helpless. Babies were firmly in that category.

"Why would that be frustrating?"

She continued kneading, determinedly annihilating the tension just in time to cause him to stiffen up again.

"I could help relieve the tension."

No point pretending that she was talking about pummelling his shoulders. It hadn't taken her long to get to the point of this impromptu reunion.

"It's not happening, Lillianna. So drop it." He shrugged her off and stood. "I've nothing at all against Evie. Actually, I find her quite enthralling." There, let her chew over that one. It'd kill her that she'd have to swallow her own catty gossip for once. "But hey, you must know that already, seeing as you're the one spreading rumours of tawdry threesomes and naughty night time shenanigans."

Her face grew hard and vicious. "I don't suppose you've mentioned the last girl you got involved with in this village."

"Why would I?" He eyed her through narrowed lids. "What does she need to know? That in the dim and distant past I had a girlfriend. Well, whoop-de-fucking-do! I hardly think that's a big shocker. And there isn't actually anything else to say about it, is there? It's not as if I know anymore about what happened than you do."

He turned his back on her and pulled himself up onto the top of the wall.

"Were you shagging Ross when you let her walk home alone?"

Crouched, he sneered back at her. Bingo! Her face lit up in triumph, she'd obviously confirmed a suspicion. "Did you think no one knew? Sammie knew. We all knew. God, it was sickening the way you two were always gawping at one another. Sammie told me all about how you used to have Ross watching you when you made out. That's really fucking sick and twisted, Kit."

"But nowhere near on the same scale as you and dear George."

She awkwardly back stepped at the mention of the Satyr statue on the Melton estate, and rightly too. Oh, there were plenty of pictures out there of assorted ladies, young and old, wrapping their lips around the old goat's staff, but what Lillianna had done with satyr George beggared belief.

Her bangles fell down her arms in a peal of discordant chimes. Thunderous, she sneered up at Kit, who sat framed against the sky. "She'd have done anything for you, and you only kept her around as piece of fluff entertainment. She told me how when you fucked, you used to be looking over her shoulder at Ross to see if he was wanking." She shook her head, so the red mass of curls flapped around her face. "There she was, confident girl, full of life and you bollocks it for her. You broke her fucking heart."

"Fuck off, Lilli."

His ex had been many things, but she'd been no saint. Okay, so maybe he could have been more considerate about Ross. Actually, scratch that. Sammie had got off on it. She'd been a total exhibitionist, not satisfied unless at least two people were watching her at all times, and preferably more.

"Or else what—you'll get me too?"

"Don't be such a cow."

"I'm simply looking out for my friend."

"You're stirring shit is what you're doing."

She breathed a huge sigh and planted her hands upon her hips. "For fuck's sake, Kit. You know what I want, do we still have to play this cat and mouse game? It's not as if you haven't been giving it out plenty while you've been abroad from what I've heard."

He stretched, scrunching his hair into clumps. "I'm not for hire anymore."

"Make it a freebie."

The rapid come back startled a smile from him. He sat down on the rock wall, so his legs dangled over the edge. Not remotely tempted but cured of any tetchiness. Guess he'd proved one thing to himself in this. He felt committed. And he did like to fuck out-of-doors once in a while. "What's up, Lilli, can't you find anyone else to treat you rough? I can't believe you've been hankering after my arse all this time."

"None of them bite hard enough." She sighed. "And it ain't your arse I'm after. If you want fingering up the jacksie you can get some bugger else to do it. I'm not wrecking my nails."

Kit laughed.

"Truce." She climbed up to sit beside him and offered a hand.

Kit warily accepted.

"So, you really are screwing Rolf Harris and Emu?"

"I thought you and Evie were friends."

"We are. That's why I'm allowed to be bitchy. I didn't think she was your type though. Guess it proves what I know."

"Nothing," he drawled.

"Fancy a cupper?"

Kit nodded, and accepted her jacket as a windshield again. "Matter of fact, I do. Thought I might head over to Doris's."

"Doris!" Lillianna's nails tapped briefly against his thigh like a drum roll. "Jeez! You're going to crash their knitting circle dressed like that!" She sniffed suspiciously at him and her eyes widened into two hazel pools. "Maybe we should stop by my place on the way and give you a hose down in the shower first."

Kit laughed and shook his head. He couldn't fault her for trying, but he wasn't setting foot in her place. He wasn't sure he'd get out again alive. Beside, the fact that he reeked of three sets of pheromones just added outlandish eccentricity to the appeal of visiting the old biddies. He was sure they'd forgive his oversight in the dress code department and his obvious post-coital scent. He certainly wasn't heading home to either Rose Cottage or Ross and Evie's place to wash it off until he was absolutely sure he was welcome.

Beside him Lillianna cackled with glee. Her pale face creased into laughter lines and her watering eyes threatening the integrity of her inch-thick mascara. "This is going to be brilliant. I am *so* coming too. I can just picture their faces."

Chapter Twelve

The jury remained out on whether the visit was actually brilliant as Kit wound his way home in the moonlight. It'd certainly been fun and novel to be ogled by six octogenarians. Laura, Doris's granddaughter, had nearly wet herself when she'd nipped over to deliver more teabags and found him posed half-naked on a pouffe in the middle of the knitting circle. The exchange between himself and Doris about how long the willy warmer she intended to knit him should be, rapidly sent the poor girl running for home.

He had the promised woollen pouch, navy with a bright red K emblazoned on the end, clasped within his hand when he bounded up the back steps to Ross and Evie's place and let himself in.

The only downside of the visit was that there were almost certainly rumours circulating the village that he was banging Lillianna by now, a few of them probably started by her in the hope of them actually coming true.

"And where have you been, lover boy?" Ross asked. He stood poised by the sink, dressed in a striped butcher's apron, brandishing a whisk, which he waved menacingly in Kit's direction.

"Tea?" asked Kit, hoping the theatrics related to something culinary and not some sort of exotic vengeance.

Ross broke into a lopsided smile, which caused intriguing little crow's feet to appear at the very corners of his eyes. "Nah, we went over to the pub to eat. If you're hungry you'll have to fend for yourself."

"I meant that's where I've been." Kit unconsciously patted his stomach, while he grinned back at Ross, aware that the sugar from the five...or maybe six cakes he'd had forced upon him was busy zinging around his body lending an extra bounce to his stride. "I went over to Doris's to catch up with her and the girls."

Ross dropped the whisk, which landed in the sink with an ungodly clatter, and brought Evie running into the room.

"You went for afternoon tea dressed like that!"

"He's been where? Where've you been?" Evie asked while her eyebrows furrowed in an expression much like Ross's.

Kit regarded them both with a shrug, and observing no unnatural tension between any of them, turned primly on the spot. "Is there something wrong with my outfit?" He looked over his shoulder at them and fluttered his eyelashes.

"Uh, you forgot half of it," said Ross.

Evie chucked him a T-shirt off the radiator, one of Ross's, which Kit shook out but didn't put on. Instead, he laid it upon the table.

"I think you should lose half of yours too. Chuck the bottoms, but keep the apron," he said to Ross. Not finished, he turned to Evie and sidled up to her wearing a smile. "Truth or dare?" Time they got this party started before any awkwardness developed.

Her expression clouded a moment, wariness bringing out the silver flecks in her grey-blue eyes. "Truth or dare?" she repeated and glanced hesitantly across at Ross.

"Truth." Ross gave a shrug.

"Dare," said Evie.

"I knew you'd be brave." Kit leaned closer to her, slipping a hand around the back of her neck to bring their foreheads together. He kept his voice low so that Ross wouldn't hear. "I dare you to give us simultaneous blowjobs."

"Have you had a shower yet?"

Kit gave a tut at her sensibilities. "No shower, but I gave him a nice flannel bath with some of Doris's rose and lavender soap."

"Both together?" She gave Ross another sidelong glance. "You're pretty big on togethers."

"One hundred percent."

She nudged Kit in the direction of the lounge and held her hand out for Ross. "I'm not kneeling on the kitchen floor. It hasn't been cleaned for about a century."

With the curtains tightly closed, and only the glow of the coal fire lighting the room, Evie knelt before the two men and reached up to unfasten their zips. Kit's fly fell, revealing his already half-hard cock. He kicked off his boots and trousers and stood before her naked without a shred of embarrassment. Ross, who was actually fully clothed, took a bit more manipulation to expose. Interestingly, he chose to leave his clothes on with the exception of the apron which he'd worn to keep clean while laying the fire.

Evie kissed him first, despite her desperate curiosity to study the contours of Kit's cock in intimate detail. She felt like a child with a new toy, still clutching the old one, unable to give up its familiar comfort but excited by the novelty of a new treasure.

Ross made no protest. He stroked a hand through her hair and let her mouth work its magic. She knew just the way to work him to make him purr—a little pressure just below the delicate slitted eye, a gentle caress beneath his balls. He clung to her, but aware of Kit's gaze burning holes into her back, Evie reached out her hand and wrapped a palm around the base of Kit's shaft.

The guys edged closer together.

Evie risked a glance up. They were staring at each other as she left Ross's cock glistening with saliva and formed an O around the head of Kit's cock instead.

He did indeed smell and taste of lavender soap. Thankfully, the floral miasma wore off quickly as a few beads of pre-come leaked onto her tongue. "Mmm," he sighed and shuffled even closer to Ross. Another glance up showed that they were kissing. Resisting the urge to stop and watch, Evie continued to alternate her attention between them, licking and sucking and using her fingers to drive them wild.

"Enough!" Ross backed away first, leaving her almost deep-throating Kit.

The temptation was there to keep on sucking, to hold him captive until he spilled his seed on her tongue, but the evening was still young, and her jaws, much as she wished otherwise, weren't made of steel.

"Truth or dare?" she asked Ross from her knees while she still played with Kit's cock.

Ross turned his back on them a moment while he stripped off his clothes. He folded them all neatly and laid them on the sofa, making her giggle and provoking a smirk of despair from Kit, who eventually barrelled into Ross while he was folding his socks and wrestled him onto the sofa scattering the pile of clothes. "Come on, Ross. Answer the lady."

Evie watched him look right up into Kit's eyes. The two of them were so perfectly matched, all toned muscle and masculine symmetry that she wanted to dive on top of them, and lie there pressed to Kit as the pair of them drove their cocks together, and she already knew what she'd be asking them to do the next time one of them agreed to a dare. She was going to have them sit side by side and stroke one another's cocks, and she was going to turn the TV on and pick up a magazine and pretend not to watch.

"Truth," said Ross.

"Is Kit really the only guy you've ever kissed?" she asked.

"Yes."

"Boring," muttered Kit, still holding Ross pinned along the

length of the sofa.

"Fine," she snarled and drew a finger up the length of his spine that made him shiver and squeak. "Is Ross the only guy you've ever kissed?"

"No." He gave her a butter-wouldn't-melt grin and dug his teeth into his lower lip. "Nor is he the only guy I've ever screwed."

"You always were a regular bloody alley cat. I daren't ask how many." Ross managed to extract an arm and throw Kit off. He rolled onto the carpet and landed at Evie's feet, which he laughingly kissed.

"Ross, it's your go," she said, realizing that yet again she was still fully clothed while they were both naked. He wound his arm around her leg and began kissing his way up her calf.

"Truth or dare?" The look in his eyes made her pause before answering. "Truth." Her hesitancy rang her voice, but Ross smiled.

"Is it true that really you're as excited by the prospect of having Kit watch us fuck as your body suggests?"

He got to his feet as he spoke and stroked his thumb tip over one of her excited nipples. A tremor of fear and longing stabbed through her insides. Evie began to shake her head. She hated being watched. It's why she re-routed Ross's passion for fucking in the rain to making out in the shower. There were no stray observers in the bathroom. Leastways, there hadn't been until Kit moved in. Not that she suspected Kit would stand back and merely observe anymore.

"Nnnn...yes." The confession left her feeling rather freaked out. A vivid blush burned her cheeks. "My turn," she gasped before Kit had a chance to say otherwise. He still lay stretched along the settee, perfectly nude. Given a black and white film and a camera, she could make thousands selling shots of him lying like that, particularly when he glanced up, and those dark eyes of his swam with secrets and zeal. "Dare?"

He nodded.

"I dare you to masturbate for me."

Kit swung his legs around into a sitting position. "Uh, uh!" He shook his head, his eyes narrowed, but a smile still playing on his lips. "Not that one."

Outraged, she squealed, jumping up and down on the spot. "Forfeit, forfeit..."

"Okay, I forfeit." Kit raised his hands in idle surrender.

"Tie him down, Ross."

"To what?" Ross's gaze darted between her, Kit and the furnishings. With the exception of the ancient radiator, there wasn't anything to tie Kit to.

Vexed by the realization, but unprepared to be thwarted, Evie scrunched up her mouth and thought. "Upstairs. Strap him to the bed." They'd all be more comfortable up there anyway and it simplified the logistics of how they were going to manage inviting him into their bedroom.

Ross saluted. "You got it." He tugged Kit up off the sofa, and planted a hand on his arse. "Come on, buddy. Let's get you looking pretty. You know you'll enjoy this."

Ross rummaged in the bottom of the wardrobe and dug out a roll of years old bondage tape he'd bought at an erotic torment fair. He used the tape to fasten Kit to the bed. Kit refused to lie down. He sat amongst the pillows at the head end, both arms bent at the elbows and his wrists flopped outwards, barely maintaining the façade of outraged disinterest he was trying to pull off. Ross wasn't fooled. While his friend might not specifically get off on being restrained, he was intrigued by Evie's determination to take the top role in the bedroom.

Ross straddled his legs as he wound the tape around Kit's wrists, securing him to the ironwork headboard. "You can always yell if you want out."

Kit grinned and snapped his teeth. "What do you reckon she's got planned for me?"

"No idea."

Snake-like, Kit's tongue pressed briefly to his top lip. "What shall I shout?"

"Don't shout, Kit. Let her have her way for a bit. We're walking a knife's edge here. It won't take much to screw it all up, and I'd rather we let things settled down naturally."

Kit tilted his head as if in consideration of the point. The way he pursed his lips together just made Ross long to kiss him, but tonight wasn't really about him and Kit. It was about the three of them finding a way to knit themselves together without setting off unwanted sparks.

"And if I don't like it?"

"Grit your teeth." Finished with the tape, Ross patted Kit's thigh. "You're a big boy, and I'm sure you've done worse for money."

"Why is it that everyone in this village thinks I'm a whore?"

Ross raised his brows, but held Kit's gaze. "The line about other men didn't help."

Kit tugged against his bonds but couldn't break free to reach out to Ross. "Is that all you're worried about?"

"Guess I thought I was unique." He traced his fingers over the curve of Kit's jaw.

"Ross, you oaf! You've always been that. Always will be."

"Don't muck this up."

"I won't."

The bedroom door creaked open. Ross shimmied off Kit's lap in order to see Evie come in. She'd rearranged her hair since they'd left her downstairs, and had pulled it up into a messy high ponytail, from which bits stuck out and hung down to frame her merry face. She'd stripped too, down to a teeny tiny polka dot thong, a pair of patent leather stilettos and the butcher's apron he'd recently taken off. She was holding the whisk he'd left in the kitchen sink.

Part of him wanted to laugh at the vision of domestic goddesshood as she dipped one knee and flashed them both a glimpse of her sumptuous rear. Kit did laugh, but his mirth quickly died when she sashayed over to the bed and rapped his thigh with the springy metal. "This is a serious matter, Mr. Skye. I'm bitterly disappointed in you. Forfeiting in the first round, what sort of wussy behaviour is that?"

"Climb aboard, babe. I promise you won't be disappointed."

"Humph!" she snorted. "The jury's still out on that. What gets him off, Ross?"

"Pretty much anything."

Kit groaned.

"Yeah. How about you sucking his cock?"

"It's been known to work." Ross crawled to Kit again and watched the muscles in Kit's stomach jump as he wrapped his large hand around his friend's cock. Already swollen from Evie's earlier attention, the thick stem stood out from Kit's bare skin, the tip vivid red and dripping the odd bead of precome. Up close, so close that he caught a hint of floral fragrance before he bestowed a gentle kiss, Ross spared a thought to how well his own stamina would hold.

"You know you'll crack first," Kit whispered.

"And if I do, I'll leave you weeping. Who exactly is the loser then?" Teasingly, he ran his tongue around the tip of Kit's glans. "Besides, who said this is all the lady has planned for you?"

"Less talk," she said, smacking his backside with the whisk. "Suck him good, Ross. I want to see his knuckles whiten. I want to see him weep."

Ross refrained from pointing out that Kit was already doing that. His friend's fists were already clenched, and within moments a nervous tick played in his jaw. He had his teeth clamped together so hard, he was reduced to breathing in sharp bursts through his nose.

Ross blew gently across the surface of the eye and Kit's thighs jerked. He licked, even more gently, and Kit's cock jerked hungry for more. He really didn't think his lover was up to much more teasing. "He's really primed, Evie."

The revelation earned him a growl of disapproval from Kit. "Traitor."

In response, Ross nipped Kit's inner thigh with his teeth, which caused his cock to further jerk and swell, and more fluid to escape the tip. Evie wet her finger in it and then slipped the digit between her lips. She held a condom in her other hand, which she rolled down Kit's shaft before positioning herself over him, her back to Kit's face.

On his knees, Ross watched her sink slowly, ever so damn slowly, inch by glorious inch over Kit's erection until she took him right to the goddamn root. A tiny part of his heart pinched slightly at the sight, but the minor pain fled a moment later when she stretched and tugged open the apron fastening at the back of her neck and let the blue and white cloth fall forward, exposing her beautiful, rounded breasts to him and him alone.

She'd rouged her nipples so they were deep crimson. "Come and let me warm you," she invited.

Ross didn't wait for a second invitation. He knelt upright before her and sandwiched his cock between the warmth of her bosom. Ross loved this and didn't get to do it nearly often enough. He kept rubbing up against her, loving the way her big, heavy breasts engulfed his cock, and how she stuck her tongue out to try and lick him when the head of his cock peeped from between her cleavage.

"Let me suck you, Ross." She clasped him around the hips, stilling his rocking, before bending to take his cock in her mouth again.

Kit bucked in protest. "Fucking untie me."

"No." She glanced at him over her shoulder.

Some of the aggression slipped from his face. "Then at least turn around and get him to come up here so I can join in."

To Ross's surprise, she actually capitulated. Unfortunately, that left him bereft of her soft comforts. Another stab of envy pierced his chest as Evie lowered herself onto Kit's prick again, having turned to face him. He'd stood in the cold too many times in the past watching Kit make love and feeling sidelined to ever want to find himself there again, especially when, in this case, Kit was the plus one, not him. They'd invited him in to share, not to take over.

"Ross." Evie flapped her hand out trying to grasp his arm.

He took the offered life line, angered with himself for letting jealousy get a grip. As multiple hands stroked his body, he realized that neither of his lovers had forgotten him.

Evie pulled him closer, her cheeks were flushed, and her body swaying to a merry rhythm, so that her heavy breasts bounced with the motion. He couldn't recall seeing her look more abandoned. Her unselfconscious enjoyment suited her. She clung to him and kissed him with lavish abandon him.

"Mmmm," she sighed into his mouth. "Help me, Ross."

He slid his fingers through her curls to rub her clit just above where Kit was fucking her. She clung a little tighter at the attention, but soon stopped him. "It has to be give and take. He's going to give—" she inclined her head towards Kit "—and we're going to take."

He realized she had a crooked view of Kit's talents. He might give off dominant, aggressive vibes, but when it came down to it, giving was what Kit did best. Using him for their pleasure wouldn't be a hardship. It wouldn't put him any place he didn't want to be.

"Ross, pay attention." She lightly cuffed him on the bicep.

Damn! He needed to stop analyzing and concentrate on getting himself laid. When it came to sex, he didn't normally let his mind wander like this. Having them both here together had scrambled his brains.

Ross looked at them, admiring the lines of their twined bodies as they undulated together. While he stroked Evie's breast, he lowered his head and licked along the nervous tick in Kit's jaw. He read Kit well enough to interpret the signs: dancing spectres in the depths of his eyes, the way his breathing had become raspy but slow. Kit was already walking the line. It wouldn't take much to tip him over. He wondered if Evie realized it.

Kit beckoned him with tilt of his head.

Ross shuffled up among the pile of pillows and traced Kit's beautiful, expressive mouth with the head of his glans.

The touch of Kit's tongue broke him. Desperate for more, he welcomed the hot caress of Kit's talented lips. Pushed himself in and out of the warm cavern and sunk into the heated darkness there. He didn't recall closing his eyes. Somehow he could still see Kit clearly and feel Evie holding on tight to his hand.

He wanted to come, and he never wanted this to end.

Both men had their eyes shut tight, but Evie's remained wide open. She couldn't get enough of seeing them together like this. Hell, watching Kit fellate Ross would've been enough to get her off, especially while he was bound and looked so outrageously sexy, but incredibly she was part of this union too, straddled across Kit's hips, his cock satisfying her hungry itch for release, while Ross, when he remembered in between gasps of pleasure, lavished further attention on her breasts.

Ross—her Ross... She touched him too. It felt as if she'd slipped into an erotic movie and was somehow able to participate. She stroked his arse and he let out a strangled cry. Kit responded with a whimper of his own and by swallowing fast. A tiny dribble of semen escaped his lips and rolled over his chin. Evie licked it away.

"Get this damn tape off me."

Evie sealed Kit's mouth with a kiss, stealing the taste of Ross's pleasure from him.

Ross released him.

The moment Kit's arms were free he flipped Evie onto her back, clamped his hands over her and held her down while he drove into her like he was possessed. Coming was all too easy, but even when they both sagged together, spent, they weren't finished with her. While Kit dealt with the condom, Ross shimmied down between her legs and roused her to another peak with his tongue. Having returned to the bed, Kit joined in by sucking her sensitive nipples. Having two men, with their four arms, two mouths, and two cocks was definitely the way to reach paradise, she decided as she sank into a lethargic sleep.

Ross woke her with his kisses and the gentle pinch of his teeth upon her earlobe at some ungodly hour. The nimble, evocative dance of his fingers over her stomach persuaded her she wanted to stay awake. It wasn't long before he lay buffeted up to her arse, his prick satisfyingly hard inside her, having hooked her upper leg over his hairy one. Unlike earlier, this joining was long and slow and drowsy. The climax from it like a languorous roll of thunder, which rather than calling a cease fire, heralded the main act.

Kit only woke when Ross pulled her onto her knees and started pounding her like a jackhammer, doggy style, so that the headboard knocked an indent in the old plaster.

"You started without me," he complained, his mouth still slack from sleep so that the words came out slurred. "Bastards."

Ross chuckled.

Evie's attention fastened upon Kit's drowsy visage. Repose took a good ten years off his age, smoothing the worry and laughter lines she'd barely noticed so that he seemed terribly young and innocent, the impression exaggerated by the fact that he had his curled fist pressed to his lips and was sucking on the bent knuckle of his middle finger.

The covers rustled as his other hand slipped out of sight. The indent of his fist knocking repeatedly against the duvet made it obvious what he was doing.

"Ross—oh, god, Ross! Slow down a minute, will you! I want to watch."

Ross's chest pressed tight to her back so that a layer of

sweat slicked their skin, as he slowed the roll of his hips to a steadier pace, allowing Evie to loosen her grip upon the headboard and flick back the covers.

"Hey!" Kit let out a bellow of protest and made half-hearted grabbing motion that fell woefully short. "It's cold."

"Just keep doing that and you'll soon warm up." Ross chuckled.

Kit's dark eyes opened, and his grip on his cock relaxed. His erection plumped up some when his caught sight of what they were doing. "Bad lovers," he snarled rolling up onto his knees. "Cruel of you not to wake me."

He traced his fingers over Evie's cheek. "You especially. Can't believe you left me out just so that you could watch me wank."

Immeasurably frustrated by the lack of gaining that privilege, Evie snapped her teeth. "You should just let me, and then I wouldn't feel the need to spy on you while you sleep."

"I've told you, tossing myself is a solitary pleasure, or else reserved for phone sex-isodes." He caught Ross's gaze over her shoulder.

Evie grinned. Phone sex was just fine. She'd make sure she didn't interrupt the next time the two of them felt like talking dirty, she'd just make sure she was in a position to keep an eye on Kit while they were at it.

He must have cottoned on to her thoughts because he pursed his lips at her grin. The black look only lasted a second before his attention reverted back to Ross. "Steady now. Let me join you."

Surprisingly, he leapt off the bed and scurried across the landing. He came back a few seconds later, his now impressive erection dressed for action and shiny with lube.

"You could have just asked, you know." Balancing on one elbow she yanked open her sock drawer and held out a bottle of lube to him. Kit took it with a smile and squirted a large blob on to two stiffened fingers. The sudden whooshing intake of breath from Ross told her where he'd directed them.

"Jeez!" Her boyfriend hissed. His motion became rather panicky and arrhythmic. "Kit! Oh, my god!"

"Easy. Just relax, you'll love it."

Evie strained her neck trying to see what he was doing. All she could make out were Kit's eyes glittering in the dark. He bore a look of intense concentration, while Ross was on the verge of expiring against her back, his movements now reduced to tremors. "What are you doing?"

Ross's verbal ability had been reduced to ecstatic sobs.

"Preparing him."

"What for?" She knew the answer, but she still had to ask.

"Something I should have done six years ago."

"Now you're just being deliberately obtuse."

"Why don't you tell her, Ross?" Kit's hand curled around Ross's shoulder.

Evie stopped craning her neck as Ross's whispered words tickled against her neck. "He's fucking me... Oh, hell that's good."

"We're not there yet. That's just the warm up. Let me give you the real thing."

She might not have felt the sensations as Kit popped Ross's anal cherry, but Evie vicariously revelled in Ross's pleasure as, open mouthed, he greedily licked and bit at the skin between her shoulder blades. She suddenly wished for mirrored wardrobe doors, just so that she could watch. "Is he inside you?"

"Almost." Ross's voice was way up high, a breathy, flighty little squeak. "Oh, Evie, I can't describe it. It feels as if he's fucking right through me into you." His cock bucked inside her at his words. Kit surged forward, forcing them all up the bed. Evie tightened her grip upon the headboard.

"That's it. Come on...easy...you can take this all."

Ross gripped her hips, keeping a tight hold so he stayed deep inside her as he tentatively eased himself back to meet

Kit's forward motion.

It was never going to last long. The perspiration dripping off Ross scalded her with its heat. Expletives flew from his lips in staggered gasps. Control, if there'd been much to begin with, completely fled the field. He bucked into her. He drove himself back against Kit, clearly lost to anything but the sensations flooding his senses.

Evie frantically rubbed her clit, determined to share the pleasure of release with him. Based on Kit's low moans he was chasing release too.

In the end, it was her climax that finished Ross off, her muscles clasping his cock tight. Completely overcome with the sheer ebullient joy of the moment, Ross cried out, before crashing against her, spent and weak. Freed of Kit's grasp, his cock now limp, Ross rolled on to his back. "If I ever wake up and find I can still walk we're going to do that again, and again...and again." His eyelids closed.

Kit gently mussed his hair and then took her by the hand. "Come on, let's shower. I think lover boy needs some rest." They coated one another in soap suds, then gave each other vigorous rub downs with the terry towels to dry off, before sliding back into bed on either side of Ross.

It felt weird to wake together the next morning. Kit's presence in the bed had overridden Ross's dislike of physical contact while he slept. There simply wasn't space for them all to have their own segregated spaces. Instead, they slept spooned together, arms and legs all entangled. Sunday followed a simple pattern, sex, breakfast, table sex, shower—Ross blowing Kit on bended knees, followed by the rumpling of the freshly made bed, then dinner and a film before an evening chock full of sex.

Evie fell into bed dead on her feet, and slept snuggled between Ross and Kit's hot, lean bodies, a position she found it damned hard to rouse herself from when the alarm started shrieking on Monday morning.

Ross rolled out of bed on the third beep and staggered towards the bathroom, making zombie noises. Evie hit snooze and pulled the duvet over her head to guard against the daylight. Everything ached, but she couldn't stop smiling thinking about what they'd done together. The alarm went off again. This time Kit silenced it. Then he gently blew across her ear.

"Stop it." Evie hunched her shoulders trying to block the irritation. Instead of backing off, Kit's lips closed upon her earlobe.

"It's time to wake up."

"It so isn't." Why the hell couldn't the working week start on a Wednesday? "You get up," she grumbled when he continued the tease.

"Babe, I'm already up."

"Really?" Despite the lethargy gripping her limbs, arousal sparked at the thought of him standing eager. Kit shuffled closer so that he spooned her back, and his cock rubbed into the crevice between the cheeks of her bottom. A low, tired groan escaped from her throat, transforming in the process into a sigh of longing. She grew wet with arousal, wet and eager, even though the fuzzy warmth of sleep still held her in a tenacious grip.

"How about I help rouse you a little?" Without pausing for a response, Kit slung an arm over her hip and brushed his fingers through the V of curls that covered her mons.

"Kit, I'm knackered." She gave another low moan, aware that she ought to get up. Maureen would give her hell if she strolled in late and could only offer a weekend of total debauchery as an excuse. Her boss, the sister-in-law of Melton Manor's owners, considered near or total death the only valid reason for not being in work and on time. "I can't be late."

"Best get up then." He hauled the covers off her and smacked her naked rump, before rolling on to his back. "Guess I'll just have to play with this little triumph of nature all alone."

She immediately rolled over. Kit lay with one hand clasped behind his mussed up bed hair, the other was stretched surreptitiously towards her half-open sock drawer, where a bottle of lube poked out from between the jumble of mismatched socks.

"I have to work."

"Yup," he agreed. "Best get dressed."

"Definitely. I can't be late."

"That is a shame."

Evie glanced down at the shiny red helm of his cock, and arousal fluttered like a wild bird through her innards, dulling the aches in her limbs and sharpening her addled mind. Maybe she had time for a quick cuddle. It'd take twenty minutes tops to shower and dress, assuming Ross ever vacated the bathroom, and another ten to drive to Melton Manor. That left fifteen minutes for coffee and toast, or savouring Kit. Despite the grumble in her stomach, there was no contest. She reached out and lightly traced the tip of his glans.

"You'll be late."

"I won't. Not if we're quick." She grabbed a condom off the bedside table and bypassing any other preamble, rolled it smoothly down his shaft. "Come and get me, tiger."

Kit gave a mock growl as Evie piled the pillows into rather haphazard mound and draped herself over them on all fours. "Don't I even get a kiss?" His chest vibrated against her back as he slid into position, sparking a triumphant hiss.

"Yes... oh, yes."

"Quick, right?" He planted his hands over hers and gripped tight.

Trembling as he repetitively filled her, driving in and out of her at breakneck speed, Evie met him thrust for thrust and revelled in their frantic, driving need. She didn't realize Ross was back from the shower until the wardrobe door creaked. Seemingly flummoxed by what he'd returned to, Ross put on his shirt and tie with his back facing the bed. When he turned, his cheeks were an unhealthy shade of red.

"Ross," Evie gasped, registering his embarrassment. "Ross, I'm sorry." She tried to push Kit away, and stretched a hand towards Ross, but Kit bucked into her twice as fast and refused to let her inch out of his arms. For the first time since their three-way dalliance had begun, she felt a stab of fear. Clearly, there were boundaries in this relationship that needed establishing. Everything they'd done over the weekend had been mutual. If it involved Kit, it involved all three of them. Neither she nor Ross had got too exclusive with him. Leastways, not like this.

"No, it's okay. We can't always all be involved. Enjoy yourselves."

She'd known him too long and knew him too well not to realize that his response was alien to what he wanted.

"Thanks," Kit muttered, and she watched Ross wince. His obvious hurt made her chest ache.

Ross turned away and hurried downstairs carrying the remainder of his outfit.

"Stop it, Kit! I have to go after him. He's hurt."

"No." Kit held her tight. "He'll be fine. It's got to be equal or it won't last out the day, and he knows that, Evie. If I'd walked in on you and Ross, I wouldn't have got all pouty, and you didn't when you walked in on me and Ross. It's got to be the same rules in all directions."

"It will be. But we've given him a shock."

"It has to be equal."

Evie snarled, suddenly infuriated by his tight grip, and his unwillingness to compromise. Ross needed her. What she had with him was far stronger and more important than the newborn bonds forming between herself and Kit in their tentative ménage a trois.

"What you were saying last night, wasn't quite so hung up on equality. Now, let go." She smacked at his hands.

"What we were—?" Kit's hold eased a little. He stopped

moving, allowing her room to wriggle free, although he caught her wrist before she scampered off the bed. "So you heard that. I wondered if you were really asleep."

"I love you," she'd heard Kit whisper to Ross as they lay still joined together, basking in the afterglow of having come from rubbing their cocks together. They'd thought her sleeping. In truth, she was dozing, but those words had seared themselves through the cotton wool in her head and tore open a hole in her heart. That Kit loved Ross was a truth that she should have known, since it was there in every look they exchanged, but hearing him say it, without a qualifier that included her, had sown a seed of doubt in her mind that continued to grow.

Kit was right. If this was to work out long term, instead of just being a passing fling, the love had to flow in all directions equally.

Kit jerked her onto the bed and rolled her onto her back. He lay on top of her so that their stomachs met, and his erection nestled comfortably between the lips of her sex. Evie squirmed, loving the weight and feel of him, and his closeness, but still angry at his confession during the night, and the way he was keeping her from Ross.

"Evie." Kit gently brushed the hair away from her face and kissed her lips. "I didn't mean it to sound exclusive. You know we haven't known each other nearly as long. You wouldn't believe me even if I made such an admission to you. It doesn't mean I won't ever say that and mean it. I want this to work, after all." His fingers curled tightly into her plump rear, lifting her, so that he slid up and down between her sex lips, tormenting her with his closeness.

She craved penetration again. But she wanted Ross to be with them. Body on autopilot, she raised her hips in greeting.

"He'll be absolutely fine, Evie. Guilt'll kill this faster than anything else. Don't let it take root."

The bedroom door swung open again, revealing Ross dressed for work, but with his zip undone and his cock poking upwards over the top of his underwear. He gave them both a rather sheepish grin. "Erm, am I welcome?"

The vibration of Kit's laughter rippled through her torso and into her limbs. "'Course you're bloody welcome, you idiot."

"Ross! How could you think you wouldn't be?" She stretched a hand out towards him as best she could while Kit continued to crowd her.

"You don't mind if I join in?"

"Only if you don't mind being late."

A shadow of doubt clouded Ross's face, vanquished a second later as Kit hooked his fingers inside the elastic of Ross's shorts and tugged him closer.

"I'll say the traffic was bad." Ross squeaked as Kit's thumb traced the curve of his glans. Kit tugged the briefs and trousers down, exposing Ross's lower half. His cock immediately swung a little higher, so that it seemed to kiss the bush of springy curls that cradled its base and extended upwards in a thin line towards Ross's navel.

"You should let your hair grow back in," Evie said to Kit, who was perfectly hairless save for his head and the morning stubble peppering his chin.

The remark prompted a frown. "No way, it'd itch like hell."

"Only for a day or two."

"Besides, if I did you'd never be able to tell us apart in the dark."

She was pretty certain she'd always be able to tell them apart, irrespective of her sight. They were built differently, smelled different, and just felt and moved in completely different ways. Bypassing the issue for another occasion, Evie stretched and shuffled up the bed a little, so that her head extended over the mattress edge into the space between Ross's parted thighs. Despite his recent shower, the perfume of him wafted over her like a fabled aphrodisiac. She licked his inner thigh, where the skin was a smooth contrast to the more hirsute outer and lower leg. Grasping him for support she stroked her hand up to his bottom and round over his hips to caress the base of his cock.

"Next time you two want to shag before breakfast, let me know so I can set the alarm for earlier." Ross ruffled Kit's hair. "God, I love you, Evie." Ross's bright blue eyes shone down at her as he rubbed the side of her jaw with one callused thumb, while she continued to lavish attention on his inner thigh and the soft weight of his ball sack.

Kit grinned. "You'd better love me too after this." He opened his mouth wide to take Ross's cock.

"Fuck, that's good." Ross replied as he guided Kit's sucking with his hand thrust into his hair. Eyes closed, a dreamy smile stretched across his lips. "Of course I love you too, you sexy bastard, much as I've been trying to deny it for years."

Chapter Thirteen

"Is she really going out with him?
Well, there she is, let's ask her."

The upbeat lyrics to the sorrowful song ran through Evie's head as she trekked over to Kirkley's tiny post office on a quest for ice cream a few days later. Kit had painted them both with the remainder of the last tub, leaving them sticky and the kitchen table permanently stained with triple chocolate sauce. Personally, she wasn't in any great hurry to taste ice cream again for a while, but the boys were both fond of it, and Kit had suggested they make alcoholic ice-cream floats, by mixing dollops of rich vanilla ice with spiced rum and cola.

Despite the teeny shop's rather haphazard business hours, it remained a hive of activity for those possessed of more sobriety than to set foot in the pub before six 'o clock. The collection of busybodies huddled beneath the green envelope of the glorious weeping willow to the right of the shop door.

"On your own today?" said one of them when Evie emerged with her tub of Neapolitan.

"Yes. Ross is at work."

This response was met with an approving nod.

"What about your lodger, he still with you?"

"Uh-huh."

"Poor you," remarked the woman.

"It must be terrible for you," remarked a second, slight woman with stark white hair. "I shouldn't like him in my house.

One would never know what he might do. I wouldn't be able to relax."

In Evie's mind, she remained draped across the kitchen table, naked, perfectly at ease, while Ross and Kit gave her a glorious massage.

The braying of muttered affirmatives to the petite woman's assertion snapped Evie from the memory.

"Oh, he's perfectly house trained. I wouldn't let him stay if he wasn't." Her glib remark earned her an array of scowls.

"I dare say he's absolutely charming at first glance." The first woman took up the gauntlet again. "It's what comes after that concerns me. Christopher Skye is a bad penny, always was. Done some terrible things, that boy."

Evie tried hard not to smirk as another memory of Kit standing over her naked, stuffing a tea towel into her mouth so she couldn't squeal while Ross smacked her bare arse reared in her head. Damned bastard, Kit, had then turned his back on her and started playing with his cock, deliberately provoking her with the fact that she couldn't see what he was up too.

Yes, living with Kit, was deeply frustrating, but, also deeply wonderful, if somewhat exhausting. She could see why he was keen to have two lovers. He'd exhaust just one. She considered her libido fairly high, but Kit's never seemed to wane, although mostly he enjoyed teasing.

"I expect you'll be glad to see the back of him. It's terrible the burden he's putting on a canny couple like you and Ross."

"Oh, I don't know. We quite like having him around."

The statement met with a line of raised eyebrows.

"Don't be silly, dear. He's no right to go intruding on your relationship."

Evie glanced warily about, heat rushing to her cheeks. Did the whole village know that he'd become far more than her lodger? Had Lillianna's words of a week ago actually made the circuit round the neighbourhood?

"Still playing his old tricks?" The question sprang from a

male throat. It possessed none of the twittering, fake concern of the women in their quest for gossip; rather it roiled with savage dislike.

Evie spun to face the newcomer, whom she vaguely recognized as someone Ross exchanged curiously polite nods with whenever they crossed paths. Tony, she believed him to be. She watched him tap a ciggy from a new packet. He didn't light it up, merely propped it behind his ear so that it lay parallel to the greying patch in his otherwise mousy-coloured hair.

"I've heard he's a good fuck." He looked pointedly at her, holding her gaze while he emphasized each syllable. "He's certainly good at fucking things up. Don't expect anything good to come of what he's up to. It never did in the past." Having etched that statement deep into her psyche, he turned and strolled off towards the A road.

Bewildered, Evie stared after him, clutching her rapidly defrosting ice cream. "What the hell was that about?"

When she turned back to the women for an answer, she found they'd all fled.

The strange encounter wouldn't leave her. Evie found herself thinking about it in odd moments, wondering what the hell Tony had meant with his words. It hadn't so much sounded like a warning as a bitter observation. It set her wondering about the way he and Ross nodded to one another, like rival cowboys in some old Western showing grudging respect in order to maintain the status quo. Ross's response to her text message didn't entirely quell her anxiety.

He's the ex of one of Kit's exes.

She guessed Kit had stolen his girlfriend in the dim and distant past, but that didn't really explain the reputation Kit had with the old biddies brigade. In the end, she called in to see Kit on her way to work.

Metal scaffolding enfolded the front and side of Rose Cottage, and a team of builders sat perched along the apex of the roof. They wolf whistled as she strolled up the drive, and pointed her around the back when her knock at the door went unanswered. Kit was in the garden, rinsing his hands under the outdoor standpipe.

Evie leaned against the wall of the old potting shed, watching silvery droplets sluice along his arms and into the cuffs of his three-quarter length sleeves. He still hadn't learned how to dress down for work. Currently he wore leather trousers topped with a T-shirt that probably cost as much as a meal for four in London. Ross had tried to lend him a pair of old combats and a pullover, but Kit had left them on the bed mumbling something about the smell making him too horny to work.

"See something you like?" Kit glanced over his shoulder at her and gave her a wide grin that showed off his crooked canines. He tugged his T-shirt over his head, so that he could soap the rest of his arms and torso without getting the cloth wet. The cold water, coupled with the nip of the breeze made his delicate nipples crinkle into two coppery points. Evie moistened her lips, thinking of biting them.

"Why are you washing outside?"

"Water's off inside, while I figure out the pipes for the utility room. That and I'm keeping the spies busy."

"Spies?" Evie glanced up at the builders on the roof, who were now back at work stripping off the old tiles.

"Not them."

Her gaze encompassed the garden, instead, but beside a couple of starlings pecking at the lawn, there was no other living thing in sight. "What are you on about—spies?"

"Spies...fan club... call 'em what you like. They've taken to sitting in the orchard to eat their lunch."

"Who has?" Now that he mentioned it, she could see an unnatural flash of blue amongst the tree branches and a pink that wasn't a blossom, but they had to have binoculars to be copping a gaze at Kit from that distance.

"It's Doris's granddaughter and her mates that work over at the riding school."

Negligent of the spluttering water, Evie shoved Kit towards the house. "Jesus, Kit! What have you been doing? They're barely legal."

"They're all perfectly legal. It's Laura's twenty-first in a fortnight. Doris told me. And when they're not here checking me out, they spend most of their time propping up the bar in the pub."

"Yeah, but still."

"I haven't done anything. Not unless washing's suddenly a crime." The gleam in his eyes told her explicitly otherwise. Not that she'd go so far as to accuse him of lying, he was merely playing loose with the details.

"Kit..."

"I get a bit lonely up here when you and Ross are at work, especially when I get thinking about all the fun things we've been getting up to..." His words tailed off. Evie stared at him, her mouth agape and her breath caught in her throat. He hadn't...the bastard...He had. "You've been...for them! So, they've seen." She had a burning urge to smack him across the face.

"Seen what, Evie?" he teased. Kit reached for a towel drying upon the Aga, but Evie snatched it from his hands and lashed him across the ribs leaving a broad red mark.

"Hey! Ow! What's that for?" He wrestled her for the towel, and finally pinned her against the wall, so that she lay trapped between the unmovable stone and the wiry unyielding heat of his semi-naked body.

"Bastard," she hissed into his mouth as his lips descended. Kit stopped short of making contact, so that his breath whispered across her lips, but there was no ravaging kiss in which to disperse her anger. "I can't believe you've done it for them, but not for me." Although a hint of playfulness rang in her voice, hurt stabbed at her chest. It seemed so unfair that he would perform for strangers but not for a lover.

Kit sandwiched their palms together either side of her head. "Done what, hmm?"

As if he needed her to explain. So, she had a fetish. There was nothing wrong with that.

Ross had suggested two days ago that she quit pestering Kit over that particular act and that they just get on with having fun, his theory being that fewer expectations would make for a less stressful relationship. In theory, it worked. Only, Kit knew what she wanted and that she was constantly biting her tongue. He teased her mercilessly, refusing to let her see so much as him touching himself, although he'd happily spend hours toying with Ross's cock without the slightest hesitation. He'd even sat with her and watched Ross masturbate.

"Are we by any chance talking about the M word?"

Evie shook her head, still vexed by his teasing. "Actually, I came to ask you about Tony."

Kit released his grip and dropped his hands to his sides. "What about him?" He rubbed at the scabby line still above his right brow.

"I bumped into him outside the post office. He wasn't all that friendly."

"Did he threaten you?"

She shook her head, eyes narrowing with suspicion and alarm at the tone of his voice. "Ross told me that you and Tony have an ex in common."

Kit rested his bum against the lip of the Belfast Sink. "Not exactly. It was more a case of I got there first. It's hardly my fault that he took so bloody long to ask her out."

"Guess he was pretty hung up on her to still be pissed at you after all this time."

"Guess so." Kit turned away and pulled his T-shirt on again. "Come on. I'll drop you at work before I head out to B&Q."

The feeling of unease between them persisted while Kit gathered his things together. "You realize you still owe me a confession in exchange for the story I told you about Ross and I getting it on in the tent," he said as he locked up.

Evie sniffed, recognizing the attempt to lighten the mood. "That was hardly about the pair of you getting it on. Hearing about your actual first time might be genuinely worth my attention."

He laughed. "Come on, Evie. Spice the journey up for me. Tell me something really dirty and maybe I'll give you a prize."

Huffily, Evie climbed into the car. There'd be a catch. He'd try and fob her off with some other reward besides the one she wanted. "Nothing to say."

"Nothing at all? Not even a nice PG-rated fantasy?"

"Nothing."

"Clearly I need to up the incentive." Kit's eyes twinkled as he checked the mirrors before reversing into the lane. "How about if you make it good enough, I'll really tell you about how Ross and I first got it on. But I'm warning you, it's not entirely pretty."

"I can ask Ross; he'll tell me without the need to barter."

"Okay, turn me on with your words and I'll let you watch."

"Watch what, Kit?" She wanted him to say it, so there could be no squirming out of the arrangement later.

"I'll shake my *thang* for your pleasure."

She kept her eyebrows raised and her lips pursed. "You've got to actually say it."

"Okay, okay. I'll wank for your pleasure."

"Great!" She grinned as sudden warmth heated her around the ears. Finally... Now, she just needed a good enough story. Unfortunately, the most adventurous sex she'd had prior to Ross and the move to Kirkley was balanced against the sink in her parent's bathroom, halfway through the most excruciating meet-the-family dinner the universe had ever witnessed. Was it any wonder that particular relationship had only lasted two weeks?

"He's back, he's back, he's back..."

Evie tentatively opened the front door later that day to find Lillianna, her hair newly dyed black and ironed Morticia Adams straight, singing on her doorstep. It was a lovely evening, the sky orange all along the horizon, and the air filled with the crisp, clean scent of the coming spring. Purple-tipped crocuses had reared their heads all along the strip of green that bordered the street. Evie peered quizzically at her friend. "Who's back...?"

Lillianna playfully slapped her cheek. "I see you're in la-la land again. It must the lack of fucking sleep your getting, or is it just the fucking? Your favourite lover boy just drove into the village. I saw him pull up at his place not more than ten minutes ago."

"I don't have a favourite... and he's only been to B&Q." Evie stared nonplussed into the twilight. "It's not like he's been away for a week. I saw him at lunchtime."

"Yeah—curious that you don't have a favourite but you know who I'm talking about."

"Drop it, Lilli. Are you coming in?"

"Nah, you're coming out."

Evie shook her head. She still needed to work on the dramatization of her sex life for Kit's benefit. Despite fitting in numerous rehearsals at work, going over events in her head and trying to make them sound interesting, the only reaction she was likely to get at the moment was a humungous yawn. "I'm all set for an early night," she told Lilli.

Truthfully, she did need one. There were muscles in her stomach and thighs she hadn't known she had a week earlier.

"Honestly, you and your dressing gown!" Impatient as ever, Lillianna pushed past Evie into the hallway, her straight hair swinging like a stage curtain over her face. "Grab your coat. Let's sort you out."

Thirty seconds later, Evie found herself crossing the green

in her slippers, clutching her coat and bag. "Where are we going?" she asked as she tried to shake off Lillianna's steel-clawed grip on her wrist.

"Molly's. You need sprucing up a bit, and I need an excuse to visit. It's Wednesday," she proclaimed as if that fact were highly pertinent. "And I had my nails fixed yesterday 'cause one of them broke, so you'll have to have yours done." She waved the evidence of her recent manicure two inches in front of Evie's face. The nosebleed effect had gone, replaced by a stylized cobweb design in black and silver, presumable intended to go with her return to black hair. "Plus, you're shagging Kit, so we kind of need to talk."

The notion of sharing the details of her sex life brought a sickly green tinge to Evie's already pale skin. "I don't do details. I've told you that before."

"I wasn't asking for them, although if you do want to share... Anyway, I notice you're no longer denying the fact that you're doing the evil with him, which must mean Ross is in on it too."

Evie stopped and planted her hand upon her hips, but Lillianna just marched ahead.

"At Molly's." She tapped her nose and gave Evie a wink. "Village green's never a good place to dish."

"I haven't noticed it growing ears."

"It doesn't need to grow 'em." Lillianna swirled around, but she kept on walking, albeit backwards. "I think it's about time you learned what certain folks have against him."

Okay, this she definitely wanted to hear. At the least, it might shed light on Tony's weird remarks.

"Eyebrows and nails, Moll," Lillianna announced when Molly opened the door of her corner cottage to them and peeped out into the now thickening gloom. "Sorry about the short notice, it's desperate." Lillianna guided Evie over the threshold and through to the conservatory, where she pushed her into the big leather chair that dominated the space. Molly followed them through, flicking off the TV with the remote on the way past. She stood in the doorway and eyed them questioningly.

"Kill the hairy caterpillars." Lillianna nodded towards Evie's brows.

Molly's narrow, heart-shaped face filled with a sunny smile as she padded across the lime-washed tiles to Evie's side. Ill at ease with the smiling torturer's approach, Evie hunched down into the chair. "I happen to like them au natural."

Molly gave a shrug and slipped the tweezers she'd picked up into her pocket, the action met with a disapproving sniff from Lillianna, who swirled away in a cloud of patchouli and gardenia with her severely plucked eyebrows arched halfway up her fore-head. "I bet Kit plucks his. He's not found of unnecessary body hair."

Evie folded her arms, remembering all too well the sensations associated with Kit's denuded body, and how noticeable the stubble around his jaw was first thing.

"And Ross definitely plucks, else how do you explain his teenage monobrow compared with now?"

"Never mind the eyebrows, these are atrocious." Molly's fingers entwined around Evie's hand and then stretched out each digit for inspection. Sorrow glowed in her mocha-brown eyes as she tutted over the destruction. "You'll have to have acrylics, there's barely any nail left." She flicked her long blonde fringe out of her heavily made-up eyes and immediately set to work pulling out the requisite bits and pieces. "I never took you for a nibbler. Normally I can spot them."

Evie glanced at her poor fingernails. A week of studiously attempting to ignore all the rumours circulating about her and the boys had reduced them to ragged stumps. Without thinking, she popped her thumbnail in her mouth and attempted to bite. The act earned her a withering glare.

"I catch you chewing these and you're in for it," Molly said as she lay out a set of fake nails on the side table attached to the chair. "Just chill for a while; this won't take long. I just need to sort your cuticles out first."

Molly set to work, soaking her nail beds. Evie allowed her attention to stray in Lillianna's direction. Her friend, who was being unusually quiet, stood by the window, with a nail art leaflet held loosely within her grasp. However, her attention was clearly on whatever lay beyond the blinds, the cord of which she twitched the moment Molly's head turned, to reveal a panoramic view into the neighbours lounge.

"You could've just called, Lilli, and stood in the dark, although the business is appreciated." Molly gave Evie a broad smile, which she barely noticed, her thoughts already back on the subject of her past sexploits and how exactly to dress them up for Kit's consumption. Maybe if she spun him something about an old temping job and seamed stockings, except he'd probably realize she was lying, and she wasn't sure he'd get off on the whole naughty secretary thing.

"Ahem!" Lillianna's sharp cough cut through Evie's thoughts. She glanced up and realized that Molly's neighbours were home. Jason and Saul were the lead singer and bass player from Kirkley's hottest band. Admittedly, their only competition was dad rock quartet *Bill and the Teds*, but the pair were certainly lust worthy, especially when they poured themselves into tight outfits and got up on stage. Currently, they were stripping off creased business suits.

"Should we be watching this?" Embarrassed, Evie dipped her chin so that her hair fell down across one eye and partially masked the view of Jason slipping off his trousers. Molly, she noticed, paid the window no regard.

"Shell pink, okay?"

"Fine, just nothing garish."

Lillianna stopped fanning the nail art leaflet and hunched against the curtain cord, her nose almost poking between the slats of the blinds as she sought the ideal viewing spot. She perched one cheek of her curvy bottom on the windowsill.

"Lilli, I'm not actually interested in watching them bumming one another." Evie's brow further creased as more gym-toned muscle was displayed along with two pairs of tight white boxer shorts. It wasn't that she wasn't curious, it was just she knew how mortified she'd be if she found out someone had been spying on her, especially given what she'd been up to recently with Kit and Ross.

"They don't," said Lillianna.

"They're not gay," added Molly. "Or if they are, they're hiding it well, considering the collection of groupies they have."

"Yeah, yuck, Evie. I don't get off on that stuff, unlike you. What's the attraction in knowing they can have fun without you?"

There were numerous attractions, none of which Evie felt like listing, including symmetry for one and satisfying some plain old curiosity for another. And that was before she considered the more taboo aspects, or exactly how big a turn on it was watching Kit and Ross make love and knowing they weren't going to push her away if she wanted to join in.

"I always thought you liked staring at men's butts." Evie set to chewing the inside of her cheek in place of her nails. Having stripped off, neither of the men seemed in any hurry to pull anything else on.

"Huh! I like digging my nails into their butts, Evie." Lillianna flexed her fingers in a clawing motion and gave a yowl. "Preferably while they're astride and think they're in control. I'm all about eyes, not arses."

Which explained her interest in Kit, who was a little too slender to have the world's finest arse, but had eyes like the souls of the world.

"Do we need to psychoanalyze your biggest fear while you're sat in that chair?" Lillianna slinked across the floor, somehow moving in steel-tipped stiletto heels, a heavily beaded dress, and with six dozen bangles up her arms, without making more than a whisper of sound. She stretched over the lower half of

Evie's chair, so she could meet her face to face at close quarters. "Terrified they're going to leave you out, are you? You wouldn't be the first."

Molly's head jerked up from its hunched position over Evie's nails. "It's true that you're having a threesome, then? It's not just some gossipy rumour."

"No—no!" Evie pushed Lillianna away and tried to get up, only to have Molly's grip tightened upon her arm.

Flummoxed, she gazed into the hazel of Molly's eyes trying to figure out the question. "Oh," she said, realizing Molly had taken her *no* to Lillianna's teasing as a denial of the relationship. "In truth...Well, sort of...ish." She sat back down with her arms folded, blushing furiously, her lips clamped together for fear of any details escaping.

"It's a full-on, stinking ménage a trois." Lillianna clacked her heels. "It's only the fact that one of them is Ross that's stopped me pulling you limb from limb yet. Never did get what Kit saw in him, and I'm not the only one." With an irate waggle, she returned to her position by the blinds. The two men from next door were now sitting side by side on the sofa in their boxers, evidently waiting for something.

Meanwhile, Molly's gaze remained fastened upon Evie, her hazel eyes bronze flecked with worry. "Oh!" she pursed her lips, as if she wanted to say more, but wasn't sure if she should, or how to go about it either. A surreptitious glance at Lillianna didn't seem to help with the decision. "I hoped it was just a rumour...for your sake. He's not just bad, Evie. He's downright evil."

So folks kept suggesting, not that any of them came out and said specifically why he'd earned such a reputation. "Really?" She tried to catch Lillianna's eye, intending to press her for the answers she promised, but her friend studiously ignored her.

"Drink?"

Molly's pleasant face set into a grimace as she spooned

granules into two mugs and dumped a teabag into a third. "I can't believe Ross has got you involved with him. I know they're old friends and Ross has never acknowledged what happened but..."

"What happened? What are you talking about?"

Horror shot through Molly's already drawn expression, causing a flight of anxious butterflies to tear about inside Evie's stomach.

"You mean Ross hasn't...or Lilli? Shit! They've not told you?"

In her alarm, Molly missed the cups and tipped milk over the work surface. Evie lurched to the rescue with a strip of kitchen towel. "You're telling me you don't know what he did?" Molly snatched up a packet of biscuits and munched her way through two without seeming to notice. "Goddamned Lillianna, that's why she brought you here, isn't it? Wouldn't dare say anything bad about him herself, in case it got back to him. Coward," she snapped loud enough for her voice to carry through to the conservatory. "And as for Ross... Jeezus, that's so irresponsible. I thought he was better than that."

She led Evie through to her miniscule lounge, which was rather overcrowded by a large aspidistra, and thrust a framed photograph at her. "This is Sammie, my sister."

Evie took a good look at the old photo, sensing a sort of reverence on Molly's part. The image was of two women in their late teens or early twenties, dressed for a night on the town in microscopic skirts and vest-type tops. Molly was instantly recognizable, despite her hair being a good five shades darker than her current bleached-blonde. Her sister had an easygoing smile, tainted by a hint of slyness around the eyes, although she was undeniably pretty.

Molly took the back the picture and replaced it on the book case. "You've never heard of her, have you?"

"I didn't realize your family was from round here."

"They moved."

Sensing impending doom, Evie mentally braced herself for the details of a road accident or drunken misadventure. Drugs were out; Kit was far too clean living for that, although maybe this would explain his obsession with green tea and muesli. Maybe it was something simpler like he'd got the girl pregnant and bailed on her. She hoped not. She didn't have much respect for people who wouldn't accept responsibility for their actions, and she didn't want a reason to dislike him.

"Just tell me, Molly."

"He killed her."

"What?"

"Oh, I can't prove it. But I know he's responsible. They found her clothes in a ditch. Wallet too."

Evie gawped at Molly, completely dumbstruck. There weren't really words to express the shock and disbelief that flattened her thoughts. Kit a murderer... Ridiculous. Sanity prevailed. She shook her head. "No. Oh, no."

"It was fine between him and Sammie while she was going along with his pervy demands, but it was a different matter once she started saying no," Molly explained.

"No."

Molly didn't seem to hear Evie's denial; she just kept layering on the dirt, thicker and thicker. Painting an image of a man so alien to what Evie knew of Kit, the dichotomy finally snapped her out of her stunned daze.

Yes, admittedly, Kit played hard and fast with his sexual morals, but that hardly made him evil. And he'd shown no indication of being the sort given to violent rages. Molly's account just didn't tally up straight.

Evie gulped a mouthful of steaming coffee to dislodge the lump in her throat. The liquid scalded her tongue, and brought stinging tears to her eyes, but also finally loosened her tongue. "You're mistaken, surely. Not Kit. He couldn't. He wouldn't. That's not him."

Molly abruptly pushed herself upright and paced around

the coffee table. "You don't know what he'd been asking her to do. It wasn't the sort of stuff you wanted passing around the neighbourhood. It was disgusting. Really crude."

Disgusting as in threesomes and anal sex, Evie wondered, though she kept the thought to herself. There'd be no placating Molly's moral outrage.

"Was he charged?" she asked, fearing for a moment that the six year stint in Japan was fiction to camouflage a stint in jail.

Molly shook her head. "The police reckoned there wasn't enough evidence. No signs of any obvious scuffles and they never found her body. They just stuck her on the missing persons register and forgot about her."

"But Kit—"

"Was the last person to see her and the only one with a motive. Of course, he denies everything. And your boyfriend backed him up."

"Ross!"

The possibility that he was somehow involved in this too threatened the contents of her stomach. Evie flailed blindly seeking a reassuring purchase, some slice of sanity, but there was only Molly and her vitriol, black tears streaking her face where her mascara had run.

Evie rose and hurried back to the conservatory. If the police hadn't charged him, there had to be reasonable doubt despite Molly's insistence.

"Did she tell you?" Lillianna turned her head as Evie pulled a tenner from her purse and left it on the leather chair as payment for her nails.

"Why didn't you?" Still fevered with shock, Evie stared at her friend. Lillianna refused to make eye contact.

"Not everyone sees it the same way as Molly."

"Do you believe it?"

Lillianna thoughtfully chewed her lips. "I don't know. I can't deny that the relationship was rocky. They were both pretty wild, but on the other hand, regardless of what I think of Ross, he's always been honest. I don't think he'd lie even to cover Kit's back. He claimed Kit was with him so he couldn't have had anything to do with it, in case Molly didn't say."

Lilli dug her teeth so hard into her lower lip that they came away stained with burgundy lipstick. "I'm sorry, Evie. I just thought you should know, and I figured they hadn't told you."

Snapshot images of Kit touching her, of the three of them entwined, were suddenly overlaid with the frozen image of Sammie smiling and her body lying naked in a ditch.

"Go home, Evie. Talk to Ross. Talk to Kit. Draw your own conclusions."

"Right." Evie glanced up and caught a glimpse of the scene playing out next door. Jason and Saul smeared in baby oil, Greek wrestling, while a woman in thigh high leather boots and a PVC cat suit half-heartedly flogged them with what looked like a suede jellyfish. "I thought you said it was kinky, not surreal."

"It's kinkier in my head. There's a bit more sand in there and some trees, and they have two nice matching slave collars, and when they're disobedient I have them lick my shiny boots clean. She—" she nodded at the woman, "—isn't exactly cut out for the role. She's much better as the naughty nurse, or the naughty schoolgirl, the naughty anything, really. She's pathetic when they make her top. One of these days, I'm going to work up my nerve and offer to give them a proper work out." She tugged the cord so that the blinds swivelled, obscuring the view. "I didn't do this to wreck it for you, Evie. I just thought you deserved to know a bit about him. I'd hate to think you got yourself into something without ever having seen the full picture."

Chapter Fourteen

Kit was sitting on the sofa playing video games when Evie arrived home. He had his long legs, encased in supple black leather, folded up before him, so that the controller rested upon his knees. Evie remained in the doorway to the lounge for several moments looking at him. It wasn't specifically nerves that held her there, more a heartfelt desire to be able to read what lay beneath his outward visage. He'd blown into their lives like a whirlwind, changing everything, reshaping everything in new and interesting ways. She loved him for it, and no number of unfounded accusations changed that; still it struck her how very little she did know about him, and how secretive he and Ross had been over the past.

"Hey," he said, spotting her. He patted the space next to him and offered up a welcoming smile. "Been out somewhere?"

"Molly's, getting my nails done." She took a tentative step forward, trying not to seem too uptight, and raised her hands to show him.

"Not bad."

"Ross not back yet?" She went back into the hallway and took off her coat.

"He sent a text. Said he's been called out to some farm to help deliver a calf. I figure he'll be awhile. I stuck lasagne in the oven." Kit came over to the lounge door and watched her pottering about at the bottom of the stairs. "Something on your mind?"

"No." Evie sucked the end of her new acrylic thumbnail. It tasted vile.

"I'll put the kettle on, shall I? I thought maybe you had a nice story lined up for me, since we've got a bit of quiet time together." The way he said nice implied dirty.

She had a story, but not one he'd appreciate hearing. Evie left him to fix the drinks and sat down at the bottom of the stairs. Really she wanted to ask Ross about the allegation first. He wouldn't outright lie to her face, even if he was being cagey. It seemed unbelievable that despite three years together he'd never mentioned that someone he knew from the village had vanished, even when they'd been desperately waiting for a house here. You'd have thought he'd want to be anywhere else. Suddenly, she wasn't sure she knew Ross all that well anymore.

She gave a deep sigh and rubbed her eyes. When she opened them up, she found Kit knelt before her, holding two steaming mugs, with a liquid sheen of concern glazing his dark eyes.

"What's up?"

When she looked down at the mugs to avoid his gaze, he rested his hand upon her knee.

"Evie? Did something happen while you were out? Did you run into Tony again?"

Hell, she'd almost forgotten Tony. Clearly he took Molly's view of the situation.

She shook her head, and relief visibly washed some of the strain from Kit's features. It came right back again as soon as she began talking. "I've been hearing things. Things about you and the past."

Kit rubbed the tip of his tongue against his upper front two teeth. "Where'd you say you'd been?"

"Molly's. Molly Dean," she replied, taking one of the offered mugs.

Kit took a nervous slug from his.

"She says—"

He fell away from her, shaking his head. "Don't. I know what she says."

"But did you?"

Horror crept across his face, followed by waves of crushing disappointment, betrayal and distrust.

"Kit, I'm sorry, but you have to realize I want to know what's going on. I kept hearing these whispers that you were a bad boy and I just thought you'd been the village teenage tearaway, but what Molly's accusing you of is way more serious. I mean, what happened?" She stretched forward to grasp his arm, but he shuffled backwards out of reach. "Tell me, please. I'm trying not to judge. I just want to hear your version of events."

He didn't answer, just stared at her like a hunted beast.

Behind him, the front door swung open. Ross loomed up, his face cast in shadow. "What's going on?" He dropped his work bag at his feet.

Kit remained silent.

"I asked about Sammie," Evie stammered. "And why neither of you thought it important to mention her."

Ross's gaze swept between her hurt and Kit's blanched expression. "Holy fuck!" he swore and pushed his hand into his hair. "I was going to tell you. There's just never been a good time."

"When the hell did you think was going to be a good time? Every bugger in this village seems to think he's responsible for her vanishing and you were waiting for the right moment to mention it."

Okay, so that outburst had just undone everything she'd been painfully trying to avoid. There was enough doubt in her words for it to sound as if she believed in Kit's guilt.

"Vanishing—that's a good one!" The little bark of laughter Kit gave caused a knot to tighten in her guts. "It's certainly the most complimentary way of putting it I've heard so far. Like I'm a stage magician and I've poofed her to some alternate dimension from which I can pluck her back for dramatic effect. Only, I don't know where she is. It'd make life a hell of a lot easier if I had the answers everyone seems to think I have." He turned on the spot and bolted out of the open front door.

Ross gawped at her. "Fucking hell, Evie! How bloody insensitive was that?" He ran after Kit.

"Wait!" Ross ran into the street. He caught up with Kit just as his lover was wrenching open the car door. "Wait! Where are you going?"

Kit clasped the top of the driver's side door, his knuckles every bit as white as his face. "I can't do this. I was a fool to come back and even think it would work. I can't make it right for them, Ross. They'll never forgive me."

"Kit, most of them already have."

"I should have walked her home. It's my fault."

Exasperated, Ross shoved Kit hard up against the metal chassis, oblivious of the neighbours and their twitching curtains. "Don't say that. It's no more your fault than mine."

Kit struggled in Ross's embrace a moment, his arms awkwardly pinned in the small of his back, while his stomach lay flush to the driver's side window. Ross leaned in closer, holding him tight and refusing to let go. Kit had run out on him before. Destroyed what they had and flown to Japan, leaving him behind to deal with the mess, and to question everything he knew. He wasn't letting it happen again.

Slowly, Kit stopped struggling. "She'll never trust me now."

"I doubt she trusts either of us at the moment. We should have told her what happened, instead of letting her hear all the crap on the rumour mill first. Me especially. I should have mentioned it before you came to stay, when it wasn't such a contentious issue. She'd have listened, and we wouldn't be saddled with this shit."

Darkness continued to creep across Kit's face so that worry lines creased his brows and formed crow's feet around the corners of his mouth and eyes. He shoved his hands deep into his pockets so that he stood with his shoulders hunched, a far cry from his more familiar confident posture.

"I should have walked her home."

"We all made choices that day, Kit. We have to live with them, because we sure as hell can't turn back time."

Kit made a noise deep in his throat that sounded suspiciously like a sob. Ross had never seen him cry. He'd seen him paled and shocked, angry even. Devastated, when the police knocked on the door with the news that Sammie was missing, but he'd never seen Kit cry over what had happened. That in itself was a mark against him in some eyes. Plenty of others had bawled over her disappearance. Folks like Tony, who'd elevated her onto a pedestal when she was neither martyr nor an angel, just a black and white image on a missing poster. Ross pulled Kit close again and felt the other man's fists tighten upon his clothing.

"Where did she go, Ross? What the hell happened to screw everything up so badly?"

Ross shook his head. "I wish to god I knew, but we went over everything with the police. People go missing all the time. Some of them just wake up one morning and walk away, leave everything: families, kids, job, mortgage. They just can't handle it any more so they wipe the slate clean and start over. It's not so different to what you did, jetting off to Japan with no warning."

"It is different. It's very different. What if she came back and saw us, Ross?"

Ross had wondered that himself. He'd gone over and over it in the early days after her disappearance, when Kit had left him too. Sammie probably had returned and seen them there making out. Maybe that had been the last straw. Kit had been the only thing keeping her in the village. She hated the place, screamed for someplace with more of a heartbeat. Simply walking away was probably easier than fighting it out with the family and certainly easier than challenging him and Kit. Sammie had always been the mistress of the snap decision. "Come back inside," he pleaded.

Kit shook his head. "You go and make your peace with Evie. You don't need me standing over you making things more awkward."

"What are you going to do?"

Kit shrugged, but the action was composed. "I might go up to the ruins, or I might just go home to bed."

"Your bed is here with us."

"Not tonight it isn't."

"Well, I'm going to come and find you in the morning."

Kit squeezed Ross's shoulder. Then surprisingly, he leaned forward and kissed him hard. "You do that."

He pulled away, and Ross stood in the dark until the tail lights of Kit's car faded into the distance.

Evie sat on the sofa cuddling Mimmy until Ross came back in. As much as she hated his lack of trust in her, she found some of her anger had faded. Truthfully, while Molly's words had momentarily given her cause for reasonable doubt, she deep down she simply didn't believe Kit was a killer. She needed to hear Ross's version of events though to feel absolutely certain.

"Kit?" she asked, curiously relieved to find her boyfriend was alone.

He shook his head.

"Do I get to know what happened?"

"He wanted some space."

"Ross, that's not what I meant." She followed him into the kitchen and watched him as he stood before the washing machine and stripped off. Beneath the bright spotlights, she could see that his clothing was speckled with blood and dung from the farmyard he'd been called out to earlier.

Ross stuffed the clothing into the drum and set it washing.

"Was the calf all right?"

"Eh? Yeah. Touch and go for a while because she got her leg stuck coming out, but it worked out okay."

Although she initially hung back, seeing Ross standing in his pants and socks made her want to hold him. He looked sexy in a vaguely ridiculous way. That and seeing Kit run and Ross follow him had shaken her. For a moment, she'd wondered if either of them would come back.

She offered him the juice carton as a peace offering, which he accepted and swallowed in thirsty gulps.

"I didn't tell you because it's not something I like thinking about, and it's awkward around Kit. You've seen how he reacts. I wasn't deliberately trying to keep you in the dark. I just didn't want to bring it up and spoil everything when we were all getting along so well."

"And now? Will you tell me now?"

A dark shadow drifted across the blue of Ross's eyes, but he nodded. "Make some drinks. We'll go sit down and talk."

It was a simple enough story, once they were settled on the sofa nursing steaming mugs of Yorkshire tea. Three of them— Kit, Ross, and Sammie—out by the ruins enjoying a sunny afternoon. "Sammie left to go back to the village to meet Molly. I think they were going out somewhere. Instead of walking back with her, Kit decided to stay out there with me. It was broad daylight and a five minute walk; there didn't seem any need to escort her. Unfortunately, she never arrived home. The first we knew of it was when the police hammered on Flora's door demanding to see Kit. Molly had reported her missing." He turned to her, and cupped his hands around the outside of hers. "Kit was devastated. I don't think he'll ever forgive himself for not walking her home."

"And you're absolutely sure he didn't have anything to do with her disappearance?" Though it felt insensitive to ask, she needed to be clear on that point.

"I'm positive, Evie. One hundred percent."

"What about indirectly?"

"Meaning what?"

"Like she was pregnant or something."

Ross shook his head. "I don't think so. She was real careful about that stuff, and she'd have told Kit. And he wouldn't have stayed with me if that'd been the case, and I was with him the whole time from the moment she left until the police arrived."

Evie cocked her head, considering that hereto unknown bit of information and what it meant. "Then technically you were both the last to see her."

He nodded.

"And when you say you were with him, what, you were just hanging out?"

He started to nod, then stopped and nervously wetted his lips. "Do you remember I said there'd only been one time between me and Kit before he came back from Japan? Well, that was it, Evie."

"You were shagging when she went missing?"

"Things came to a head that afternoon. We'd been pussyfooting around each other for ages, both too afraid to make an actual move. It was okay while we were doing the threesomes thing, but then Kit starting seeing Sammie and it started getting awkward. I think he thought it'd be different, that she'd jump at the chance of a three way relationship, but it was never actually going to happen." His eyes glazed a little, as if he were seeing flashbacks of the past. "I lost count of the number of times I watched the two of them make out, but it never progressed to me joining in. She liked teasing me, and she was a rampant exhibitionist, but that's as far as it went. For all her talk, when it came down to it, her tastes were spectacularly vanilla."

His hand fell upon Evie's leg, his fingers curling. Evie squeezed his hand between her thighs, reassured, but still curious. "Why didn't you both just admit to what you were doing?"

"Because it wasn't like it is now. It wasn't comfortable between us. It was awkward and new. And it felt wrong. That and admitting it to the police was bad enough. I'm not sure the rest of the village knowing would have helped. There were a few vocal villagers like Molly and Tony who actually accused him of murdering her, but most of them were just disgusted at him for letting her walk home alone. Telling them he'd done it so that he could indulge in gay sex with his best mate would only have further damaged their opinion. And now, I don't think anything short of actually finding her will make things right."

"I assume people have tried to find her?"

"Don't start digging, Evie. I know you like puzzles, but this one is best left."

She saw his point. Absolutely. But that didn't stop her scanning through all the missing persons sites on the internet the following morning. Of course, all she turned up were more tales of woe, but they gave her a better perspective on what Kit surely felt. She kept trying to imagine what it would be like if Ross simply never came home one night, but the ache that started in her chest at the very notion of it stopped her exploring the idea.

"Were you crazy?" she asked the absent Sammie. "Why the hell would you walk out on Kit and Ross?" She couldn't envisage one good enough reason for ever doing so. They were far too bloody scrumptious.

At lunchtime, she armed herself with green tea and another tub of ice cream, and went in search of Kit.

Chapter Fifteen

"I know you're in there." Evie stood on the doorstep of Rose Cottage, peering through the letterbox at a marginally improved view of the hallway since her last visit, although there were still cables hanging out of the walls. There were no builders on the roof today.

Abandoning the notion of politeness, she went round the back of the house and climbed through the sash window into the kitchen. Kit sat hunched on a window ledge in the rear bedroom. "What do you want?" he asked.

"Sorry." She waved a thermos of freshly brewed tea and the ice cream tub at him.

His jaw remained set, lips tightly pursed. Then the tiniest flicker of a smile quirked the edge of his mouth. He took a slug of tea. "Spoon?"

Evie pulled a teaspoon out of her purse, polished it on her sleeve and handed it over. "Did you sleep here?" She threw a glance at the horrid iron-framed bed that sat in the centre of the room. It looked as if it'd done time on the set of a Hammer horror film or three.

Kit dug the spoon into the ice cream, turning it upside down in his mouth to lick it clean. "Can't say I did much sleeping. The ceiling's got a ton of cracks in it."

"The bed at home is too big without you. I've got used to snuggling and Ross won't unless you force him to. He thinks I can see into his head or something, if we're touching."

"Can you?"

"No more than you can see into mine."

"How'd you know I can't?"

"Because you haven't jumped me yet." The notion of Kit having psychic abilities made her more nervous than it ought. He might not be able to read her every thought, but Kit was damned good at interpreting her physical responses. Considering how little time they'd known one another, he had a remarkably good grasp of how to push her and when. As for his responsiveness between the sheets, well, she could almost believe there was a supernatural ability involved.

"Maybe I just like stringing you along." Kit loaded the spoon and held it out towards her. When she stretched forward to lap it up, he jerked the spoon away from her lips, and held it just a fraction out of reach. "Ross tell you all about it, did he? About how screwed up with guilt I am."

"He explained your side, yes. It seemed only fair after Molly had given me hers." And planted all those doubts, she might have added.

"I don't actually want to talk about it. I'd rather talk about you, and whether you're prepared to share a story with me yet."

Considering how much she'd learned about him now, she could hardly deny him a little of herself. Still, there was a part of her that wanted to flee the notion of exposing her innermost thoughts. She'd gone over and over the tale she'd constructed for him the previous day while eating her porridge, but it had seemed flat. Besides, it was a lie, and barely stirred her to mild interest. It would impress Kit even less. It'd probably set him yawning after a minute and a half. Instead, she'd have to share something deeply personal and hope he'd understand. Hell, she'd even come prepared with props.

"Evie?" His fingers trembled, causing the laden spoon to shake.

She closed her hand around his wrist and held him still as she devoured the ice cream. The cold raised tingles as it slid down her throat, an excitement that further sparked at the heat in his gaze as she wiped the smear of dessert from her lips. "Maybe." She hedged her bets. "Or rather, I don't have a story. My sex life was boring in the past. But you said a fantasy would be okay."

"I did."

They both stood so still for a moment that she could hear their breathing, two discordant whispers in the echoey room. Exposing herself like this just didn't come easy. She'd follow someone's lead, be expressive in the heat of the moment, but talking things over like this simply filled her with shame. She'd sound foolish...perverse...really darned perverse. He might laugh, or worse—be horrified.

"Go on," he prompted. "Or should we get comfortable first?" As he ogled the bed, a grin transformed his sullen visage back into that of the warm and loving man she'd let into her relationship. Molly's accusations had never really broken her trust in him. They'd just planted seeds for doubt, which she'd stupidly allowed to grow.

Eschewing the bed, she remained by the window. "It's a bit sad...tacky, maybe."

"Let me be the judge. Just tell me."

Evie swallowed deeply. "It's after dark, and I'm somewhere I shouldn't be."

"What sort of somewhere?" It was like a magic switch. Suddenly, Kit was alive again. His dark eyes glowed with curiosity as he unfolded his legs from the window ledge and set his feet upon the floor.

"An old building. I get caught. There's this man." She closed her eyes falling into the scene: an ill-lit corridor with a slippery, highly polished parquet floor. Dressers stood at regular intervals, housing silver cups and rows of gleaming trophies. "He's older than me, and scary, but he's beautiful too. Refined, and yet at the same time wild underneath. He's furious when he finds me walking about and he grabs me by the wrist."

She locked her own fingers around her lower arm and squeezed so that the flesh ached. "He drags me to this other room. A classroom."

She paused, waiting for Kit to snort at the admission. School fantasies, especially finishing school were so passé. She'd been telling herself that for long enough. Unfortunately, attempting to deny its power only seemed to increase the taboo appeal of it, in much the same way that any sort of denying herself something made her lust after it.

But this wasn't just about being naughty. It was about wanting what was wrong and exposing herself.

"All the other girls are there," she continued.

"Dressed like you? What are they wearing?"

"Uniform. White blouses and grey skirts with short knitted cardigans, and we've hats too. Boaters, with red and white ribbons."

Ashamed, she hid her face, but couldn't resist peeping at him from between her fingers. Kit didn't remark upon the outfit, but he looked at her as if he were making a mental assessment. Was it her imagination or did his gaze linger over her breasts? Evie didn't even wear a skirt for work, but she'd chosen one today, slightly longer and straighter than the pleated one of her fantasy, but nevertheless reminiscent of it. The top she'd chosen buttoned down the front too. Kit's attention lingered upon the top pearlescent button. Just a hint of the valley between her breasts showed above it.

"I'm a virgin," she blurted and coloured just like the real thing. "I don't know what it's like, but I think about him all the time. He's the only male teacher."

"And you've made him angry. Does he punish you?" Kit's voice was soft as a whisper.

She nodded. "But not in the way I'd like."

"Meaning he won't fuck you."

"No...yes."

Her conflicted response raised a low chuckle in his throat,

but it didn't feel like he was laughing at her, merely that he appreciated the duality of her answer.

"He makes me expose myself. I have to stand on a chair in the middle of the class and lift my skirt."

Heat swept across her face. Evie ground her teeth into her lower lip, knowing that her skin was blazing. She screwed her eyes closed, not sure if she could actually bring herself to go on. This was too personal. She'd never contemplated sharing it with Ross, though the whole idea of it turned her on so much she was reduced to squirming on the spot, to provide some friction for her sensitized and achy clit.

Kit's clothing swished as he moved. He came to rest just behind her, so that his breath stirred the wisps of hair that had escaped her ponytail.

"Lift your skirt, Evie."

His words, hissed into her ear, and caused a further pooling of moisture in her sex.

"I can't," she sobbed.

"Can't or won't?"

"Kit, I need a minute. Give me a minute."

He eyed her curiously, but didn't stop her fleeing. Evie ran to the bathroom, where she raked through her purse for the item she'd brought with her. God, she hoped he understood. Hoped he realized what she was trusting him with, and that she was asking him to trust her in return.

Kit was absent when she returned, but he entered a moment later. She didn't know where he'd got them from in this old crumbling ruin of a house, but he'd pulled on a gown and mortar board over the top of his clothes.

"Where were we, before I was unfortunately called away?" His smile warmed her from the inside out. Then, he was no longer smiling, but scowling and stern. "I believe you were going to give us a demonstration of your lewdity."

"Yes, sir. Please, sir." Further flames licked across her cheeks, but it felt good to lapse into the role. She sometimes role-played with Ross. They'd invent little scenarios in which they'd met in the rain, or he'd pick her up in a bar and take her to a hotel room and do her. Then they'd drive home separately and pretend nothing unusual had gone on.

"You're a disgrace to yourself and to this school, Miss Latham." Kit gave each sound a distinctly sarcastic inflection, taking on the persona of a stern tutor so well, his version completely meshed with the construction in her head. "Come now. You weren't being so shy among the trophies. Show the other girls what a rampant little slut you are."

The way Kit said "slut" made it more of a purr than an insult.

"Raise your skirt. Take down your knickers, and show them what you've been doing."

"No. I can't."

"Show them how disrespectful you were of the rounders baton."

God, he caught on fast. Kit half tugged, half pushed her towards the centre of the room, where he kicked over a metal bucket and made her stand on it. "Don't defy me, Evangeline. You'll do as I ask if you know what's good for you." Good grief, did he actually wink at her as he said it? "I'm sure you'll prefer my methods to that of your peers. You know we encourage the girls to discipline themselves at this establishment, and I don't think you'll care for twenty-three wood-backed hairbrushes warming your backside. I understand that's the current punishment."

It was, and she'd been the fool to propose it, never for a moment imagining she'd be the one forced to lie exposed, her arousal becoming increasingly evident as the smacks warmed her, and readied her for a good fucking that would never come. No, better that she did as Sir asked. Better she expose herself to this more minor punishment. And maybe by doing so, she'd tempt him to scratch the itch she'd been desperately trying to soothe when he'd caught her.

"Don't make things worse by standing here faking embarrassment. I heard your groans."

"But, sir." She leaned towards him as best as her precarious balance would allow. "I was thinking of you, and I wasn't abusing the bat. Belinda had just left it there when we came in from games earlier."

"Don't argue with me. Raise your skirt and take down your knickers."

Evie faltered, so enthralled by the image Kit had conjured that she almost wanted to pursue what he was suggesting, and what he presumably thought they were heading towards. Her sex felt all squirmy and wet. She was opening like a flower unfurling its petals, her body preparing to welcome him, and already tightly gripping what she'd put in place.

"But, sir."

Kit's face darkened with rage.

"You know I can't," she blurted. "Because I'm wearing it. Like you showed me the other night. I couldn't help it. I liked what we did. Can we do it again... please?" She dug her teeth into her lip.

"My office, now!"

Evie hopped down off the bucket, and Kit half dragged, half pushed her over to the bed.

"What are you wearing? What exactly are you implying, girl?" Kit's eyes crinkled with confusion. She prayed she hadn't thrown him too much, switching the scenario from something he seemed surprisingly sure of to something very different. He'd understand soon. She just prayed he wouldn't be shocked in the way she suspected Ross would be. This wasn't something she'd ever had the nerve to ask of him, though the fantasy had first arisen due to his coaxing and suggestions that they explore a little rear entry.

No, Ross would have been deeply shocked, and she'd never wanted to rock the boat. Things were comfortable between them. They each had their kinks. Ross loved water and getting them wet, and she loved watching him masturbate. It was balanced—intrinsically fair. Even with the addition of Kit the equation still balanced. They shared him equally.

"Show me. Now."

Evie tentatively grasped the hem of her skirt and began slowly dragging it upwards, exposing one inch of thigh after another, after another.

"Up," Kit demanded, going so far as to shove a hand between her tightly clasped thighs. "And stand up straight. What would Miss Bellows think of your deportment?"

She wasn't wearing panties, but nor was she bare.

Kit's breath caught. He blinked and then his shoulders relaxed. "So that's what you were about in the bathroom. I'm surprised at you, Evie. I thought you were such a good girl. Where have you been hiding it? Not in your toy drawer."

He'd been through her toy drawer! She was about to protest the intrusion, but he snapped back into character. "What's the meaning of this?"

"Is it not buckled right? I did it just like you showed me."

"Like I showed you?"

Her knees felt weak. What was he thinking? Was he horrified? Kit pressed a fingertip to the tip of the stubby black dildo attached to the harness she wore, and gave her a curiously indulgent smile.

"You haven't lubricated it properly. I'm sure I was particularly specific about that."

"Oh! I'm sorry. I forgot. I do still have it."

"Where?"

"My satchel."

"Get it."

God, he was going to allow it. They were genuinely going to do this. When she'd fastened the straps of the harness in the bathroom, she still hadn't believed things would play out this way.

Kit took off his clothes as she stumbled around trying to lay her hands on the bottle of lube. He was stretched out upon the bed, perfectly naked save for his mortar board when she finally climbed up beside him.

"All Ross's coaxing to let him fuck you in the arse inspire this?"

Mute, she nodded.

"Go slowly. Take your time."

Kit clasped the iron foot rail, balancing on his knees, while Evie removed her skirt before slathering lube over the stubby dildo. She hadn't dared buy anything bigger. This had been an embarrassing enough party purchase. Still, its circumference was easily the size of four of her fingers squashed together.

Kit arched as she rubbed it against his anus.

"Evie!"

"Yes, sir."

"I hope you don't mind an audience."

"What?"

He pushed back against the persistent pressure and crooned as the dildo found its mark. Evie watched the black cock slide in and out to the motion of her hips, and his odd remark bypassed her thoughts. To begin with he let her set the pace. But it didn't last. He wanted more. Harder...faster. "That's it. That's right. Do me good," he barked while she smoothed her palms over his back, noticing how the knots of tension there dispersed a little every time she slid forward. "Yes, Evie!"

"Tell me how it feels."

"Good."

Having anticipated more than a one word answer, she felt floored by his monosyllabic reply. No wonder that he enjoyed Ross doing this. Suddenly, Kit pushed upright. He leaned back against her, forcing the black cock deeper. He ground his bottom against her groin, providing a welcome dart of pleasure as the motion tugged at her swollen clit, before he reached back and entwined his arms loosely about her neck. "Kiss me," he sighed. His breathing was erratic as they kissed.

"Stroke me." He was in control again, if indeed, he'd ever lost it. "They're still watching. Show them what you can reduce me too."

Again the reference to onlookers, but in the fantasy they were supposed to be in his office.

"Do you see them, Evie? Do you see them watching us? They want to be us. They dream of performing like this." She spied them then, little black dots in the distance. She and Kit were facing the window, and his fan club sat perched amongst the treetops. Laura and four others, staring at them as she stroked her hand up and down his cock, and all the while the dildo connected them.

Over and over Kit had refused to stroke himself for her pleasure, but in many ways feeling him for herself was better. It wasn't so visual, rather it focused on textures. Smooth flesh, the taut skin over the head of the glans. He bit his lip, and rested his head against her shoulder. His eyes closed. Slowly, his breathing deepened.

"How long have they been out there?"

"From the start."

Evie shuddered. What she and Kit were doing was personal, not something she wanted shared with the entire population of Kirkley. Word of their antics would quickly pass around.

Her hand stilled upon his cock.

"You're in control. A little shame is healthy," Kit coaxed. It didn't stop her longing for a curtain.

"It wasn't supposed to be this real."

"It feels fucking real to me." He laughed and the sound caused ripples of delight to run down her back.

"Why aren't you bothered? Are you so used to performing that you don't care who watches or what people think?"

"They all think I'm Satan anyway; a little sexual deviance won't make a ha'p'orth of difference."

"Kit!" She grasped the base of the dildo and pulled free of him. Here they were, back to the issue of Sammie again. Was she a phantom now destined to haunt them for eternity?

"Run out on me now and you forfeit everything," he warned. "Us, and what we both have with Ross."

One hand on the buckle that held the strap-on in place, Evie paused.

"Stay, and finish what you started."

"Kit, I'm not even turned on anymore."

"Aren't you?" He turned to face her. "Well, let's see what we can do about that." One touch—his index finger traced over the very tip of one nipple, and despite two layers of fabric she felt it as though he were caressing bare skin. Her womb clenched, every muscle tightened. Kit unfastened the buttons of her blouse so that the edges parted to reveal the soft curves of her breasts. "Take it off. And the bra too. Come and fuck me naked."

Evie bit her lip. She couldn't revel in their perversity like he could, she could only think of those girls watching, judging her.

"I can see this is going to take some more focused persuasion." Instead of leaning forward to engulf one nipple as she'd anticipated. Kit rolled on to his back, and propped himself up a little on his elbows. He looked perfect—washboard abs, the hairless simplicity of his body. His cock lying across his abdomen, the skin of it darker than that of the rest of his body, and dashed with blue veins like an oriental vase. Kit covered his balls and erection with one hand, and then made deliberate eye contact with her. "You have shared. And I wouldn't want you to think me a liar."

Slowly, he began to masturbate.

When Evie watched Ross perform, it often seemed that there remained a barrier between them. The same sort of distance that separated actors from their audience. With Kit, that distance seemed lessened. He stroked himself with absolute confidence, seemingly without regard for how he appeared to her, and he looked at her the whole time.

Evie watched his pupils swallow up his equally dark irises. His mouth fell slack. She wanted to photograph him, to capture this image of him for eternity: his expression, the way his hair fell across his brow and the way his hand curled around his shaft.

"Fuck me," he mouthed.

She didn't wait for a second request, but obeyed him, their observers forgotten. Kit could make the whole world disappear. It just stopped existing when he focused his attention like this. Nothing beyond the here and now mattered.

He mewled as she entered him. They rocked together gently, like an empty swing swaying in a summer breeze. "That's it, Evie. You feel so good inside me." His thumb swept up around the tip of his cock, not touching the eye, but lightly tormenting the skin around it until his breaths became indulgent gasps.

"I want to see you come," Evie admitted.

"Yeah." His actions seemed to find extra focus, until he was sprinting towards the finish. He didn't stop, even as the semen pooled upon his stomach. Evie dipped a finger in it and smeared it across his parted lips. Then she jammed their bodies together and kissed him hard.

Kit unbuckled the harness and hooked it over one of the iron bedposts. "We'll be keeping this. I want to see you use it on Ross." She shook her head, but something told her Kit would prevent it being awkward, and that Ross wouldn't balk at the idea in the same way she'd anticipated if she'd asked before Kit had tumbled into their lives.

"Come here." Kit lay down again. He had her shimmy up the length of him, until she sat astride his head, clinging to the bars at the foot end of the iron bed. Kit's tongue lathed her clit so that his chin gleamed with a little more moisture every time he tapped her bum to make her lift up so he could take a breath. He tongue fucked her, and he tormented her clit, alternatively sucking and petting it, until her heart raced so fast she thought it would leap free of her chest. When it came, her orgasm gripped her tight, squeezing her, enfolding her, and then letting her float. Evie clung to the bedstead, unable to move and aware that there were tears rolling down her cheeks.

When she did finally move it was only because her muscles protested the position. Kit hugged her to him so that her head rested upon his chest and pulled the bedclothes around them.

"This is where I first had Ross."

"Not up at the ruins?" Evie cocked her head up to look at him, but his gaze remained fixed upon the scarred ceiling.

"We started out at the ruins. Kissing. Hands inside each other's pants. Got ourselves all hot and bothered. We'd both made out up there with girls before, but doing each other there in broad daylight seemed a little too risqué. There are things that people will accept stumbling across and there's stuff they get up in arms about."

"Are you suggesting Kirkley's inhabitants are anti-gay?"

"I think they're anti-gay sex in their back gardens. Just catching the pair of us kissing would have set them all in a proper tizzy. So we came here."

Evie's fingers traced the letters of Ross's name across Kit's lower abdomen. "Tell me about it."

"Ross was nervous. He had sunburn from sitting outdoors for days on end, but he still managed to look bleached. And he had all this gorgeous hair. It must have come down to his waist. I recall wrapping it around my hand as a means of holding onto him as we kissed."

"Had you kissed guys before?"

Kit shook his head. "It was odd at first. It was like kissing a girl, except he needed a shave so he was all sandpapery and coarse. Oh, and all tongue."

She'd seen pictures of Ross with his hair long, but he'd already cropped it short by the time they'd met, and as much as she tried to picture Ross and Kit as younger men, her imagination refused to comply. The image cemented in her brain was that of them as she'd first seen the together as lovers, when she'd walked in on them in this house, two full-blooded men, neither afraid of touching each other or of being a little rough.

A chuckle rumbled through Kit's chest. "He kept saying 'it's unreal, man. It's unreal'. He was all hands but he didn't know where to put them."

"But I suppose you did?"

"I'm not saying I knew any better than him, but I like to think I was a little better at hiding my lack of experience. I know I was better at hiding my nerves."

Evie rolled across him and straddled his hips, the thought of Kit and Ross in bed together for the first time making her horny all over again. "Go on."

"I got on top, a little like you are now, and I held our cocks together while we rubbed up and down each other. When I couldn't take anymore, I went down on him. You'd think he'd never had a blowjob before he came so fast."

"And then did he do the same for you?"

"Uh-uh! I didn't exactly trust him to suck, not considering how much his teeth kept chattering, and actual penetration was out of the question."

"But?" Her brows quizzically furrowed.

"I know, considering what we've just done, but, I wasn't so comfortable with the idea then. Japan and being steaming drunk once too often changed that. We didn't actually properly fuck, until... well, just before you turned up."

"That was your first time?"

"Second...well, third, technically."

Evie petulantly pinched his nose between her curled fingers.

"Anyway." Kit brushed her off. "We did the old public school boy thing and I came thrusting like a maniac between his thighs. I think Flora was actually home by that point. God knows what the poor dear thought of the bed creaking."

A strong mental picture of an old lady in a chintz shawl standing downstairs looking up at the ceiling filled Evie's thoughts. "Probably thought her good for nothing nephew was busy disgracing another poor girl."

"Might account for the dirty look she gave me when the police turned up and said Sammie was missing. The police actually searched the house. I don't think Flora believed it'd just been Ross and I upstairs. Gay?" He shook his head. "She knew me too well for it to even occur to her."

The haunted look had returned to his eyes. Evie stroked his jaw. "She wasn't aware of your penchant for threesomes involving your best mate, then?"

"We did that away from home."

She nodded her understanding. "But…so, the three of you never really happened, then?"

Kit gave a regretfully headshake.

"I think I asked Sammie about a dozen time. Guess I lived in hope, but I knew she wasn't up for it after the explosion I got at the first time. She was a serious monogamist at heart."

Evie pressed her palms to his chest. "I thought I was too."

"Does it bother you that you're not part of a compact little breeding unit anymore?"

She scowled and swiped at his face. "What a horrid thing to say."

Kit caught her wrist. He toppled her and stretched over her, holding her down. "It's true though. I've heard all the gossip about you and Ross. Folks don't start predicting weddings and babies without cause."

"I thought I wanted to settle down," she confessed. "It was mostly me, rather than Ross."

"And now?" She felt his cock stiffen where it lay sandwiched against her leg.

"Things are a little different. I can't marry both of you."

He leaned into her and rubbed their noses together. "Oh,

I'm sure it's legal somewhere." He changed tactics and kissed her instead until she moaned as his erection brushed the lips of her pussy. The ache in her cunt surprised her a little so soon after an orgasm, but she wanted him, and she guessed she'd grown used to having two lovers. However, Kit did nothing more than tease, and eventually he sat up and fished about for a T-shirt.

Evie followed his lead. "When you came back from Japan, did you know about me?" she asked.

He padded across to the window ledge and resumed his earlier seat, sighing at the molten remains of the ice-cream. "I hadn't had any contact with Ross, hadn't a clue whether he was with anyone or not. I kind of hoped he was, because he's a good guy and doesn't deserve to be alone, but on the other hand I hoped it wasn't serious."

"But we were serious."

"Yes, but I didn't know that before seeing you together, and you'd already got in the shower with me by that point."

"And that changed things?"

"Evie, it changed everything. I knew you understood Ross when you did that and that you cared about pleasing him. I just had to hope you liked me well enough to let me get close to you both."

She slowly digested the explanation, churning it over to see what sort of hummocks it made. "I like you," she said eventually, turning to face him. "I like you a hell of a lot, particularly when you're not being moody. And Molly, Tony, and whoever are all morons for thinking you'd ever hurt someone in that way."

"Like," mused Kit. His lips brushed the edge of her jaw. "I guess it's too early to push the boat out a little further than that."

She knew exactly what he meant, and maybe she did love him, but it was far too early to admit that.

Chapter Sixteen

Kit didn't come home that night. He claimed he was staying at Rose Cottage to make sure the new roof didn't leak, but Evie suspected there was more to it than that. She lay on the bed listening to the rain pound against the window, wondering what sort of turn their relationship would take next. Was Kit trying to give her and Ross space or time to adapt?

Ross came home soaked. His clothing plastered to his skin and his hair darker for being wet. "I hear you sorted things out with Kit." He stood at the end of the bed and shook like a dog, splattering everything with water droplets, before tugging her off the bed into his arms. "Come outside with me."

"What for?" she asked, still thinking of Kit and their earlier coupling.

"Puddle jumping. And maybe some other jumping." The same answer he'd offered on numerous other occasions. They'd frolicked together in plenty of puddles, but they'd never yet made love in the rain. Ross desperately wanted to, but the thought of such exposure made her shiver, and he'd never pushed the issue.

"I don't know, Ross," she teased, although not entirely feigning her reluctance. "It's cold and I've got my pyjamas on."

"Evie—you know I'll soon warm you up." His enthusiasm tugged mercilessly at her. Ross grinned as two wet patches spread across the front of her pyjama top from their embrace, revealing the dark areolas of her nipples. "God that is so sexy.

Let me see them really wet." He leaned forward and palpated one nipple with his tongue, leaving the fabric even wetter, and her nipple perked up and excited, eager for more. "Yes...oh, yes."

Ross suddenly pushed her away. "I'll give you a thirty second start. If I catch you, you're mine."

"And if you don't?" she called, already edging away from him to slip her feet into her trainers.

"I'll wash the dishes for a week and you can take naughty photographs of me pleasuring myself."

Excitement fluttered in her chest at the prospect of sitting at the centre of a sea of photographs of his rampant cock in close up, and arty framed images of his pecs and shoulder blades.

"Go!"

Evie was in the living room when she heard him call. She ran through the kitchen and down the back steps into the garden. Taking Ross at his word, she avoided the street and prospect of him claiming her on the village green, and headed for the gate at the bottom of the garden that lead into a copse of woodland instead.

The rain felt cold against her face. It trickled down her neck and ran into the neckline of her top. The thin fabric of her pyjama bottoms quickly turned transparent and clung to her body like a second skin. Evie darted amongst the trees, conscious of not veering too far off the path in the dark. It was slightly drier beneath the bowers, and the air smelled of mulch and pine needles.

Ross came crashing through the undergrowth behind her. Evie kicked hard and managed to stay ahead, until she snagged her foot on a tree root and came crashing down in a pile of sodden leaves.

Ross dived upon her.

Evie squirmed beneath him until he caught her arms and pinned her wrists either side of her head. Then she lay still and panting, a tempest raging inside her. They were outside. It might be dark, but it was still early. There'd still be folks about.

Ross switched his grip to one hand, freeing his other up to explore her body. Her clothing was virtually transparent now, save for a few garish patches of colour where the rain had yet to soak through. He roughly fondled her breasts, then wriggled his palm beneath her and hooked his fingers around the drawstring waist of her pyjama bottoms and tugged them down.

He pushed one cold finger inside her and stroked at her hot inner walls. Then two fingers, which he withdrew slowly and ran upwards to scissor around her clit and coax it from its hood.

"Ross," she hissed.

"You're hot for this. Don't try and deny it."

She couldn't, even though the wet leaves stuck to her back, and the cold drizzle made her constantly conscious of the fact that they were outdoors and exposed.

"You're not going to scream, are you?"

Evie shook her head. Sometimes when they fucked, she couldn't help making a noise, but she'd bite her tongue in two before she drew attention to them like that out here.

"Good." He dragged her bottoms down a little farther, so they lay coiled in wet folds around her knees. She felt his cock nudge her belly, and then prod purposefully between her thighs, until he found his goal. Unlike his fingers, his rod was hot as molten steel. He pierced her with his heat, driving as deep as the position would allow, until their hips lay stacked upon one another and every movement provided welcome friction for her clit.

Ross took his weight on his arms, using his strength to hold her down as he slid into her and stroked back again, repeatedly filling her until he forced mewls from her throat.

"That's right." His lips grazed the side of her neck. "Let me hear how much you want it. You love me fucking you, don't you, Evie? You're insatiable. You just can't get enough of my cock to satisfy you." She tried to lift herself against him, longing to feel the play of his muscles beneath his skin and the thump of his heartbeat pounding against her chest.

But whatever game they were playing didn't involve closeness and kissing, instead it was about power and dominance. Him holding her down and taking what he wanted, as swiftly or as slowly as he wanted it. The fact that his actions aroused her to distraction was seemingly incidental, though undoubtedly deliberate. She wondered how much of this was provoked by whatever Kit had told him on the phone about their earlier encounter. There was no escaping a little jealousy.

"Ross! Gawd, ease off a bit. We'll be seen."

"I don't care if we're seen. And nor do you really." Kit had told him, or at least he'd mentioned the fact that they'd been observed. Evie fought to release her wrists and managed to get one free so that she could caress Ross's face. "Let's go inside. You can hold me down just as well on the kitchen floor."

"Yeah." Ross pulled back onto his knees. "But it won't be the same. And I did tell you what I was going to do when I caught you. Maybe you should have stayed inside if you didn't want me to shag you out here."

His thumb split the lips of her sex and dragged across her clit, making her writhe. Ross peeled off her pyjama bottoms and trainers and tossed them aside. Evie squealed as he exposed her entire lower half, but Ross's hands swept reassuringly up and down her legs. "I don't know why you're so scared. You look fantastic naked. All these soft curves. If anyone sees us the only thing they're going to be thinking is what a lucky bastard I am to have you." He lifted her legs up straight and cradled them to his sides. "Watch," he hissed.

Evie lifted her head a little and watched him rub the plum tip of his cock against her labia, drawing circles around her entrance. Much as she longed to run indoors, her body craved the deep press of his cock again.

"Say yes, Evie."

Ross pulled off his shirt and chucked it onto the pile of clothing beside them. Raindrops chased across his pecs, and formed rivulets amongst the soft V of hairs between his nipples, that narrowed down towards his naval, only to thicken again at the base of his cock.

"Yes," she whimpered.

Ross surged into her immediately, so their bodies slapped together and her breasts bounced with the motion. Ross's palms closed around their thinly veiled weight and roughly moulded and massaged them. She climaxed quickly, the sharp pleasure tingling across her cold skin, barely dispersing before he was bent over her again, and had locked his mouth with hers.

Evie entwined both her arms and legs around his back.

Swift and eager he moved, his glans tugging at her already sensitized flesh every time he reached the brink. "Oh, I've been waiting for this. You've no idea." The words of praise, of thanks continued to spill from his lips. "Ever since that first day when I saw you in that sheer sundress and the rain turned it into tissue-paper plastered to your skin. Oh, Evie. I could fuck you like this five times a day, every day, and never have enough."

She believed him, every word of it, though she suspected he'd find some method of including Kit into their wild couplings. "Hard," she breathed into his ear. "Fuck me faster and don't slow down."

"Yeah." His chest expanded with his next breath and his weight slammed into her, driving her across the pile of leaves and up against the tree base.

Evie braced her hands against the bark. "I mean it. Don't stop."

Every stab of his cock warmed her from the inside out. Perspiration burst across their skin where their bodies lay moulded together, wetting the places the rain didn't reach.

"Oh, Evie!" He sucked air through his teeth on a backstroke and froze, his eyes closed, and jaw protruding with the strain. "I can't..." he gasped, thrusting forward again so that his cock convulsed deep inside her. A swift roll of his pelvis set off a second orgasm for Evie. Unlike the fire-flash blink of the first one, this one drummed like the rain and jerked her hips, while her insides clenched tight around his spasming cock, until they both gradually quieted.

They lay pressed together, listening to the sounds of the forest for several minutes, neither quiet ready to move. "I love you. Thank you." Ross dropped a kiss onto the tip of her nose and then carefully rolled off her. He helped her regain her feet, and they stood looking at one another. Ross held her hand and swirled her beneath his arms. He backed her up against the bark of the oak tree squatted on the ridge behind them. "Mind if I carry you home, my merry water nymph?"

"I think dryad is more appropriate," Evie replied as she tried to extract leaves from her hair. She gave up after the first three and stooped to collect her clothes instead. They were wet and streaked with dirt. She wrinkled her nose at the prospect of forcing her legs inside their covering. Ross tied his shirt around her middle instead.

"I did say I was going to carry you home." He did just that. Stumbling a little over the uneven ground, he carried her straight upstairs and ran a hot bubble bath that they both climbed into. "I think we should have Kit's name added to the lease," he said as they sat snuggled together surrounded by fluffy white foam.

"Is he going to want that? He has Rose Cottage."

"But we can't all move in there yet. There's no proper bathroom for starters. I'd rather we persuaded him to stay here a bit longer first. I don't like him staying over there on his own. He's already had one...accident. Heavens knows what could happen if anything more major occurred."

Evie noticed Ross pause, but didn't remark upon it. She didn't like the idea of Kit staying alone in that big house either, but she suspected he'd refuse the offer of a joint tenancy. He seemed intent on working his way into their relationship at his own pace now they were over the initial hurdles. And maybe he was right. Perhaps separate retreats would serve them better for awhile until they really got to know one another. Besides, as had been demonstrated on two occasions already today, there were times when only having two of them around served their purposes better than being a constant triad.

"Maybe we should just all think in terms of moving into Rose Cottage when it's restored, and give ourselves some breathing room for a bit."

Ross tugged the plug chain up with toes. "Yeah, maybe you're right. It is nice to have some just us time."

While it was nice to have some us time, it was also nice to have Kit home with them in the evenings, but increasingly he seemed to be putting in long hours remodelling Rose Cottage. Ross too seemed overburdened at work. Spring had arrived, and with it, extra duties around the local farms in addition to the seemingly never ending queue of sick pets. Tourists started flocking to Melton Manor again so that even Evie was thoroughly worn out by the evenings. Sex started sliding into a secondary role to companionably chilling out playing video games or watching a movie together. Once or twice, they'd even spent the night over at Rose Cottage, huddled together for warmth on the twisted iron-bed.

With them all spending so much time away from home, Kit had begun taking Mimmy with him for company. For her part, the rapidly growing kitten had well and truly taken to the rambling old house and the execution of its fauna. She'd been delivering Kit a nice half-chewed mouse or baby bird every lunch time for the last week.

"Anyone home?" Evie called before she hurried in carting a shopping bag, although she knew the answer from the lack of cars on the drive. "Good."

Having showered and made a cup of tea, she settled in the living room to paint her toenails. The boys might not have been missing their love-making, but she was feeling increasingly antsy; young male visitors to the big house had been turning her head all day, and it wasn't a make out session with her vibrator she craved to still her wandering eyes. That meant taking a few minutes to put on the glitz and work out a seduction strategy for when her two boys did eventually crawl home.

Smiling, Evie smoothed the hem of her new dazzling white sundress. It was composed of three silky thin layers that hung to just above her knees, and embroidered with tiny red poppies. In combination with her new open-toed sandals it was sure to capture Ross's interest. She was hoping that what lay underneath would nurture Kit's attention. It'd hurt like hell, but she'd had her bikini-line waxed almost bare. She stuck her hand inside the leg of her panties and smoothed a fingertip over the baby soft skin, raising a tremble of excitement that left her wet and eager. Sex was certainly going to be interesting. Maybe this was the reason Kit preferred to be nude down there. Evie dabbed a finger in her moisture and brought it to her lips. The scent and taste of her own body further caused her insides to liquefy. Maybe a quick preparatory orgasm just to take the edge off her need, so she wasn't completely gagging for it when they got home would be a good idea.

Only the doorbell rang.

With a sigh, she hobbled off to answer it.

Inwardly, her heart further sank when she recognized the caller as Lillianna, and recalled what had happened the last time she'd made an impromptu visit. "I'm not coming out. I'm not speaking to Molly or Tony or anybody else, and I'm not making an apology for hogging them both."

Lillianna paid her no regard. She pushed her way inside and barged into the living room. "Have you seen it? They keep showing it on the local news." She snatched up the TV remote and flicked channels until she found a news station.

"Seen what?" Evie slunk in behind her. Balanced on the edge of the sofa, she took up the little nail varnish brush again.

"The bit on the homeless women in York."

Evie wrinkled her nose. "Just got in. I haven't had the TV on. What's so exciting?" A feature on homelessness, while worthy, didn't strike her as a topic normally all that dear to Lillianna's heart, but the other woman was literally buzzing with it.

Evie finished her nails, barely looking at the screen as the newsreader rattled through the other stories: forthcoming budget, more over turned lorries on the A1 and a bit on llama farming. Meanwhile, Lillianna hung on every word. "There." She jabbed her finger at the glass when the homelessness report began.

"What?"

"There."

Evie followed her finger as it tracked one of the figures around the screen. "Yeah, it's a person. What am I supposed to be seeing?"

"It's Sammie, you dope. Sammie Dean. Molly's sister. Kit's ex. You know, the vanished lady."

"Really?" Evie squinted sceptically as the figure shown huddled in a sleeping bag in the doorway of some shop.

"Not her, you dunce," Lillianna squealed, adding a palm print to the numerous fingerprints she'd already placed upon the glass. "Not the sleeping bag woman, the charity worker. It's her."

Having only seen a few old photographs of Sammie, Evie couldn't honestly claim to recognize her. This woman, who admittedly appeared to be called Samantha, had very short hair and a much harder face than she recalled from the pictures. In all honesty she would never have recognized her as Kit's missing girlfriend. "Are you sure?"

"I'm damn sure, I'm sure." Lillianna planted her hands on her hips, in her favourite straight-talking, no nonsense pose. "Molly's been dancing around doing circus tricks. She's just driven off to go and meet her."

"Really?"

"She got the charity deets from the TV people."

Still a little disbelieving, Evie nonetheless let a small smile split her lips. If Sammie had turned up, then they could wipe away the doubts hanging like the sword of Damocles over Kit's head. "What did you come to tell me for, you idiot?" she bellowed. "Why aren't you over telling Kit?"

"Isn't he here?" Bangles rattled as they slid along her raised arms.

"No. He's working on the house. Come on." Evie strapped on her sandals and headed for the door. She was definitely going to have a night to remember after this revelation.

Kit sat knee-deep in plaster dust with a chisel in his hand. "Lillianna... Evie." A distinct roll of relief infused his voice on seeing Evie come in behind the other woman. "To what do I owe the pleasure?" He'd finally relented and bought a set of overalls, but somehow he made even the dust-covered baggy jumpsuit look sexy. Lips pursed into a bemused line, he paused to rub grot out of his eyes as he waited for a response.

Evie poked Lillianna in the back.

"Sammie's turned up," she squealed and dived on Kit, crushing her face to his dusty chest.

Kit froze into position. "What?"

"Alive," Evie added, realizing he might think they meant her body, although, maybe that wouldn't have tallied with Lillianna exuberant puppy dog zeal. "She's in York working for some charity or other." Still a little sketchy on the details, despite the news report, she looked to Lillianna for further confirmation.

Her friend beamed. "Molly's gone to meet her. Tada...tada...tada." She did a little jig.

Kit dropped his tools, but doubt continued to cloud his face. "Seriously. She's okay? It's not a mistake?"

"It's her. It's real. It's real. It's real." Lillianna flung herself at him, entwining him in her skirts, which shed a few sequins onto the floor that winked among the rubble. Kit accepted the second embrace and the rather sloppily given kiss she smeared across his lips, but his eyes, those deep pools of longing, remained suspicious.

"Evie?"

"It's true, Kit. Leastways she's shown me the TV clip, and Molly's convinced. I mean, she'd recognize her own sister."

Even she recognized the doubt in her own words, doubt that was instantly reflected in Kit's gaze. Instead of whooping at the good news, his brows drew into a troubled frown. He walked across to the window, shaking his head. "Does Ross know?"

"I've not told him. I don't think so."

Oblivious to solemnity, Lillianna continued to thud her heels against the floorboards. "We should all go out and celebrate. Champagne. Slap up meal. The works."

"Lilli." Torn between supporting Kit and calming her friend, Evie tried to stretch herself between them both.

"I'm not celebrating anything." Kit folded his arms across his chest. "One blurry TV broadcast means nothing. How can you be sure after six years, not far off seven? I don't suppose anyone has actually spoken to her yet. Find out where she went and what the hell she's doing on TV? No." He walked back to the rubble and picked up his tools again. "It could be anyone."

The clang of the hammer driving the chisel into the old plaster momentarily stopped Lillianna's jiggling, but his refutation failed to quell her exuberance. "It's her. It's her. It's her-er-er! What's it gonna cost you to have a little faith," she sang.

Evie remained by the window watching their awkward dance. It reminded her of a flamenco performance, full of passionate flurries, attacks and retreats, Kit so reluctant and Lillianna at once enticing and berating him for his disbelief. For her own part, she wished Kit's scepticism didn't make her hackles rise over what had happened all over again. She had doubts of her own about this sudden reappearance; it was hardly surprising he felt the same way. Anxiously, she bit her thumbnail, causing the acrylic overlay to fall off.

"Lilli," she coaxed, seeing exasperation creep into Kit's expression alongside the fear. "Why don't you go over to the pub and let the folks there know? I'm sure they'll all be thrilled to hear, and we could join you in a bit."

"Well..." Lillianna gave her dubious frown.

"Lil."

"Yeah. Yeah, okay. You're right. We do need to spread the word. I'll catch up with you in a bit."

Back outside, Evie escorted Lillianna all the way to the gate that adjoined the lane. "Don't worry about telling Ross, I'll let him know. But I'll let you have the joy of telling Tony."

When she returned to Kit, she found him standing in exactly the same position as when she'd left. Only now there were tears poised ready to spill down his cheeks and his black hair lay spiked up off his head, where he'd clearly raked his hands through it and the dust had held it in place. They stared at one another, not sure what to say.

"I didn't know her, Kit. I can't be sure. All I've seen are a few old photographs."

"It doesn't feel right." He surreptitiously wiped the tears from his eyes. "Why would she suddenly just appear like this? If she ran off to get away from everything, surely she'd avoid advertising herself. She had to realize there'd be a chance of someone recognizing her and making a fuss."

"Maybe things have changed enough so that whatever drove her away then doesn't matter anymore," Evie suggested. "Molly's the only one of her family still around." She shook her head trying to figure it out. "Maybe it was something with her parents. Haven't they gone abroad? So, there'd be no chance of them seeing it." If only there were an obvious culprit to point a finger at to explain why she no longer felt the need to stay hidden. The problem was no one had ever identified a reason for her disappearance, which is why so much of the blame had fallen on Kit's shoulders. Outsider. Last to see her, and a known sexual deviant, at least amongst Kirkley's quiet community. He'd been an altogether easy target.

"It still doesn't make sense." Kit scrunched more spikes in his hair. "I daren't believe it, Evie. I can't face the prospect of getting excited only for Lillianna and Molly to be wrong."

Ross arrived forty minutes later, following a text from Evie and having off loaded his afternoon patients onto his partners at the practice. He wrapped his big arms around her and lifted her off her feet. "Thank god." His relief was short lived. One look at Kit confirmed all still wasn't right. Their embrace was much briefer, more of a solemn patting of backs.

"He's been like this since he heard," Evie explained once they were out of earshot of Kit. Ross had insisted on boiling the kettle. Apparently, it was recommended medicine for any trauma. "He's afraid it's all going to amount to nothing and that there's going to be another backlash against him. You don't think Molly's making this all up just to cause trouble, do you?"

Ross shook his head. "No. You've spoken to her. You've seen how choked up she still gets over it. I don't think she'd resort to that sort of deception."

"But Kit hasn't been around before. I know some people are still being funny with him, but there's plenty who are accepting him too."

"Nah, Evie." He accepted the offered over glove to lift the whistling kettle from the hob, and began pouring their drinks. "If it turns out it's not her, I reckon it's just a genuine mistake. Either way, I think we should head home after these and wait for news there. I don't fancy being here if it's bad news."

She was about to ask why, when she recalled that the police had originally come here looking for Kit when Sammie had first disappeared.

"I've already tried to get him to come home, but he just keeps saying that he has work to do and that he's not wasting the evening sitting around twiddling his thumbs, not even if the twiddling involves sex or video games."

Ross's jaw dropped. "You're telling me he said no to sex. Jeezus! He really is worked up."

"Well, I didn't actually... Oh, never mind. How is it you're a whole lot less doubtful?"

Ross loaded the mugs onto an empty paint tray and nodded her ahead to open the doors. "If it was just Lillianna spouting off, I'd dismiss it, but I don't think Molly would go tearing off without getting an address or something else concrete first. She saw her parents zipping off too many times, whenever there was a suspected sighting, and coming back disappointed. It never did them any good."

"They moved away now, haven't they?" Although, maybe Molly had rung them and they too were racing towards York to claim their missing daughter.

"They went to Spain about eighteen months back. Molly refused to go, accused them all of abandoning her sister. Truthfully, I think they did the only thing they could to maintain their sanity. Kirkley held too many bitter memories, and there wasn't any prospect of a proper resolution."

Kit drank the tea, but he refused to come home with them. "I've told Evie. I'm not sitting around. I'd rather work. It's better than drinking myself into a stupor."

Maybe there were other things troubling him too, like finally finding out why Sammie had run off all those years ago.

"Tell you what. Let's Evie and I go and get fish and chips for us all," Ross suggested, something that at least gained a nod of approval. "We can bring them back here and maybe by then we'll have heard something."

The fish and chips, wrapped in numerous layers of paper, were burning Evie's lap when they were stopped from entering the lane to Rose Cottage by a row of cones and a police vehicle parked width ways across the road. They both got out, leaving the meal to cool on the seat. "What's going on?" Ross called to the officer sitting in the car, who signalled one minute. He appeared to be on the radio.

"Oh, thank god!" Lillianna came tearing out of the concealed entryway on the right that led to one of the farms. She threw herself at Evie and Ross, squeezing them both tight. "I thought you might still be in there. But you're safe." She backed away a little, bent over and took several laborious breaths, before resorting to an inhaler.

"What's going on?" Evie asked.

"Rose...alight...fire." Lillianna gasped. "Trying...to put...it out." She took another puff of her inhaler and sat down in the lane. "Can't remember the last time I used this?" she said once her breathing had calmed. "It's the cottage."

She didn't need to elaborate, the smell of smoke drifted towards them on the night breeze, along with large fluttering bits of ash. Something large was burning.

Ross obviously made the connection at the same time. His arm dropped like a lead weight from around Evie's shoulders. "Kit's still in there." He sprang away and pushed off the top of the car bonnet to get past.

"Hey!" the officer yelled and finally emerged from the car to give chase, breathlessly shouting into his radio as he ran.

Numbed, Evie watched them disappear in the fog bank up ahead. "We went for chips. Kit stayed behind. How? We've not been gone that long?" She began walking, circling around the abandoned police car to get into the lane.

"Evie, wait!" Lillianna caught up with her. "We should keep back. It's not good up there."

The fog cloud grew denser as they neared the cottage. Ash swirled like confetti in the air and stuck to every surface. The smoke itself had a bitter taste and dried their throats. Regardless, Evie pressed on, her coat held tight across her mouth and nose. She reached the rear of the first fire engine, and almost ran into Ross. He was sandwiched between two burly police officers, resisting their pleas for calm, his curses, regularly punctuated by calls for Kit.

There was no answering cry, only the horrid crackles and fizzing pops of flames burning through dried timbers, and then the roar of water as the fire engine crews directed their hoses. Upstairs, one of the cottage windows blew out and shattered, making both women yelp. They scuttled back towards the hedgerow on the far side of the lane. "What happened, Lilli? Tell me."

"I don't know. I'm not sure. Everyone was at the pub celebrating, waiting for you, but then a rumour started circulating that Molly was back and it hadn't been Sammie after all but some other woman. It all got a bit crazy then, some folks had had a bit too much and they were getting mouthy. I left the pub at that point and went over to Molly's, but there was no sign of her. Her car isn't even back. I tried sending her a message, but I've not had a reply. And I tried you. Again, no response, so I thought I'd walk back up here and find you. Only I got halfway across the green and someone told me the place was on fire. I tried to ring you again, and I sent a message, but you know what the reception's like around here."

True to her words, another few paces into the field and Evie's mobile phone started chirping with a message alert. She gazed at the text neither seeing nor comprehending it. Instead, tears streamed down her cheeks, forming rivulets in the tight mask of smoke particles that already coated her face. This couldn't be happening. It wasn't real. Fate couldn't tear him away from them like this. They'd only just got comfortable with one another. Ross had even suggested they consider booking a holiday together.

"He's still in there," she groaned, sagging to her knees among the damp grass. "He wouldn't come with us…refused to believe… And Mimmy's in there with him." The notion of the kitten being trapped in her basket tore another hole in her already breaking heart. Both her strays. They'd both arrived the same night; now they were going to depart together.

No! She couldn't let herself think like that. They'd survive, both of them. Somehow, they'd be all right.

"They have to get them out." She clawed at Lillianna's skirt, and buried her face in its magenta and black folds, sequins digging into her cheek. "Have to. Have to get them out."

Chapter Seventeen

After Ross and Evie left, Kit down tooled and watched their car tail lights fade away. Evie had been clucking around him like a mother hen, when all he'd really wanted was a moment alone to collect his thoughts. Sammie found...alive and well. He couldn't believe it. He didn't believe it. She'd been missing too long, and the details of her absence were too deeply engraved upon his soul for him to accept anything but absolute proof that anything had changed.

Kit wandered through the empty rooms to his favourite perch on the windowsill of the back bedroom, only to find condensation clouding the small mullioned panes, which had run down and formed a large puddle on the sill. Frustrated, he flung a rag on it, and collapsed onto the bed instead, causing a plume of feathers to puff skywards. Mimmy immediately pounced, disturbed from her favourite hidey-hole beneath the bed by the growl of the springs. Distractedly, he watched the kitten caper, swiping at the speckled feathers with her paws.

Maybe he'd come back as a cat in his next life. It seemed a pretty easy life, and no one made a fuss about you going on the prowl. Not that he currently felt remotely sexual. What he really wanted was someone to hold him tight and not let go regardless of how much he abused them. He needed that sort of absolute faith, that sort of unwavering love to prove that everything was still okay, and that the world wasn't about to turn topsy-turvy again.

Kit dug in his pocket for his phone. He scrolled through the call list searching for Ross and Evie's home number. Maybe if they held him, one either side, he'd feel safe. Stuff fish and chips, he wanted them back. His thumb hovered over the dial button. He didn't want to sound needy.

The sound of shattering glass startled him into a seated position. Kit ran onto the landing just in time to see a second missile sail through the already shattered window that provided illumination on the turn of the stairs. The smell caught in his nostrils just before the new glowing missile shattered on impact. What was that? Petrol? He stopped himself short of the lower landing, his arms braced upon the banisters as the fuel caught and the flames fanned out in a huge arch below him. Kit made a hasty retreat. Already, fiery tendrils were racing across the landing and down the aged wooden stairs.

"Shit!" One of the loose electrical wires sparked. And then the lights went out.

Something had provoked this. What had he done?

The woman hadn't been Sammie, he concluded. So, they were coming for him with flames and pitchforks. He needed to get out of here and run.

Kit ran back towards the bedroom, improvising an escape route out of the window. If he threw the mattress out first, the landing would at least be soft. Mimmy shot between his feet as he opened the bedroom door. "No!" he called after her. "Stupid cat."

Kit chased across the landing after her and followed her up the half-rotten stairs to the attic. She carved a long gouge in his hand when he tried to extract her from one of Flora's old hat boxes. "Ow! Damn, you stupid moggy." He sucked at the wound, in which blood had begun to pool, then made a second grab for her. This time he hung on, despite her claws. "Hey, it's okay. We don't have time for this. We need to get out." There were no convenient hatches onto the roof. That was damned inconvenient oversight. He'd phone a Velux windows rep tomorrow if he got out of here alive and there was a house left to install them in. Fire brigade, he thought, hurrying downstairs again. No, he needed to get out first.

The few seconds it had taken to grab Mimmy had wrought extensive damage to the landing. What little wallpaper there was now hung in fiery curls. Thickening smoke obscured the route back to the room he'd inhabited. It was the only room with sash windows that still opened; the others had long since succumbed to layers of paint and wood filler. A few of them had been nailed shut from the outside.

Kit inched his way along the passage. Flames seemed to line every groove between the floorboards, rows upon rows of pretty orange petals that he had to dance around. If it had been more than a few feet he didn't think he'd have made it. He paused halfway, gasping for breath and wondered if he'd have been better staying in the attic and trying to knock a hole in the new roof. Having it fixed had clearly been a terrible mistake.

He laughed, although it came out as a dry cough that morphed into a sob. Mimmy's wriggling intensified at his distress. "We should have had a puppy," he told her. "At least dogs are loyal, and they understand the concept of giving comfort not just receiving it. Keep still, will yer."

A crack sounded above and plaster began raining from the ceiling. Kit darted, avoiding the falling debris, but he skidded, jarring his ankle. Pain fired up his leg, and on instinct he flung Mimmy through the door to the bedroom and reached out for support, only for every nerve ending in his body to join the chorus of agony as a jet of flames scorched his hands. Kit drew breath to scream but no sound came out. The smoke dried his eyes and got into nostrils. He followed Mimmy into the bedroom, and kicked the door closed behind them. There, he collapsed, as the world began to spin.

His hands were blacked and dotted with vibrant speckles of red. Kit bit down and made his muscles propel him forward, even though he could feel the fluid seeping between his fingers. Crying, and choking, he crawled his way to the window. It hurt like hell to manipulate the catch. Kit sacrificed an abandoned mug to the cause, bashing it against the stiff lock until it released.

Air gusted into the room as he raised the sash. There was no time to manipulate the mattress now. And he wasn't sure he could do it. He pulled the ends of his sleeves down over his hands, leaving just the tips of his fingers sticking out, then the grabbed the yowling kitten again. Ignoring both her squirming and the bite of her claws, he tucked her as best he could inside his jacket and zipped it up. "You'll thank me later, pussy cat."

Kit shimmied out of window and tentatively lowered himself from the sill. He didn't remember hitting the ground, only being roused from his prone position amongst the trees in the orchard by a man in a large helmet.

"How is he?"

Ross turned his head from the partition window separating the treatment room from the waiting area to find an unfamiliar figure stood a few feet away. She stared expectantly at him, her hands raised to the disinfectant dispenser. Another two more familiar figures bustled up behind her. "Molly. Lillianna." He nodded. Only then did he make the connection. "Sammie!"

She inclined her chin a fraction. "Hello, Ross."

She'd changed. How the hell had they recognised her from a television image? Here she was in the flesh before him and he could only see the vaguest similarities to the girl he once knew. She was still blonde, but where once her hair had fallen in a silken cascade across her shoulder blades, it was now cropped almost to the scalp. And by God, there'd never been much to her, but she had to be three stone lighter. "Sammie?" he hissed again, still not quite believing it. All those years of wondering and here she was in front of him as if there'd never been any trouble.

"We heard what happened," said Molly, coming forward to stand between him and her sister, making herself into a human shield. "Lillianna said that Kit was trapped inside. Is he going to be okay?"

Anger surged inside him. They had no right. Molly had made Kit's life hell for years with her accusations, and as for Sammie, she had a huge apology to give and a hell of a lot of explaining to do before she learned anything from him. Her selfishness had saddled Kit with a lifetimes worth of guilt. More than that, Sammie was the reason Kit was lying in a hospital bed.

As for Lillianna—her interference had damn near split them up, but he acknowledged that hadn't been her intention. She was simply trying to protect Evie by presenting her with the facts.

"His hands are grim," he began, avoiding eye contact with any of them. Ross turned back to the glass divide and the activity around Kit's bed. "I don't know if they'll ever be right again. The burns are pretty bad. They're going to get plastics to look at them." They had Kit wired up to a drip.

"I'm sorry," Molly said.

"Do they know how the fire started?"

"No," he said firmly, hoping she understood the conversation was over. Kit had babbled something to the fire officers about petrol and a smashed window. They were looking into arson, but the two primary suspects were already accounted for. Molly had been off meeting Sammie, and Tony had never left the pub. Kit kept saying he didn't want any fuss, that he wanted the whole episode forgotten, but he was high on a cocktail of pain meds.

"Drink?" Molly asked.

Ross shrugged.

"I'll help," said Lillianna. The pair of them walked off towards the main entrance, leaving him alone with Sammie.

The scent of her perfume wafted over him, light and fruity with a sharp after bite, as she moved to stand beside him. "I had to go, Ross. I can't explain why, but I had no choice."

"Would it have hurt to tell one person that you were okay?"

He didn't want to hear her story. At this moment, he didn't want to understand. Her past choices had nearly stolen Kit from him forever. Six years while Kit hid in Japan had hardly passed in the blink of an eye.

"I never meant to hurt him." She pressed a hand to the glass, another liberty at which he ground his teeth.

"But you did." His words must have pierced the glass, for Evie waved to him, and gave him a rallying smile.

"He's doing okay," she mouthed. "You can come in."

Ross left Sammie in the corridor and headed into the private room. They'd been told only one visitor at a time by the original nurse, but no one protested his entry. Kit's hands were swaddled in dressings, and he was connected to an intravenous drip, but he was sitting upright and now his skin was clear of soot, he didn't appear nearly so ill. Ross threw his arms around his neck. "You fucking idiot. The cat's not worth your life. What were you thinking?"

Unable to pat his back in response, Kit gave him a gormless grin. "I didn't want another disappearance on my conscience. One is enough for any man. I'm okay, Ross. The doctors aren't too concerned. Leastways they're not talking about the prospect of taking skin grafts off my arse."

Kit's attempt at humour brought tears to Ross's eyes. "I love you, you stupid bastard." He nuzzled against Kit's shoulder, not conscious that he was crushing him until Evie tentatively eased them apart.

"They are however, pushing enough meds into me to make up for all the times I've refused them." Kit rolled his eyes at the drip. "I don't suppose you could have a word with them about my preferences for natural methods."

"No, he can't." Evie patted Kit's leg through the sheet. "They're probably the only reason you're sitting upright and aren't screaming like you were the whole way here in the ambulance."

Kit raised his brows, feigning scepticism. "Did I scream?"

"Like a girl," said Ross. "But don't worry, we won't put it about."

"I bloody hope not. I'm not planning on being away from home that long." Ross starred at him a moment, then let a smile crack his lips. If Kit was thinking of sex, then he really wasn't that badly hurt. He crushed his lips to Kit's, thrusting his tongue deep. He didn't care who saw: Sammie or the various members of staff. He wasn't going to hide their relationship anymore. No one would get away with thinking they were simply sharing Evie. They'd make it plain it was a proper three-way relationship. As if to prove that, Evie rubbed up against his shoulder. He wrapped an arm around her back and drew her into the huddle, kissing her too. "Shall I wait to mention the lease?" he asked.

Evie thumped him.

"Is that Sammie?" Kit sank back against the pillows, his gaze focused on the woman standing in the corridor. "I want to talk to her."

"Tomorrow," Evie barked. "When you're okay."

Kit did eventually talk to Sammie, but not until the next day. If she gave him anymore details about her disappearance than she'd admitted to anyone else, Kit didn't let on. When asked, he just smiled and said he was satisfied, and that he only wished she'd felt she could have trusted him better then. And no, actually, he wasn't a dad; he made a point of informing Evie while Lillianna was also present, just to nip that particular rumour before it started. Lilli liked to be at the forefront of any gossip, but she also liked to be right.

The police came to speak to him too, but Kit refused to name potential suspects or press charges. He explained what had happened and left it at that, keen to put the past behind him. Flora's legacy was a wreck, little more than a smouldering, blackened shell, but he asked as the officers left how soon he could start repairing it.

Chapter Eighteen

"Blinking hell! It's like a funeral parlour in here." Kit laughed at the abundance of cards, flowers and get well soon balloons taking up space in the living room. "Amazing what rescuing a cat does for one's reputation." He nudged one particularly garish offering of a black sequined heart and smiled at Lillianna's "get well and smoochy" message inside.

Following Sammie's brief reappearance, the villagers had rallied round, each more eager than the last to express their sympathies over Kit's injures, and to dismiss any suggestion that they ever thought he had anything to do with Sammie's disappearance. An assertion Evie had learned to accept with grace.

Not that any of that mattered now. Kit was finally home, and so was Mimmy. The little kitten had suffered a bad dose of smoke-inhalation during the fire, but she was now fully recovered, thanks to Ross's partner at the veterinary practice, who had thoroughly cleaned her up and taken her home to nurse, since Ross and Evie had their hands full travelling back and forth to the hospital to visit Kit.

Evie left Ross aiding Kit to remove his coat, and padded through to the kitchen to shove a pizza in the oven. The current plan was for the three of them to curl up on the sofa and watch a movie together. Only, when she returned, the boys seemed to have forgotten their coats. Ross's lay on the carpet, and Kit's still had one arm in his jacket. Evie hung back in the doorway, watching, as her lover tenderly rained down kisses upon Kit's upturned face. "Making up for lost time?" she asked.

Neither of them replied.

"Keep kissing me and you're going to have your work cut out for you," said Kit. With his hands still covered in swaddling bandages, he was neither in a position to push Ross away or draw him closer. "I'm not sitting up all night with a raging hard-on that I can do nothing about. It's been bad enough in hospital. I'll come and slap you in the face with it until you wake up."

"Promises, promises," Ross scoffed. He finally helped pull Kit's other arm free of his coat sleeve. "You know I'm feeling a little frisky in that regard myself." Ross rolled his hips so that his loins pressed tightly to Kit's abdomen, in response to which Kit gave an anguished groan.

"Evil," he cursed.

"What did you say about Evie?" Ross glanced over his shoulder and caught sight of her standing in the doorway. "Coming to join us?"

She took a few steps forward, but still didn't intrude. It was great to have Kit home again, but she wasn't sure the three of them getting frisky quite so soon was such a good idea. Ross apparently thought otherwise.

"Damn, you're hot like this, Kit. I love the fact that you can't do a blooming thing. I can do whatever I like and you can't stop me."

"Who says I can't?"

Evie laughed at the challenge in Kit's voice. She was pretty certain he'd come out on top of this power play scenario, even taking into account his injuries. However... "Ross, he's still—" She was going to say injured, but Kit cut her off.

"—just fine. I'm just fine," he said, and the purr that escaped Ross's throat as Kit's mouth closed over one nipple attested to that fact. "Who says I need hands to get either of you off?"

"Kit. The doctor told you to take it easy."

"Yeah, and he also told me that Margaret Thatcher was the best thing that ever happened to this country, and that he thinks he's emo son is gay."

Evie came and perched on the arm of the sofa beside them. "You should still—"

"Yeah, yeah. I get it. Take it easy. Work up to things gradually. I'll not do a thing. I'll just sit here. That okay?"

She nodded, but the moment she'd done so, Kit exchanged a secretive look with Ross, and the latter slipped off Kit's lap and knelt between his spread thighs. "Ross, no!"

"Please," murmured Kit, a plea she hadn't the heart to argue with. "All rest and no play makes Kit a growly sourpuss." He pouted.

Evie raised her hands in capitulation. Ross immediately dived on Kit's belt, and helped him wriggle far enough out of his trousers and underwear that the fabric bunched around his knees. His erection swung free of the restriction, the head already ruddy and ripe for a touch. Ross wrapped a large hand around the base of Kit's cock and applied tongue to the head.

Thirty seconds of watching his head bob was enough to crumble her resolve. Evie clambered onto the sofa beside Kit and lavished kisses upon him. God, she'd missed this, even in the few short days they'd been apart.

"Evie." Kit nudged her away with his words. "I want to watch him. I want to watch you." There was no need to ask for further clarification. Evie shuffled off the sofa again, and stood a little to the right of Ross so that Kit could see them both without the need for movement.

"Which bit of me do you want to see first?" She coyly pressed her palms together and touched her fingertips to her lips.

"Lose the denim. You know I hate the stuff."

Evie looked at him from under her eyelashes as she tugged down her zip, then she turned around to shimmy out of her three-quarter length cut-offs. The lace of her panties skimmed across the surface of her buttocks, rising up as she bent, no doubt giving Kit an impressive vision of her curves. Ross, she noted, when she turned to face them again, had adjusted his position so that he could keep one eye on her too. He was also struggling one handed with the buckle of his belt.

Clearly the moment demanded more than just the pleasure of giving.

"Want some help with that?" She released his fly and ran her cupped hands up and down the length of his smooth shaft. He was just as primed as Kit and leaking shiny beads of precome that she rubbed into the taut skin. Evie rolled onto her side on the carpet and wriggled into the space between the two men. The warmth of Ross's body, coupled with the soft brush of the thick hairs around his loins felt great against her palms. So close to him, she revelled in the scent of his body, that earthy smell that made her want to snuggle up close to him and coat herself in it, as if to mark herself as his. His cock bobbed eagerly the closer she got, but she eschewed touching him there, choosing to tickle the underside of his balls with the very tip of her tongue instead.

"Oh, man. Evie! I can't suck while you do that."

"Sure you can," she whispered close to his skin, knowing the stroke of her breath would tantalize him almost as much as the lick.

"I can't."

Ignoring the plea, she did it again, and somehow he managed to keep it together enough to continue fellating Kit, his body moving back and forth with the rhythm of his sucks. However, when she ventured toward the delicate nerve-endings around this anus, he jerked rather more violently, and clamped a hand upon her stomach. "Evie, no! Really no. This is about Kit's pleasure, not mine."

"Isn't it about us all pleasing each other?"

"She's right, you know, Ross," Kit interjected. The sofa

springs creaked as he strained forward trying to catch a glimpse of what was going on, but she doubted the angles involved allowed him much visibility. "Evie, how about you swivel yourself up here beside me and let me put my tongue to work too."

Having just claimed this was about them all being equal, she could hardly refuse him on the grounds that he was supposed to be resting. Evie climbed onto the sofa. It took a moment or two of wriggling to negotiate the contortions involved in positioning herself so that Kit could reach her cunt without the benefit of using his hands, and so that she could still reach Ross well enough to suck him. She concentrated on doing that, rather than continuing to tease his puckered hole. Nevertheless, Ross seemed to be on a hair-trigger, his cock bobbing high, the skin stretched taut like that of a ripe plum. He groaned, despite having his own mouth full of Kit's cock, and he was soon coated with a fresh glow of sweat.

For her own part, she tried not to concentrate on what Kit was doing with his tongue, although, he made that extremely hard. Kit had a way of touching her clit that seemed to pool warmth just behind her naval, that would then zip downwards turning her hardened clit into the centre of a magical explosion. She jiggled her hips, thinking about how good it would feel if one of them were to fuck her while the other licked. They hadn't done that yet, but she was making mental notes for future possibilities. Right now, though, they were seriously making her buzz. Her thigh muscles involuntarily spasmed and clamped either side of Kit's ears. He laughed, and the sound of his mirth amplified the sensation of ascent. This was going to be over very quickly.

Kit pushed Ross's head clear of his cock. "You two didn't have to be abstinent in my absence, you know."

"How do you know that?" Evie glared at Ross, wondering when he'd told Kit.

"He didn't say anything. It's blatantly obvious. You're both hyper-sensitive."

"Ugh!" was the only response they got out of Ross, whose hips continued to piston. Evie returned to sucking him and seed flowed onto her tongue mere moments later. He sagged back onto his haunches, still panting hard. "Sorry, guys."

"No problem," said Kit from his position wedged between Evie's thighs. He raised his head, revealing his chin, glistening with the wetness of her body. The two men's gazes locked.

"What is it?" she asked. They reminded her of two stags locking horns. She eased herself around until the sofa fully supported her back.

"Come here." Kit pushed himself upright using his elbow and nodded at his lap. Evie dipped her head, assuming he meant for her to take Ross's place sucking him. "No. Astride." Kit's smile shone in his eyes—challenging, daring her.

"Wait." Ross started rooting around in Evie's purse for condoms.

"Equal," said Kit, demanding her attention again. "I'm clean, and I assume you two are and that there's some contraception going on somewhere given that you're constantly at each other without any apparent concern for the consequences."

"Hang in there." Ross rushed over, having already ripped open the foil packaging.

Evie stayed his hand, before he could roll the sheath down Kit's shaft. "He has a point, Ross. I want to feel him naked. Don't you?"

"I... I guess. Maybe not at this precise moment."

Although judging by the perkiness of his cock, it wouldn't be long before he was considering it.

Evie slid onto Kit. He was as smooth as butter and pleasingly stiff. They took it steady, her taking charge since Kit's movements were limited by his injuries. It wasn't long before Ross was pressing up against her back, his hands seeking her breasts and the puckered teats of her nipples. Only half-hard, his cock rubbed along the crack between her cheeks in time with the motion of her rising and falling. This was surely the mirror of what Ross had been imagining that first night when Kit had stood in the kitchen doorway watching them. He must have thought of his lover joining them. Perhaps that was the reason he'd called Kit's name as he'd come. He'd never intended the gasp to be a warning. It had been a simple admission of his thoughts.

"Kiss me."

Ross met her demand, his tongue thrusting deep into her mouth, duplicating the motion of his fingers, two of which stroked through her damp curls to find her clit. They scissored briefly around Kit's thrusting cock, before returning to the source of her pleasure.

"Come for us, Evie."

"Yes, do." Kit's eyes fluttered closed and his neck arched back. "Before I beat you to it."

Ross rubbed her clit a little harder and pushed a finger into her arse. The combined sensation from three points of stimulation set her soaring. Ross nuzzled her neck as she came, while Kit gasped against her chest as his cock spasmed inside her.

They held each other close.

"I love you," she gasped, and she knew they understood she meant them both.

About the Author

Madelynne Ellis has a healthy obsession with a certain Japanese rock-star, drinks decaf out of preference, and likes scaring the wobblies out of people at gothic horror weekends. A multi-published author in both traditional print and digital formats, Madelynne's aim is to deliver scorching, character-driven stories that both enchant and torment. To learn more please visit www.madelynne-ellis.com, or send an email to madelynne@madelynne-ellis.com.

GREAT CHEAP FUN

Discover eBooks!

THE FASTEST WAY TO GET THE HOTTEST NAMES

Get your favorite authors on your favorite reader, long before they're out in print! Ebooks from Samhain go wherever you go, and work with whatever you carry—Palm, PDF, Mobi, Kindle, nook, and more.

SAMHAIN
PUBLISHING

WWW.SAMHAINPUBLISHING.COM

CPSIA information can be obtained at www.ICGtesting.com
Printed in the USA
LVOW041847281111

256816LV00001B/101/P